Praise for Gena Hale's Novels

Sun Valley

"Don't miss *Sun Valley*. It will reinvigorate the iron in your blood."
—Catherine Coulter

Dream Mountain

"Nonstop adventure, gnarly intrigue, lots of laughs . . . and a hunk. What more could you ask?"
—Catherine Coulter

Paradise Island

"Intrigue abounds in this action-filled romance that will leave readers on the edges of their seats."
—*Booklist*

"Absoring, exhilarating, and entertaining—action-packed romance thrillers don't come any better. This is the kind of joyride for which bedside lamps were invented. I'd say Gena Hale has Arrived—with a capital A!"
—Judith Gould

"Prepare yourself for a breathtaking ride."
—*Romantic Times* (Top Pick)

"An exciting contemporary romantic suspense novel that will thrill the audience with its nonstop action."
—Harriet Klausner

"Complex and tension-fill̲ed . . . on all counts."
—*us*

Also by Gena Hale

Paradise Island
Dream Mountain

SUN VALLEY

Gena Hale

AN ONYX BOOK

ONYX
Published by New American Library, a division of
Penguin Putnam Inc., 375 Hudson Street,
New York, New York 10014, U.S.A.
Penguin Books Ltd, 80 Strand,
London WC2R 0RL, England
Penguin Books Australia Ltd, Ringwood,
Victoria, Australia
Penguin Books Canada Ltd, 10 Alcorn Avenue,
Toronto, Ontario, Canada M4V 3B2
Penguin Books (N.Z.) Ltd, 182–190 Wairau Road,
Auckland 10, New Zealand

Penguin Books Ltd, Registered Offices:
Harmondsworth, Middlesex, England

First published by Onyx, an imprint of New American Library,
a division of Penguin Putnam Inc.

First Printing, June 2002
10 9 8 7 6 5 4 3 2 1

PUBLISHER'S NOTE
This is a work of fiction. Names, characters, places, and incidents either
are the product of the author's imagination or are used fictitiously,
and any resemblance to actual persons, living or dead, business
establishments, events, or locales is entirely coincidental.

For Catherine Coulter,
with much love, admiration, and thanks.
Every time I look at the stars,
I think of you and smile.

Prologue

Neala Delaney had just thrown most of her won't-wrinkle clothes into two suitcases when the door-bell to her apartment buzzed. *Not now. I don't have time for this.*

She ran over and hit the intercom. "What?"

"It's me. Buzz me in."

She swore and hit the button with her fist. When her unwanted visitor got to the door and knocked, she yanked it open. "No."

"Neal, darlin'—"

Before her uncle could say anything, Neal slammed the door in his face—or tried to. His big foot got in the way. "Whatever it is, I can't."

"Neal, we need to talk." The big Irishman grimaced when the edge of the door rammed into his foot a second time. "Sweet Jesus, girl, will you leave off? I'm serious!"

She let him in, only because it would take too much time to find her baseball bat and break his legs. "I've got to finish packing. There's still some of your whis-key in the kitchen, I think. Help yourself."

He didn't. He checked the windows and closed all the blinds instead. Worse, he didn't ask her *why* she was packing.

Neal squared her shoulders. *I'm not going to ask. I know exactly what will happen if I ask.*

She successfully ignored him, until he followed her into the bedroom. "I need you to pick up a package for me."

"Call UPS." She slammed one case shut and locked it.

"It's not that kind of package," he said, and told her about the senator's wife.

By the time he'd finished, she gave up sorting through her lingerie and simply dumped the contents of the entire drawer into the second suitcase. "Why don't you go get it yourself?"

"Sure and I would, but I'm in the middle of this Richmond mess. I can't risk breaking my cover. You, on the other hand—"

"No." When he opened his mouth, she whipped up one hand. "*No.* I have to get out of here, fast. As in *yesterday*. End of discussion."

"Please, Neal." He tried to put his arm around her, but she ducked under it and sidestepped him. "It'll only take an hour. Two at the most. I swear on my sainted mother's grave."

She snorted as she went into the walk-in closet for more clothes. "You mean you still remember where you buried *that* body?"

"Look, darlin' girl, just do this one wee bit of a thing for me tonight." His voice wobbled a little when he added, "I'm begging you."

When she reemerged, she gave him the eye. "Don't you 'darlin' girl' me, old man." She tossed the might-wrinkle clothes she carried on top of the lingerie. "I'm not Laney, I'm not stupid, and I'm not doing any more of your dirty work."

"This'll be the last time I ask."

"Yeah, right." She had to sit on the second case to close it. "That's what you said when you talked me into dating that Iranian ambassador." She reached down and flipped the locks. "You remember. The one who wanted me to join his harem."

Her uncle winced. "National security was at stake."

"With you, national security is *always* at stake." She grabbed three pairs of shoes at random from her shoe tree and dropped them in her carry-on. "And what about that time I sang 'Happy Birthday' at that Colombian drug lord's party? It was *your* brilliant idea for me to sit on his lap so my wire could pick up everything. I nearly got raped."

"The DEA was very grateful to you for that."

"The DEA didn't have to wear turtlenecks for a month to hide the bruises." She rubbed the side of her throat, remembering how strong the drug lord's soft, pampered hands had been. "And how about that roach-coach Mexican cantina you booked me into last summer? The one those smugglers burned down during my second act?"

"I admit, Immigration rushed the gate on that one." He gave her a sheepish look. "You saved a lot of lives, using your microphone to talk those people out of there."

"And smoke inhalation kept me from singing for the next six months." She zipped the carry-on closed with a single jerk. "I'm through being your gopher. Find someone else, Uncle Sean."

"All right." He looked thoughtful for a moment. "There's always Laney, I suppose—"

"What?" Neal grabbed the front of his shirt. "Absolutely not. Don't even think about it."

"Now, darlin'." Sean patted her fist, then eased it away. "I know you watched out for her when you were girls, but she's a grown woman now."

Neal pictured her sister's sweet, open face, and felt the familiar blend of love and protectiveness welling inside her. "Laney shouldn't be let out on the street without a bodyguard."

"She tries to see the good in people."

Meaning Neal didn't. She grabbed a handful of cosmetics from the top of her vanity. "Make that two bodyguards."

"Well, maybe you're right." Her uncle paused a beat, then added in a nonchalant way, "But since you're in such a hurry, I'm sure she won't mind helping her poor old uncle out."

"Knock it off. Laney has no idea what you do, and it's going to stay that way." She hesitated, then dropped the makeup into her cosmetic case. "Look, I'd go, but I've got problems. This jerk I'm working for—J. R. Martin—is a major wise guy, and he wants me in his bed. Then he plans to rent me out to his buddies. His *Chinese* buddies. And guess what? He's not going to take no for an answer."

"I know." Sean shuffled his feet when her head snapped up. "We've had Martin under surveillance ever since you started working there. Actually, if you're willing to, you can help us—"

"No." Neal was emphatic. "J. R. is a lot scarier than those coked-up Colombians were."

"So is Shandian, and as it happens, your boss is working for them."

"What?" She sat down on the edge of the bed, knocking off her carry-on and one of the suitcases. "J. R. is involved in this?"

"Up to his eyebrows, darlin'. Who did you think his Chinese friends were, anyway? Martin's been fronting Shandian's contributions to the senator's campaign fund—among other things. You get the evidence for us tonight, and we can get all of them at once."

She thought for a moment. No matter what he promised, if she left, her uncle *would* ask Laney to do the job. Laney, who didn't have a deceitful bone in her whole body. She put her hand in her pocket and pulled out a coin. "All right. Call it."

"Heads," Sean said.

Neal flipped the coin and watched it land on tails. *No. I can't do this to Laney.* Before her uncle could see it, she shoved it back in her pocket. "Heads—you win. I'll do it. But this is the last time, I swear to God. After this, I am retired. Unavailable. *Invisible.* Got it?"

Her uncle gave her a big, satisfied grin. "Got it."

Neal had no problem getting into the senator's suite at the Falconcrest Hotel. Wearing her slinkiest, most expensive cocktail dress, she sauntered directly up to the penthouse floor. The master code-key card Sean had given her had worked like a charm on the door. Yet once inside the suite, she found she was alone.

So where was the blonde?

Maybe something had gone wrong. Something always seemed to go wrong with her uncle's schemes. Cursing under her breath, she started searching the bedroom. The sound of a door opening and closing made her dive for the closet.

Neal looked through a slit in the bifold doors. A petite, classy-looking woman walked into the bedroom and went to the mirror. She looked at herself, then pressed a hand against her stomach.

She's not armed, and she's blond. Has to be her. Slowly Neal opened the doors and stepped out. "Hi, there."

The small woman gave a small shriek as she jerked around. "Who are you? What are you doing in here?"

"I'm Neal." She held out her empty hands so the woman could see she wasn't armed. "Sean Delaney sent me."

"Yes. Yes, of course." Her tense shoulders slumped as she propped herself against the vanity table. "Forgive me; I'm—I'm very nervous about this."

To say the least. She'd seen kangaroos with less hop. "That's okay, Mrs. Colfax."

"Karen, please."

"Okay, Karen." Neal watched the other woman check her diamond-studded watch. "Do you have the package for me?"

"It's in the other room. We have to hurry; he's on his way back to the hotel." Karen lifted a thin hand to her face, and Neal suddenly spotted the outline of a bruise under the other woman's flawless makeup. "If he finds out about this, he'll kill me."

"He—" Neal went still as she heard the suite door open a second time.

The senator's wife grabbed her arm. "In the closet!" She pushed Neal in, then followed.

"Doesn't he know you're here?"

"No. I'm supposed to still be at the governor's banquet."

They both listened as the outer door to the suite closed. Two men began talking almost at once, and Neal's stomach twisted as she recognized one of the voices. Beside her, Karen trembled violently.

"The Chinese wanted that tech embargo lifted, Senator. You shouldn't have voted against the bill."

"Turning that kind of technology over to a communist government is sheer insanity, J. R." There was the faint sound of ice hitting glass, then liquid pouring. "Here, have a drink. We'll talk about this."

Glass abruptly shattered, making both women jump. "There's nothing to talk about anymore, Phillip. You were paid to vote yes."

"You don't understand the situation." Phillip Colfax didn't sound angry anymore. He sounded confident— and amused. "I am a United States senator. Shandian can make all the campaign contributions they want, but they don't control me. Neither do you."

"Brave words for a man who takes two million dollars from the tong and reneges on his promises."

The senator chuckled. "The tong will pay me a lot more to keep quiet."

Another sound of glass shattering, this time not as loud. "Dead men don't talk much."

There was an ominous silence, then: "Don't you threaten me, you piece of shit. Get out."

*   *   *

Twenty-four minutes later, Neal and Karen stood over Phillip Colfax's body.

The senator's wife stared at the knife in her husband's chest. "Not like this. It can't happen like this. Not now."

The senator had probably been dead before he'd hit the floor, but Neal bent and checked for a pulse anyway. She could still smell the whiskey he'd been drinking, and shuddered. "I'm sorry, Karen." The petite woman didn't respond.

Neal glanced to one side and saw some small glass shards glittering on the carpet by the door. She looked up, and saw the broken lens of the security camera for the first time. "There's a camera over the door. He must have smashed the lens." She let her breath out slowly. "That's it, then." She went over and picked up the telephone. Someone had to call the police, might as well be her.

"Wait." The petite woman turned away from the body. "We have to talk about this."

"About what?"

"What we tell them."

"It doesn't matter what we tell them." Neal parked the receiver on her shoulder and pointed up. "Everything is on tape."

"Not everything. There's no audio, just video. And he broke the camera before—before—" She stared down at her husband.

"We still have to call someone. He's a *senator;* a lot of important people are going to be a little upset that he's dead. People like the President of the United States, for one."

"You don't understand. We can't involve the local authorities."

"Why not?"

As the senator's wife told her why she couldn't call the police, Neal slowly replaced the receiver, leaned back against the wall, and closed her eyes.

Why didn't I tell him it was tails?

Neal understood why Karen was so afraid. Unfortunately, the government would never be able to prosecute the Chinese without the evidence. J. R. would probably get off, too. It wasn't right. He should be the one to pay for this.

A radical thought suddenly formed in her head.

"There's another way." Neal went to the penthouse suite window and stared out at the night. Lights from the surrounding skyscrapers glittered, cold and distant. "Give it to me and go. They'll think you still have it. I'll cover for you."

"No, it's too dangerous."

"I'll call it in to the police as soon as you leave." She paused. "Someone has to tell them J. R. Martin murdered him."

Karen's expression went blank for a moment. "You can't."

"It's the only way." She felt a surge of guilt, then ruthlessly squashed it. "They need a witness, and it can't be you."

"But surely your agency—"

"I'm not an agent, Karen. I'm not even supposed to be here—I was just doing a favor for my uncle. Under the circumstances, they're not going to do anything to help me. Or you."

The senator's wife looked down at her husband's slack face. "He's a powerful man. He'll have you killed."

"If I agree to testify at the trial, they'll put me in protective custody." She hoped. "I'll be safe until my uncle can straighten this out." Neal guided Karen toward the door. "Go."

After the petite woman slipped out of the suite, Neal locked the door. Her hands were shaking, her heart pounding.

I can do this. I have to do this.

Careful not to step in the blood, she went over and crouched down beside the dead man. It took two tries before she was able to pull the knife out of the senator's chest. Blood gleamed on the serrated blade, so she held her other hand under it to catch the drips as she walked back to the bathroom.

After she threw up, Neal washed the knife thoroughly with soap and hot water. When she returned to the living room, she put the knife back on the table, exactly where it had been before. She took a long look around the suite. Only a vase of flowers lay smashed near one wall. There was no other hint that anything violent had happened here. That had to be fixed. Using only her elbows to avoid fingerprints, she deliberately knocked over two chairs and a table, and broke a lamp.

There, all the signs of a violent struggle.

She took a deep breath, pressed a hand to her churning stomach, then went over to the telephone.

The 911 operator answered on the second ring.

"I need help." Neal didn't have to fake the terror in her voice. "I've just witnessed a murder."

Chapter 1

Will Ryder shoved his chair back from his desk, knocking over a reading lamp and two framed photos of his parents as he got to his feet. If any of his men had been in his office, the look on his face would have cleared them out in a second.

"You want me to do *what*?" he shouted into the phone.

"Baby-sit her." The overseas connection cleared enough to carry the answering snap of impatience in CID General Kalen Grady's voice. "Keep her out of sight. No trips to town, no phone calls, and no visitors. She'll need round-the-clock protection. She's also good-looking, and knows how to use it, so watch your men. Do something to keep her occupied. Teach her to ride a horse."

As if Will had nothing better to do than to play nanny, riding instructor, chaperon, *and* bodyguard. "You are out of your mind."

"It's no big deal. You could do this in your sleep."

"In my—" He let out a short, humorless laugh. "Kal, I've got three hundred heifers and fourteen mares ready to drop, strays all over the mountain, and two hands down with the flu. The last time I slept was in November."

"Sounds like you can use a little vacation."

A vacation. When he had to work sixteen hours a day to make sure his men got one day off every week.

Will closed his eyes and silently counted to ten. His father had always claimed that helped keep him from blowing his top, but then, Dad had never had to deal with the federal government.

And that government was in a hurry. "Talk to me, Will."

"I can't help you out." He took a bottle of aspirin from his desk drawer, shook out two, and dry-swallowed them. "Give the job to a couple of your boys. They've got the necessary training—I don't."

"I can't risk it right now. I've got a leak some-where."

Will slowly sat back down as the implication set in. "Christ, what a frigging mess."

"Exactly. You're the only person I can trust to keep her safe." His old army buddy waited a beat. "You still owe me for what went down at Abyada Sada."

"You're calling that in?" Will stared out the big bay window at the western pastures. Irregular patches of dirty snow still mottled the soil, but it was retreating. New grass shoots streaked the wide fields with dense swatches of pale green. "For a woman?"

"She's the only witness I've got. I don't have a choice."

Neither did Will. Kalen Grady had taken a bullet for him when their platoon had crossed into Kuwait at Abyada Sada during the Gulf War; he definitely owed him part of a lung and probably his life. It didn't make him happier to finally pay off the debt—not knowing he'd have to put up with some city girl for the next two months.

"Well? Will you handle this for me?"

"You mean, will I let you blackmail me into doing this? Yeah, all right. When is she getting here?"

"Her plane landed about thirty minutes ago."

Neal walked into the nearly deserted passenger ter-minal at Big Timber airport. Unlike its large, modern-ized counterpart in Helena, Big Timber's daily traffic consisted of privately owned twin-engine aircraft, commercial freight shipments, and the odd commuter flight.

Notices for local stock sales and rodeos crowded the bulletin board in the lobby. To one side of the baggage claim area, an unclaimed crate marked JOHN DEERE sat gathering dust. On the other side, three men dressed in coveralls and sheepskin-lined jackets were wrestling to get what appeared to be a small engine block on a pallet jack through the exit door.

"Mary, Mother of God," Neal muttered as she watched them. "I've landed in the Twilight Zone."

She grabbed her suitcase off the revolving luggage belt, and set it down by her feet. Two male ticket agents on the other side of the lobby openly gaped at her.

She glanced down. She'd gotten warm on the plane, so she'd unbuttoned her coat. Nothing had popped out, so why were they staring? Didn't they have women around here?

The two men in suits and expensive trench coats who'd trailed her from the plane at last caught up and flanked her. "I'll take the suitcase, Ms. Delaney," the heavier man said.

She handed it over. "Exactly where are we?"

"Montana." Agent Bruce Bowers stared at her chest until a harsh sound from his partner made him look away. "You'd better go change in the ladies' room. We'll wait."

Neal had put on the cocktail dress expressly to irritate her keepers, so she had no intention of changing just yet. "I'll do that at the hotel, when the rest of my luggage arrives."

"You're not going to a hotel," Agent Wayne Selbrook said. "We've got you situated at Sun Valley, a cattle ranch just west of here, near the mountains."

"A *cattle* ranch." Neal chuckled and shook her head. "Very funny. Come on, tell me which hotel." Neither man said anything as she looked from one to the other. "You're not kidding." Her grin faded. "Are you crazy? I can't stay at a *ranch*."

Selbrook, who had very clean hands and a cheesy mustache, frowned. "You don't get an option on where you go, Ms. Delaney." He gave her his be-a-sport look. "It'll be fun. You can relax, maybe get in some horseback riding."

"Me? On a *horse*?" Neal's voice squeaked, but only for a second. "Not even if you drugged me."

Something came out of Bowers's mouth that sounded suspiciously like "That can be arranged."

When they walked out of the terminal, the frigid air penetrated her thin coat as easily as if she'd been completely naked. A startled breath left her, and she watched it form a visible white puff. Slushy snow crunched under passing tires while freezing droplets dribbled from the icicles edging the roof above her head.

"This isn't Montana. It's the North Pole." She yanked her case out of Agent Bowers's hands and made a neat about-face. "The joke's over, boys. Take me back to Denver. Please."

The agents exchanged a long-suffering glance before they maneuvered around her and blocked her path.

"Ms. Delaney—"

"No." Her patience, along with most of her body heat, had dissipated. "I don't want to hear about it. I don't care. Let his goons shoot me in the street. At least I'll die where people don't have to live in igloos."

"Stop exaggerating the situation, Ms. Delaney." Agent Bowers repossessed her suitcase. "It's not that bad. Spring's arrived early this year."

"How do they know that?" Neal eyed a cabby, who had gotten out to scrape a hole in the thick layer of frost covering his decrepit taxi's windshield. "Are the icebergs retreating?"

The federal agents flanked her again and marched her out to their rental car.

As Neal huddled in the back, she silently cursed her

uncle. She hadn't been able to contact Sean since the night of the murder, and this whole federal-protection thing was getting out of hand. "Guys, look. I'm sure this . . . *ranch* . . . is a perfectly wonderful little vacation spot. But I personally don't do the cowgirl thing. Really. I need to *talk* to somebody about this."

"You know the rules, Ms. Delaney." Selbrook pulled out into the exit lane from the lot. "You can't make any phone calls."

"You can dial the number for me."

Selbrook drove from the airport toward an ominous-looking line of mountains. Neal knew she needed the FBI's protection until the trial got under way—but a cattle ranch? Horseback riding? In subzero temperatures?

Maybe it was only temporary. Maybe they planned to move her to someplace more suited to her thermal comfort zone. Like Venezuela. "How long am I going to have to be at this place? A couple of days?"

"You'll be staying there until the trial begins."

"That's not for two *months*!" The squeak in her voice was back with a vengeance. "Oh, no. No. I can't do eight weeks in winter wonderland. Call your boss."

Bowers glanced back at her. "He's not available at the moment."

Her temper flared. "Then have someone *find* him and *get* him on the phone, because I'm not spending the next two months hanging around a bunch of cowsicles!"

Both men went back to ignoring her.

This was ridiculous. She'd seen how key government witnesses were protected on television. They lived in hotel suites. Took bubble baths. Played cards. Watched cable. Ordered from room service.

She'd been looking forward to that last part. She *adored* room service.

Not once had she ever seen a show about federal witnesses being forced to go horseback riding, around cows, in the snow. And hadn't she endured enough over the last six weeks? Being stuck in that cheap motel outside Kansas City while the feds decided what to do with her had nearly driven her crazy. She'd already sworn she'd never eat take-out food again, not even if she was held at gunpoint.

She glanced out the window at the wet road. *Okay, so the snow's melting, and the landscape is pretty. Who's to say when the next blizzard hits?*

Over the next half hour, she renewed her persuasive efforts on Agents Selbrook and Bowers. She tried charm. Pleading. Not even good old bribery worked.

"It's against the law to bribe a federal agent, Ms. Delaney," Selbrook reminded her. "Besides, you don't have any money."

"I can borrow some."

When he didn't respond, Neal sighed. She hated making threats—they violated her basic philosophy of Live and Let Neala Have Her Way, and almost always induced hostility on the receiving end—but it was clear her escorts had no intention of cooperating.

"Gentlemen. I've tried to be nice, but here's the bottom line: If you make me stay here, I won't testify at the trial."

Now Selbrook glared at her reflection in the rearview mirror. "Ms. Delaney, do you have any idea how angry J. R. Martin is with you right now?"

"Who cares? He's behind bars, so he can throw all the tantrums he wants." Neal saw Bowers shake his head and leaned over the front seat back. "He's *not*?"

"Martin jumped bail two days before the Denver papers ran that photo of you standing over the senator's body."

"Oh, great." Neal clunked her brow against the back of Bowers's headrest. "Well, you guys still have that security tape."

Selbrook's awful mustache bristled as he glanced in the rearview mirror. "No, actually, we don't."

"It's disappeared." Bowers popped a stick of gum in his mouth and began to chew with gusto. "Your

testimony is the only evidence we have left against
Martin."

That genuinely spooked her. But she tried to turn
it to her advantage. "Sounds like you people should
be keeping me happy, then. My idea of happiness is
a nice, roomy suite at the Marriott, preferably overlooking the heated pool."

Selbrook heaved a sigh. "Ms. Delaney, you were
found alone in the suite, standing over Senator Colfax's body. We *do* have photographs of that."

Neal recalled the reporter who'd taken a few shots
from the door of the suite before the cops had chased
him off. "And your point is . . . ?"

"If you don't testify against Martin," Bowers said,
"we can charge *you* with first-degree murder."

Before she could respond, Selbrook pointed toward
a truck stop that had appeared on the horizon. "Let's
stop up here and get some breakfast." He glanced at
Neal in the rearview mirror. "You'll feel better after
you've had something to eat."

*I'll feel better after I get back to Denver and brain
my uncle.* She sat back and formulated a new plan.

She had to get away from Dumb and Dumber.

"Mind if I use the ladies' room?" Neal asked as
they parked beside a hay truck and a semi.

"If you change out of that dress while you're in
there." Selbrook climbed out, then ducked his head
back in. "And don't spend all day redoing your
makeup, either."

As if he didn't spend an hour a day trimming and
grooming that ridiculous tuft of hair sprouting under
his nose. "I'll try to restrain myself."

After Selbrook gave Neal her suitcase and locked
the trunk, she turned and stumbled deliberately on a
rock. He caught her, and while she pretended to fum-
ble for her balance, she deftly removed the car keys
from his jacket pocket.

"Oops. Sorry." She curled her fingers tightly around
the keys to keep them from jangling, grabbed her case,

and headed for the rest room. "I'll just be a minute. Be a dear and order me some french toast—hold the powdered sugar—and a pot of tea." When Bowers would have shadowed her, she threw a flirtatious smile over her shoulder. "I think I can handle this by myself, but if I need rescuing again, I'll whistle."

Red-faced, Bowers snapped his gun and hitched his belt up. "Hurry up."

She went to the rest room, but she didn't change. Instead, she climbed on top of one of the toilets and peered through the small, dingy window. Five minutes passed as she watched, but there was no sign of Laurel and Hardy. Neal climbed down and grabbed her case.

She might just pull this off, after all.

An hour later, Neal stood in the center of an empty highway, kicking the rental car's tire and yelling, "Who takes out a car with only two drops of gasoline in it?"

It was actually her own fault for not checking the gauge; she'd been right there, parked only a few feet from the gas pumps. But getting away from her keepers had been more important than anything, and at least they couldn't chase her now.

Until they got another car. Or a dog team and a sled.

Neal scanned her surroundings. Not much to see, really. The road. Dead grass. Snow. Fences. Mountains in the distance. That was it. And it felt like the temperature was dropping.

I've got to get out of here.

It took considerable effort to push the car until it stretched across both lanes. By the time she finished making her impromptu roadblock, she was shaking and covered with icy sweat. Taking off her coat only made that worse. The sound of an approaching vehicle was the only thing that kept her from crawling back into the car.

Instead, she folded her coat over her arm, braced

herself against the frigid wind, and began waving at the pickup truck headed toward her.

Here goes nothing.

A flash of red caught Will Ryder's eye two seconds before he saw the car he was about to plow into. His boot slammed on to the brake pedal, and the truck went into a skid.

"Goddamn it!"

His day had already gone from wrecked to ruined. After the phone call from Grady, his foreman had dragged in two battered, sullen hands. Evan made them admit how they'd gotten drunk the night before and beaten the hell out of each other. Firing them had forced Will to cancel the rest of the crew's days off until he could hire replacements. More phone calls made him even later leaving the ranch for town.

Now this fool was going to get them both killed.

Melting snow kept the roads slick, and anything trying to stop on it was susceptible to fishtailing, so Will had plenty of practice coming out of a skid. Once he'd managed to stop without smashing into the car or rolling into the drainage ditch, he threw the truck in park and shut off the engine.

A woman wearing a red coat stood to one side of the car. No, not a coat—but a *dress.*

A very tight, glittery, low-cut red dress.

For a moment, all he could do was stare. She was wearing a dress. A cocktail dress. In Montana. In *February.*

The obviously deranged woman sauntered over to his truck. She carried a large suitcase and a coat folded over her arm.

Here comes trouble, his dad would have said, *looking for a place to happen.*

Will climbed out of the truck and slammed the door. "Lady, what do you think you're doing?"

She halted in midstride, and looked bewildered. "You mean, besides turning into a frozen entree?"

He swore as he strode over to the car. "You don't park in the middle of a highway."

"I didn't park. I broke down." She gave him a singularly adorable smile.

"Why didn't you put on the emergency flashers?" Without waiting for an answer, Will reached in and flipped them on to avoid a repeat of what he'd just been through. "You've got to get this heap off the road now."

"I'm sorry, I didn't think of the flashers. I would have moved the car to the shoulder if I could have, but it's too much for me." The tall, dark traffic-stopper shaded her eyes with one hand to have a better look at him. "Could you . . . ?" She made a small, helpless gesture.

Once Will pushed the sedan off the road and safely onto the shoulder, most of his temper had evaporated. He turned to deal with the owner, and got his first good look at her face.

Whoever she was, she was a beauty. Long, curly sable hair spilled around an elegant face. Flashing dark eyes met his, while her full red lips curved. The smile did a better job than the dress, but only because he refused to look below her collarbones.

Like something out of a movie. God, she's gorgeous.

"You okay? Any bumps or bruises?"

"Oh, no. I'm peachy." She flashed the megawatt smile again. "Just peachy."

Her skin was exactly that color—light, rosy gold—and maybe just as smooth. Realizing how much he wanted to touch her and find out made him knot his hand into a fist. "What's wrong with the car?"

"Silly me." She rolled her eyes. "I ran out of gas. You're a Godsend, you know; I was praying someone would stop and pick me up before I had to be defrosted in a microwave." She put down the case, turning her back on him in the process. Which was when he discovered her dress was backless to the waist. The sight of all that smooth exposed skin made his teeth clench.

She'd get picked up, all right. Then beaten up, raped, and probably murdered.

"Put your coat on." He took it from her, and their arms brushed. Touching her was a mistake. Her skin *was* soft, and smooth, and sent a jolt of heat straight to his groin.

She shrugged back into her coat. "I would have walked to the nearest gas station, but I'm afraid I'm a little lost, too."

"Either you're lost, or you're not. There's no 'little' about it." He moved in closer, watching the way her expression changed. *Wary,* he thought. About time she realized how vulnerable she was, out here alone, dressed like that. "Where were you headed?"

"Civilization, assuming it still exists out here." She looked down as he began buttoning up her coat, then peeped up through her long, curly lashes. "You're not lost, I hope?"

He finished the job, then pushed his Stetson back on his head. "Lady, I live here."

"Really." She drew the word out as she scanned their surroundings. Her dark curls danced as she shook her head. "My condolences."

His temper returned full force as he moved away from her and pulled out his cell phone. "Have you got Triple-A?"

She glanced at his truck. "Um, to be honest, this isn't exactly my car."

He stopped dialing. "What?"

"I sort of borrowed it."

"You stole the car? Dressed like that?"

"I did not *steal* it. I borrowed it. From a couple of friends." She looked down at her buttoned-up coat. "And what's wrong with the way I'm dressed?"

"Nothing, if you like getting frostbite."

Her chin went up at that. "I'm from Colorado."

"Colorado. Right." He redialed the garage, and told his mechanic to send a wrecker out for the car. Ms. Survivor was practically shaking out of her thin coat by the time he finished the call. "Here." He shrugged out of his sheepskin-lined parka, draped it over her shoulders, and gave her a push toward his pickup. "Get in my truck."

As Will opened the passenger door, she pulled his parka closer around herself before stepping up. Her thin, high-heeled shoes slipped on the running board, and he grabbed her from behind to keep her from falling.

"Easy does it, Calamity." He'd felt the way she'd recoiled when he put his hands on her, felt the way she was trembling now. *Not as tough as you want me to think you are.* Once she was settled, he buckled her in. "Sit tight."

He went around and got in behind the wheel, then started the engine back up. His passenger still shivered violently, so he turned the heat on high and adjusted the vents for her. His movements made her jump a little.

"Thanks." She eyed him, gnawed at her lower lip, then looked out at the road.

Will could almost smell her fear. It should have made him back off; instead it aroused an instant, nameless response inside him. One that was so primitive and possessive it bordered on predatory.

He performed another, slower inspection. This close, he could smell her skin. No perfume, just her— warm and spicy, the way purple sage smelled in full bloom during the summer. Her skin was so clear that he could see the delicate blue veins at her wrists and temples.

The heated air from the vents fluttered through her hair, and a stray curl got caught between her lips. Before she could smooth it back, Will reached over and gently pulled it free. Her hair should have been coarse, stiff with hair spray and whatever else females put on their heads these days. Instead, it felt like silk. As he released the curl, he wondered how the rest of it would feel, filling his hands.

Bet she'd do more than jump.

Unlike most of the women he knew, she wore plenty of makeup—gleaming lipstick to match the dress, rose blush on her narrow cheekbones, black liner around her dark eyes. All very skillfully applied, but he didn't like it. He wanted to see what was underneath it. Would she be just as stunning after a dunk in a trough and a good scrub to get all that goop off her skin?

She'd be wet. Wet and mad and ready for taming and why the hell am I even thinking about it?

She shifted a little farther away, and broke the spell.

What was the matter with him? No matter how nicely she was packaged, the woman was trouble. Probably a car thief. Definitely the only car thief in America who wore a cocktail dress to work. Maybe it was the latest trend in Colorado.

Colorado. Denver.

Will sat back and closed his eyes for a moment. Fate had a real sense of humor. "You're the nightclub singer," he said. "From Denver."

Now it was her turn to be surprised. "How did you know that?"

Kalen had mentioned she was good-looking. That was like saying the Crazy Mountains were a couple of hills. He'd have to put Sun Valley off-limits to his men, too, or they'd end up killing each other over her.

"I was coming to pick you up." He looked down the road, but saw no sign of the FBI agents who should have been escorting her. They must be the "friends" from whom she had "borrowed" the car. "What are you doing out here by yourself? You're supposed to be waiting for me in town."

"I got tired of hanging around Dumb and Dumber."

At his blank look, she added, "Special Agents Selbrook and Bowers. I'm Neala Delaney. Call me Neal." She held out her hand. "And you are . . . ?"

Going to shoot Kalen Grady in the head the next time I see him. "Will Ryder." *Delaney. Black Irish. Definitely trouble.* He took her hand, and his eyes narrowed as he felt another jolt. Static, that was all it was. Static she was carrying around with all that hair of hers.

"So why were *you* elected to pick me up, Will Ryder?"

Because he didn't have the sense God gave a wayward steer, he thought, and released her hand. "Someone left a message about you."

"Really." Neal gave him a sideways glance. "Do you local cattle barons always run out at the drop of a hat to pick up strange women?"

"Cattle rancher." Irish *and* she had a mouth on her. "We try to be neighborly." A mouth he didn't want to think about anymore. Will abruptly put the truck in drive and made a U-turn.

She sat up straight and grabbed the edge of the bench seat with both hands. "Where are we going?"

"Sun Valley."

"Ah, the cattle ranch." She considered this—and him—for a moment, then did something odd. She dug her hand into her coat pocket, searched, and pulled out a coin. Under her breath, she muttered, "Heads I go, tails I stay."

She tossed the coin up, then caught it. Will saw that it landed on heads, then watched her put it back in her pocket. "Looks like I'll have to pass on the ranch. Can you take me to the nearest phone instead?"

"You decide things by flipping a coin?"

One of her dark brows arched. "Only the important stuff."

She'd obviously gotten a mild dose of hypothermia. Or he had. "You're one peculiar woman."

"Am I?" She shrugged, as if it didn't matter. "Mr.

Ryder, I need to make some phone calls and arrange some alternative transportation. What's the nearest city—Helena, right? Can you run me over there instead?"

He couldn't help the laugh. "Helena is a two-hour drive from here."

"Oh." She frowned, thinking. "Is there someplace closer?"

"There's a bus stop nearby," he lied. "You can pick up a ride from there to Lone Creek."

She looked out as another elderly pickup truck passed them. "This Lone Creek place—they've surpassed the telegraph there, I take it?"

His mouth curled. "Yeah. They have indoor flush toilets, too."

"Excellent. Drop me off at the bus stop, if you would." She sat back, as if it were all settled.

He was tempted to ride her directly into town and dump her off at the first phone booth. She could call whomever she wanted, and even buy herself a bus ticket to Helena. But that would throw a wrench into Kalen's plans.

"Put your seat belt on," he said, and headed for Sun Valley.

Neal didn't realize anything was wrong at first. It was enough to be inside the warm truck and headed toward freedom.

Snowcapped mountain ranges rose along both sides of the horizon—bigger and broader than anything she'd seen back in Colorado. Open pasture stretched for miles in every direction, edged with dense swaths of lodgepole pine. There were no telephone poles or electric wires, no speed-limit signs, only weathered wood-post fencing stretched with endless miles of barbed wire, and drainage ditches that ran down both sides of the highway. Wildflowers were growing around the dwindling patches of snow.

She'd been in worse spots before.

If only she weren't so tired and cold and scared. If only she could speak to her uncle and explain things. If only she'd been able to convince the suits to take her back to Denver.

But J. R. was out of jail, back in the street, and knew she was the state's key witness.

So he knows. So what? I can find a way to avoid him.

Her baby sister's chuckle echoed in her mind. *Mother of God, Neal, sometimes I think you'd rather throw yourself in front of a moving truck than admit when you're beat.*

Meeting Will Ryder had been like getting hit by a truck. Or the Incredible Hulk. Neal stood five-feet-ten in stockings, but Ryder had at least seven or eight inches on her. It must have come from whatever Scandinavian blood he had, along with the pale eyes and nearly white hair. But instead of the fair skin that naturally went with his coloring, he had the deep tan that came from years of working outdoors.

Then there was that body of his. Big. Muscular. Not a single ounce of fat on him. Roof-beam shoulders over a weight lifter's chest, tapering down to a flat abdomen and long, tree-trunk thighs. The kind of build that made women sigh, and other men wear off molar enamel.

She glanced at him as she recalled her first impression: *Jesus, is that a Viking? In a cowboy hat?*

Sitting behind the wheel of his truck, he'd looked impressive. Up close he was absolutely intimidating— he towered over her, dwarfed her. She'd never felt that kind of physical impact. It made her want to turn and run as far and as fast as she could.

And the way he'd looked at her, after he'd gotten her car off the road . . . His face had lost all expression, and his eyes had narrowed. Behind that intense focus was something powerful, something he kept on a very short, tight leash. And for a moment there, she wondered if the leash would hold.

Maybe there's a little Viking in that cowboy, anyway.

Her mother hadn't liked blonds for some reason, which was why Laney was a redhead and Neala a brunette. *Italian sax player,* Bridget had said once when Neal had demanded to know more about her absentee father. *Blood as hot as his temper. Just like you, Neal.*

Still, even Bridget Arlen would have appreciated a man put together like Ryder.

Neal, on the other hand, wasn't too sure what to make of Will Ryder. Who had left the message about picking her up? Abbott and Costello? What else had they told him?

"So why the dress?" Will said suddenly.

"I left my favorite goose-down caftan back in Denver."

"Truthfully, why are you wearing it?"

"Truthfully?" He nodded. The poor man simply didn't know who he was dealing with. Then she found herself telling him the truth. "Agent Selbrook doesn't like it. Have you ever met Agent Selbrook?"

"No."

"Lucky you. He buys my clothes, and his idea of high fashion would offend a bag lady."

"I don't think much of high fashion myself," he said. "You always dress to aggravate men?"

"Occupational hazard," she said, and laughed in spite of herself. "Don't tell me you have something against red."

"Only if the person wearing it is turning blue."

Neal sighed. "Point taken."

She glanced at the hand he had resting on the top of the steering wheel. There were calluses on his palms and innumerable small scars on his fingers. No wedding ring, and no light band of skin to indicate a recent vacancy in the bedroom. His fingernails were clean and trimmed, but one had recently been torn down to the quick. "Ranching must be a lot of work."

He grunted. "It pays the bills."

They passed by a pasture dotted with slow-moving, black-and-white animals grazing on mounds of hay in the snow. Just as she'd suspected. Cowsicles. "How many cows do you own?"

"Cattle, not cows. At last count, four thousand, two hundred and thirty-three head. We probably lost ten or fifteen to the last storm."

She tilted her head to one side and considered the cattle in the pasture. "How do you lose something that big? Wait—you mean they're dead?"

"Yeah. Winters are hard here." Grim lines formed on either side of his mouth. "We sometimes lose five to ten percent of the stock to bad weather."

She might not know anything about ranching, but she knew how much she had to pay for filet mignon at the market. "That must really hit you in the wallet."

"It's not the money. They're *my* animals." He made it sound like he had four thousand–plus oversize pets. "I don't like losing what's mine."

Not a very modern attitude, and still she liked him better for it.

"Couldn't you put them in a barn or something?" He laughed, and she turned away from the window. "What?"

"Lady, ten barns wouldn't be big enough to hold my herds. Besides, they're range animals; they'd rather be outside."

That meant that somewhere around here there were four thousand cows—no, cattle—wandering around. One more reason for her to check into the nearest Marriott. She peered through the windshield at the empty highway ahead of them. "Are we almost there?"

He didn't look at her. "Just about."

A few minutes later, Ryder slowed down and made a right turn onto a small dirt road leading off the highway. Neal scanned the cluster of buildings in the distance.

"What's that?"

The side of Ryder's mouth curled. "A ranch."

"Not much to look at, is it?" Neal tried to sound bored, while her heart nearly jumped out of her chest. Where there were buildings, there were people—and telephones. She might not have to resort to a bus ride after all.

No reason to mention that to Ryder, though.

As they got closer, she saw no signs of people or telephones. There was plenty of fencing—it lined both sides of the narrow road. It sagged in some places, with posts pulled out of the ground and coils of barbed wire hanging where it had snapped. The road led directly up to what looked like a huge garden gate, minus the white pickets.

"You people always put fences and gates around your ranches?"

"Lady, this is Montana. We put fences around everything." Will stopped the truck, got out, and opened her door for her. "This is where you get out."

Reluctantly she took his hand and climbed down. A quick glance didn't reveal any benches or bus stop signs. "Are you sure this is the right place? I don't see any signs."

"Sign's up there." Will pointed up as he went around the front end and climbed back in behind the wheel. "You can walk the rest of the way to the house. I'll stop by to see you tonight."

"The house?" Neal stood and watched as the cattle rancher reversed, then drove back toward the highway. "See me tonight? But I'm not going to . . ."

An ominous feeling settled over her as she looked up to where Ryder had pointed. The sagging sign above the gate was so weather-worn and faded that it took a moment to make out the lettering.

SUN VALLEY RANCH.

In a soft, lethal voice, Neal began to call Will Ryder every filthy name she could think of.

Chapter 2

Two thousand miles away, army CID Colonel Sean Delaney knocked over his crutches and a Styrofoam cup of coffee as he reached across a desk to grab General Kalen Grady by the lapels.

"You did what?"

Grady locked his hands around Sean's wrists. "I had Neal moved to Lone Creek. Let go and we'll talk about it."

"Talk about you using my family as bait?" The big Irishman shook him off. "After what happened with Laney, I told you, never again."

"Laney drew Tremayne down from the ridge and confirmed for us that he was still alive. You know we had to have his testimony to prosecute the Shandian executives involved in the Dream Mountain operation." Grady calmly mopped up the mess, then sat back in his chair. "All Laney did was provide a necessary distraction for Tremayne until we could wrap up our investigation."

"And what's Neal supposed to provide for you, Grady? A big bull's-eye for the Chinese?"

"The Chinese don't know where she is. Besides, she'll have protection twenty-four hours a day."

"You know how Shandian operates. She'll be a sitting duck twenty-four hours a day." Sean ignored the crutches and limped back and forth across the room, one big hand pressed against the back of his neck.

"Why are you doing this? She's willing to testify at the trial. All you have to do is pick up the gammy son of a bitch, put him in jail, and throw away the key."

"I would, but J. R.'s jumped bail."

Sean stopped pacing. "What?"

"Gone. Went to ground an hour after they released him on a million-dollar bond."

"So that's what you're doing—using Neal to draw him out into the open. The same way you used Laney to flush Tremayne." Sean shouldn't have been surprised. He knew Kalen, knew how his boss's mind worked. "Did you call one of Martin's knee-breakers yourself, General? Tell them where to find her?"

"Not yet. Now let's talk about our friends in the tong. In spite of the fact that they're unhappy with J. R. for killing Senator Colfax, they're more concerned with reclaiming what T'ang Po's son smuggled out of China. Did your contact get the goods from him?"

The irony of the situation wasn't lost on Sean. He was supposed to have what the CID most wanted, when the truth of it was sitting right under their bureaucratic noses with Neal. "Ah, so now you're wanting something from me."

Grady folded his hands. "I want Shandian."

"So do I. And my niece back in one piece." Sean paused. "Surely we can work this out to our mutual benefit."

The general's face lost all expression. "Don't try horse-trading with me, Irish. Not unless you want to be court-martialed before those retirement papers go through."

Sean sighed. It had been worth a try. "You'll get the goods."

"You have them in your possession?"

"Not yet." If Grady knew where they were, he might just forgo the trial and shove Sean in front of a firing squad. "Soon."

"The attorney general wants those indictments. I can't count on J. R. until we get him back in custody and work a deal. Colfax's wife has been missing since the night of the murder. T'ang's front man is plugging holes faster than I can make them." Kalen ran a tired hand through his dark red hair, then gave his most experienced field operative an unsmiling look. "Get me the goods, Sean."

"Fine." Sean picked up his crutches and used them to get to the door. "Like I said, you'll have them soon."

"Where are you going?"

"I'm on medical leave, remember?" Sean patted his thigh, which had already healed. "Old fart like me needs to spend time with pretty, young physical therapists, not chasing Chinese thugs. I'll see you next Monday."

Grady made a call as soon as Sean left. "Put a man on Delaney. Now. Twenty-four-seven . . . I don't care about the medical leave; he's faking it. . . . Yeah. Probably so he can go after the girl. I want reports every six hours. And let me know the minute he leaves the city."

Neal continued to swear until the sound of the big pickup had faded away.

Jerk. He'd never intended to take her to a bus stop for a second, and yet he'd never said a word. She looked around at the emptiness, and shivered. At least he'd left her with his parka for the long walk up to the ranch house.

"The hell with you, Ryder," she said under her breath as she adjusted her grip on the suitcase handle. "I don't need you to get out of this mess. I don't need anyone."

Neala went up to the sagging wooden gate. She would have kicked it open, but her feet were too numb. Fumbling with the unfamiliar latch on the gate made her break two nails and use more bad words. As soon as she got the wretched thing open, she heard an engine and saw another pickup truck hurtling down the drive, straight at her.

Doesn't anyone drive a four-door sedan around here? How do I stop him? Of course. Neal picked up her suitcase, then calmly shoved the gate shut and latched it. *I think I'm getting the hang of this place already.*

The driver hit the brakes, sending twin fountains of dirty slush into the air on the other side of the fence. The front end came to a shuddering stop a few inches from the gate. A sour face under a filthy straw hat popped out of the driver's-side window.

"Open the gate and get out of my way, woman!"

"No, I won't." Neal walked over and planted herself in front of the gate. "You work here?"

"Not anymore." The old man spit a stream of brown tobacco juice on the ground. "Sum' bitch boots my boy for a little harmless hell-raising, no way *I'm* gonna keep working for him." He shifted the truck into gear. "Now open that gate, and move your fancy ass!"

The head disappeared, the truck backed up, and the engine revved.

If he busts this thing down, I'll probably end up paying for it.

Neal tugged the gate open, stepped aside, and watched as the truck roared past her. The old man took a hard right and drove off in the direction she'd walked from.

Oh, damn, why didn't I ask him for a ride?

She was briefly tempted to sling her suitcase after him, but decided all she had the energy left for was getting warm and getting something to drink.

"Two jerks in a row. Being an ass must be some kind of residency requirement."

There was a big house at the end of the drive—big and old and somewhat neglected. In fact, the closer she got as she walked, the less welcoming the house looked. The exterior badly needed a new paint job, and there were more weeds sprouting from the muddy snow than anything else. Grime clouded every window, and the front porch screen was torn in several places.

"It'll be nicer inside," Neal said, hoping the genie of nightclub-singer wishes was listening. She climbed up to the porch and went in.

It was silent and dark inside, and the light switch beside the front door didn't work. Gaps in the curtains allowed some dim sunshine in, enough to see the interior. Comfortable furniture and an entertainment center decorated the front room, but conspicuously absent was a television set.

Whoever lived in the house didn't cook, judging by the hoard of open take-out food containers jumbled on the coffee table. At the sound of her footsteps, a couple of roaches crawled back into a half-open pizza box.

"House pets." She wrinkled her nose. "How charming."

The smell of neglect permeated the chilly interior. It was a shame no one had bothered to dust the beautiful oak furniture and vacuum up the dirt from the plush carpeting. She walked back through the house, noting the sad condition of the draperies covering the grimy windows. The formal dining room table had a swatch of blue canvas covering it, upon which used car parts and a healthy amount of black grease had been spread.

Is this a house or a garage with nice furniture? Maybe the kitchen will be in better shape.

It wasn't. The kitchen table was covered with dirty plates and partially full coffee mugs, stacks of old, unread newspapers, and unopened mail. Grease and food splatters marred the beautiful hardwood floor. Used pots and pans cluttered the counters. She couldn't see the sink, but she assumed it was under the towering pile of more filthy dishes. The cabinets were empty except for some boxes of breakfast cereal.

Somewhere behind her, an unseen small body bumped into something, then squealed and scurried away.

Neal slowly turned in a full circle. "Stay here? For two months? I don't *think* so."

As she searched for the phone, she bumped the table, sending a stack of newspapers to the floor. When she automatically bent down to pick them up, a spider as big as her hand raced out and jumped on her shoe. She screamed, kicked it and both shoes off, and ended up on top of the kitchen table, hyperventilating.

"Get away from me! Get!"

The spider slowly crawled back under the papers.

Once her hands stopped shaking, she pulled her lucky coin out from her purse and flipped it.

"Heads I stay, tails I go."

It landed on tails, proving there *was* a God. It was decided, then. She'd get a drink of water, change her clothes, make her phone call to Sean, order a taxi, and then get the hell out of Dodge.

"Mr. T'ang?"

He had not gotten used to being addressed in English, and it took T'ang Yin a moment to compose the appropriate reply before he punched the intercom button.

"What is it?"

The young American girl he'd hired as his personal secretary responded quickly. "Two gentlemen from the Denver office are waiting to see you, sir. They won't give me their names, though." She sounded vaguely uncomfortable.

T'ang's wife, Kuei-fei, arched her smooth brows. "This one is even stupider than I thought, husband."

Since his wife had spoken in Chinese, T'ang wasn't

worried about the girl taking offense. "Send them in, Miss Watkins."

T'ang Yin had been in his new position as director of the Shandian Corporation for less than a week, so he felt it prudent to remain on his guard. He had not wanted this job in the first place. The organization was in a shambles, still reeling from the debacles caused by his two predecessors, Chang Yu-Wei and Fai Shuzhi.

Chang Yu-Wei had brought a multitude of disgraces upon himself, first by fumbling the acquisition of the SOAR biocomputer prototype, then attempting to swindle two governments into buying what he himself did not possess. As a result, an important party member had been forced to commit suicide.

Fai Shuzhi had done little better. Although he had founded a new alliance between the tong and the leaders of a Middle East extremist group, his nephew's bungling of the ore-smuggling operation and the revelation of the bogus "rhodium strike" at the Dream Mountain mine had seriously damaged the fledgling Chinese space program. Thanks to Fai Shuzhi's ineptitude, millions in lost materials and design setbacks had shut down the launch of a covert surveillance orbiter.

It was no surprise T'ang Yin wanted no part of Shandian. Only an appeal to his honor from the head of the tong had finally swayed him.

"Greed will not infect you, my nephew," T'ang Po had stated. "Nor will limited vision. You are the only man I trust to rebuild what has been so imprudently squandered. Consider my offer carefully. You can retrieve the honor that has been taken from us. Make Shandian strong again."

He agreed to meditate on the matter, and once home had presented his dilemma to Kuei-fei.

"Po is testing you," his wife had said. "He does this by placing you in a position where two others have failed. He does not wish to risk his son, Jian-Shan, of course."

T'ang was sorry he had reminded her of the great

bitterness in her life, and moved to comfort her. She allowed his embrace for a short time, then stepped out of his arms.

"Perhaps we can use Shandian to our advantage. I do not care to relocate to America, but it is a minor annoyance. I would advise you to accept, my husband."

As always, T'ang had followed Kuei-fei's advice.

The two men who entered his office bowed at once. One closed the door and secured the lock, while the other offered an anonymous-looking briefcase.

"You have acquired the tape?" T'ang asked in their native language, and waited only for the nod before opening the case and removing the VHS cassette. "Play it for me." He handed it to one of the men.

The man eyed Kuei-fei, who sat in a graceful pose on a chair beside her husband's desk. "Now, sir?"

"Yes." T'ang took out a dozen black-and-white photographs. "These are of the crime scene?"

"Yes, Director."

He studied the various shots of the dead man, then handed them to Kuei-fei. However, it was the security tape that proved most startling. It showed some fifteen minutes of the empty interior of the U.S. senator's suite. He fast-forwarded it to the point when a woman in a beautiful red dress entered. Newspaper photos didn't do Neala Delaney justice, he thought, and watched her disappear into a bedroom. The senator's blond wife, Karen Colfax, soon followed. Both women appeared together a moment later, standing and talking just inside the bedroom door. They abruptly vanished just before Senator Colfax and J. R. Martin entered the suite. The two men spoke, then argued. Martin subsequently smashed the lens of the camera. T'ang rewound the tape to the beginning, then paused it at the point when Neala Delaney entered the room.

She was darkly beautiful, he thought, studying her tall, voluptuous form. The type of woman a man bought and kept for himself, but only with a great deal of money. Slowly he advanced the tape, and made note of her specific movements. She appeared to be nervous, judging from her facial expression, as she searched the suite.

"Who is she?" Kuei-fei leaned close. "The senator's mistress?"

"Neala Delaney," the man said. "She is employed by Shandian—indirectly. I believe she is a singer in one of J. R. Martin's nightclubs."

T'ang watched Neala as she went back into the bedroom. He doubted Colfax would risk giving even his most favored mistress a key when his wife was staying at the hotel with him. "How did she get in?"

"We do not know, Director. She was present when the police arrived, and claimed Martin killed the senator."

T'ang watched as Karen Colfax entered, and saw that she, too, was visibly nervous. When both women appeared together, all they seemed to be doing was talking. A pity there was no sound on the tape. "She may be a friend of the senator's wife."

"I do not think that is the case, my husband. Colfax was part of the extreme conservative right. He would not allow his wife to associate with such a person," Kuei-fei said.

He gave his wife an approving nod before addressing the men once more. "Where is the Delaney woman now?"

"According to our information, the FBI have her in custody and have placed her in the Federal Witness Protection Program." Another file was handed over. "From our contact in Washington."

"I see." T'ang put the folder aside. "And the senator's wife?"

"We have no information on her whereabouts, Director, but the woman's family has filed a missing-persons report."

Kuei-fei rose and went over to the VCR to stop the tape, and gave him a significant look.

"That will be all," he said to the men. "You may go."

"Should we pursue the Delaney woman, Director?"

T'ang shook his head. "I will contact you when you are needed."

Kuei-fei waited until they departed before she secured the door and replayed the tape. She stopped it at the precise point when Neal entered the suite. "She could be working for the Americans as a courier. Dressed as she is, no one would question her presence."

"She could be working for the Irishman," T'ang conceded. "He used another woman before—at Dream Mountain."

"The Americans are trying to manipulate J. R. Martin. We must find this woman." His wife regarded the screen for a moment. "I think you should call Po at once, Yin."

T'ang Yin placed the overseas call immediately. It was the middle of the night in China, but he made no apology to the tong leader as he explained the situation.

"Do you know where the FBI has taken her, Yin?"

"According to our contact, she was moved to"— T'ang Yin flipped through the file, then paused as he recognized the name—"Lone Creek."

Po gave a brief, dry laugh. "The plot within the plot unfolds."

Yin thought quickly. "Since one of our operatives is already in place, I will make the proper arrangements at once."

"Excellent. Eliminate her so that she poses no further risk to our friend Mr. Martin. Keep me informed of your progress."

Kuei-fei smiled at her husband as he ended the call, and hung up the extension phone she had been listening on. "You did well. But we must not have the woman killed. Not yet."

"No, not until we know why she was speaking to

the senator's wife." T'ang rewound the tape to watch it again. "Then she dies."

After two hours, Neal sat down on the dusty sofa in the front room. She would have cried, but she was too cold and too dehydrated.

Calling her new accommodations *spartan* would be flattering. There was no electricity. The phone was dead. Everything was covered with dust. The bathroom had been left in a vile state.

Neal had grown up poor. She could live without room service. She could clean up the kitchen and the bathroom—maybe. With some supplies, she could even stay here and put up with the loneliness, the emptiness, the isolation.

What infuriated her was the simple fact that she couldn't get herself a drink of water.

She'd tried. None of the sinks worked. The refrigerator was empty. It didn't make sense—she'd seen abandoned cups of coffee everywhere. If you wanted to make coffee, you needed water. Then she'd spotted the old-fashioned hand pump in the kitchen.

She'd grabbed the handle and started working it up and down. And up and down. And up and down. It rattled. It screeched. It moaned. It did everything but produce a single drop of water.

And the harder Neal worked, the thirstier she got.

"It's just because I *can't* have a drink," she said out loud, and pounded the sofa cushions with her fists. Dust rose around her in a faint cloud, making her sneeze. "Okay, maybe it's the lack of HEPA filters, too."

She became so thirsty that she went back into the kitchen and gave the pump another try.

"This can't be happening to me," she said ten minutes later, and let the handle drop with a clang. She'd clutched it so hard her palms felt bruised. "All right, think, stupid. It's a ranch. Ranches have cows and chickens and pigs and stuff. Cows and chickens and pigs need water. All I have to do is find them."

She looked through the window at the empty, dead-looking pasture behind the house. A long shadow came from another, separate structure beyond the side walls.

Will Ryder had told her his cattle were kept out on the range, but she'd bet pigs and chickens preferred indoor accommodations.

She forgot how cold she was as she headed for the back door—which, she discovered, was blocked by two bulging plastic bags. Something had been gnawing at them, too, judging by the small, ragged holes weeping bits of garbage.

"Jesus." Gingerly she stepped over them. "Doesn't this guy believe in garbage pickup? Or exterminators? Or the bubonic plague?"

It took a few minutes to pick her way through the slushy mud at the back of the house over to the barn. A dusty bale of hay propped the door open.

"The things I do for my country." Neal lifted her skirt and climbed over the bale. The sharp ends of the hay scratched her hands and arms, and she swore. "To think I used to *want* to go on hayrides."

The interior of the barn was dark, crisp, and pungent. Neal's nose wrinkled as she waved a hand to ward off the smell and a couple of flies.

"Whew, yes, definitely some cows and chickens and pigs in here."

As she stepped off the edge of the bale, her foot caught a pole of some kind and sent it flying. The resulting clatter of metal on more metal made a tremendous crash. Neal staggered back, both hands out, and ran smack into something big.

The something big smacked her back, square in the shoulder, with something cold, sharp, and toothy.

"Oh." She turned and saw an enormous rake swinging from a rafter hook. "I hope they don't expect me to maintain the yard."

Something made a huge, horrible noise, bellowing practically in her ear, and Neal fell to her knees, covering her head with both arms.

"Okay! Okay! I'll rake leaves!"

Something snorted. She got up and peered through the darkness. The glittery shine of a single eye winked at her.

"Nice monster. Good monster." She put down both hands to push herself off the ground. "I'll just be going back to the house now."

There was a shuffling sound, and the eye drew a little closer. Neal froze, feeling a waft of damp, warm breath pass by her cheek. Then something tugged at her hair and tried to pull a handful of it out of her scalp.

"Hey. Cut it out!" This thing might be bent on eating her, but nobody messed with her hair. She flung a hand up and promptly got nipped. "Ouch! Knock it off; I'm not a chew toy!"

As she stumbled to her feet, her eyes finally adjusted to the darkness, and she recognized the outline of the head in front of her. "Hi, there. Good cow. Nice cow."

The not-so-nice cow tossed its huge head and released another disagreeable bellow. In no way, shape, or form did it even resemble *moo*. It shuffled past her and knocked into one of the stall doors.

"How did you get in here? You climb over that nasty hay, too?" Neal crawled backward on her hands and feet until there was a foot of dirty straw between her and the cow. "I don't suppose you know where there's some water, do you?"

The sound of her voice made the cow turn its head and twitch its ears. It huffed at her, then banged into the door again.

"Never mind." She scrambled to her feet. "I'll find it myself."

Other than the cow, which appeared to have wandered in from the range it was supposed to be happy living on, the barn was completely deserted. As she checked each empty stall to be sure there were no more surprises waiting for her, the cow continued to batter the one stall door.

"What's in there that's got you so excited?" Neal went over to the stall and gave the evil-eyed bovine tank what she hoped was a friendly smile. "A stash of Evian, perhaps?"

Elsie's broad pink tongue emerged and swept over her nose before she opened her mouth and made another angry, non-mooing sound.

"Whoa. Excuse me." Neal reached over and unlocked the door latch. "Forget I asked." She watched as the cow entered the stall, and immediately plunged its face into a trough. There must have been something to eat in the bottom of it, because Elsie arched her head back up and began to chew. "Save some for me, will you? The grass doesn't look too appetizing."

While the cow was occupied, she took a quick look around. There was another black iron pump, a little bigger than the one in the kitchen, standing on a small raised platform at the back of the barn. This one had a tin pail sitting under its spout.

Water?

Afraid to hope, Neal tiptoed toward the pump. Elsie stopped chewing and bellowed again. Maybe the bad-tempered cow was as thirsty as she was.

"Keep your pants on. I mean, your hide on. I get a drink first; then you can have some."

There was no water in the empty pail, but she saw a single drop clinging to the open end of the pump. Eagerly she seized the handle and worked it up and down.

A clear stream gushed from the pump.

"Eureka!"

She pushed the tin pail aside and bent to plunge her face under the pump, letting the stream of water pour over her chin and cheeks and fill her mouth. She could feel it erasing her makeup, but quenching her thirst definitely outranked maintaining her personal appearance.

"Ahhhh." She closed her eyes as she drew back and swallowed with delicious greed. Who needed makeup out here, anyway? "Now, that's more like it." She went back for more.

The water supply dwindled for a moment, until she groped blindly for the handle with one hand and started pumping again. The water was ice-cold, and had a slight mineral taste to it, but Neal thought it was far superior to the best brands of bottled water. The straw and dirt under the spout quickly became a mud puddle. Finally she'd had enough to take the edge off her voracious thirst, and she filled the bucket.

Elsie promptly showed up to claim her share.

"Help yourself." Neal stepped out of the way and wiped the water from her face, then laughed as the cow snorted and drank. "Okay, we'll make that *your* bucket."

She noticed a bright yellow plastic tag someone had punched through Elsie's ear and bent to read it. There was a number—745—and the letter *S*. The only other marks she saw were a couple of shiny scars on the cow's left shoulder, which looked like a *D* stacked on top of an *L*.

Neal glanced through the barn door. "Are there seven hundred and forty-four more of you wandering around out there?"

When she was finished drinking, Elsie began nibbling at the dirty straw beside the pump.

"Yuck, no, honey, don't eat that stuff. I'll get you something else." Neal knew she couldn't feed the cow canned beans and pickle relish. The sad-looking dead grass out in the pasture beyond the barn looked unappetizing. There was nothing else edible around.

"What is it, exactly, that you eat?" Neal tried to remember what was on the labels in the supermarket. *Beef, sirloin, maverick . . . grain-fed*. She slapped her palm against her forehead. "Grain! You want some grain, right?"

Elsie whuffed out a breath, scattering some of the straw.

"Sounds like a yes to me."

There was no grain to be had in the barn, so Neal made a trip to the kitchen and brought back an armful of the cereal boxes she'd found in the cabinet.

"What do you think?" she said, and showed Elsie the cereal. The cow nosed the box she held out. "I don't know if this is your brand, but let's give it a shot." Carefully she poured out a handful. "Taste-test time," she said, and held out her hand. The cow eagerly lipped her palm and started chewing. "Good? Great." She went into the stall, tipped the container, and poured more into the bin that seemed to be for that purpose. "Here you go, honey."

Elsie followed her into the stall and went right to the bin. Neal stood watching her eat for a moment, and felt ridiculously pleased with herself for figuring it out.

"Just don't get used to me being your waitress, okay? I'm outta here, as soon as Ryder gets back."

The cow lifted her head and stared at Neal as she chewed. She didn't look too convinced.

Chapter 3

Will heard about the federal agents whose car Neala Delaney had "borrowed" soon after he arrived in Lone Creek. One of the truckers he knew caught up with him at the feed store, and relayed a message from the two stranded strangers he'd brought into town.

"They was looking to find you, Mr. Ryder. I left 'em over at Molly's 'bout an hour ago."

Will signed the invoice for the shipment of mineral supplement he'd ordered, and handed it back to the clerk. "They mention anything to you about their car?"

"No, sir, though they did put in a call to a rental place on one of their cell phones. Having a car delivered direct to Molly's this morning, from what I heard."

If Neala Delaney had stolen their car, they wouldn't be able to report it without getting the county sheriff involved. But why were they waiting on him? Will nodded to the trucker as he headed out of the feed store. "Thanks, Joe."

The federal agents were still at Molly's Diner when Will walked in a few minutes later. Both men sat in a booth by the front windows, drinking coffee and finishing up the remnants of two hearty meals. As if they hadn't a care in the world.

What had Neala called them? Dumb and Dumber?

"Agent Selbrook?" At the nod, Will unclenched a fist long enough to shake the suit's hand. "Will Ryder, from High Point."

"Wayne Selbrook. Have a seat, Mr. Ryder." He gestured to the other agent. "This is my partner, Bruce Bowers."

Molly brought over the coffeepot and a mug for Will. The middle-aged woman's dark-tinted, oversize glasses glinted as she eyed the two agents with open curiosity. "You want the usual, Will?"

"Coffee's fine, thanks, Molly." He waited until the woman had served him and returned behind the counter before addressing Selbrook. "Heard you ran into some trouble out at the truck stop."

"Nothing we couldn't handle," Bowers said.

"I see." Will looked from one man to the other. "Where's the girl?"

"She's, uh, trying to escape," Selbrook said, and drained his mug.

Bowers chuckled as he wiped his mouth with his napkin. "Not for long."

Will sat back. "You two don't appear to be real concerned about it. Why aren't you out rounding her up?"

"We needed a break, so we let her steal our car." Bower grinned and loosened his belt. "No big thing. She'll run out of gas on the highway."

"What if she decides to go from there on foot?"

"Even this broad's not that stupid, but if she does"—Bowers shrugged—"maybe walking will help her cool off."

"Alone? In this weather?" Will regarded both men through a faint red haze. "This how you usually handle your star government witnesses?"

Bower started to say more, but a glance at Selbrook shut him up. To Will, Selbrook said, "She's a bit resistant to the idea of staying at your ranch, Mr. Ryder. We thought we'd teach her a lesson, you know, give her a little scare."

"After listening to her whine all morning about wanting to stay at a hotel, she deserves that and then some," Bower said, and shoveled a forkful of eggs into his mouth. "I've been hard-pressed not to knock her on her tight little ass since we got this assignment."

"That so?" Will didn't think much of men who used their fists on women. What he did think of were the three hitchhikers who had been found murdered out by that particular stretch of highway over the last two years. All young. All women. All alone. "Why did she give you boys a hard time about staying at my ranch?"

"You know how these high-maintenance women are." Bowers waved his fork in an expansive gesture. "Nothing makes them happy—and I mean *nothing*. She started in on us about this place from the minute we landed at Big Timber. Wanted us to take her back to Denver. Said she couldn't stay in a place where the water comes out of the taps in cubes."

Both of the agents laughed at that; then Selbrook noticed Will's expression and cleared his throat. "Did General Grady brief you about where to take it from here?"

"Yeah, he told me." Will finished his coffee. "I don't care much for this."

"There's no real danger involved. The general is more concerned with keeping her on ice until the trial. Besides, she's pretty tough; she can take care of herself."

Will didn't express his feelings on that subject. Someone's nose or jaw would end up broken in the process. "What about you two?"

Bower drained his glass of orange juice, and muffled a belch. "As soon as we turn her over to you, we'll be heading back to Denver. All you have to do is make sure she stays put until we need her in court."

"Doesn't look like she enjoys staying put, now, does it?"

"We'll be finished here in a few minutes and go

round her up as soon as our car is delivered," Selbrook assured him.

"Don't waste your time. I already picked her up and took her to Sun Valley." He got to his feet. "You two are leaving, right? Going back to Denver?"

"Yeah, that's pretty much it for us," Bowers said, sounding surprised. "Why?"

Will grabbed the heavy man's tight shirt collar, cutting off his oxygen, then jerked him close. "I don't like idiots who treat defenseless women like stray dogs." He released the purple-faced agent, then dropped a couple of bills on the table. "Now get out of my town."

"You stay put, Elsie."

After she latched the door on Elsie's stall, Neal checked her watch. It was only ten A.M. Ryder wouldn't be back for hours. The only thing with wheels on the property was an ancient tractor, and that had a gutted motor and two flat tires.

What if he doesn't come back?

Neal stalked back up to the ranch house. She'd drive herself crazy waiting for him to show up. She might as well make the place habitable for one night, just in case he didn't.

Thank God for Agent Selbrook's lack of fashion sense, she thought as she traded her expensive cocktail dress for some of the bag-lady clothes he'd bought her.

After she changed into clothes suitable for the task, a determined search turned up a few rags, some pine cleaner, and a welcome can of insecticide. Getting the entire house back in shape would take a few days, so she chose the tidiest of the four bedrooms and concentrated her efforts there.

"If all else fails, I'll go sleep with Elsie."

By the time she'd swept the floor, killed a few roaches, stripped the bed of its musty, unused linens, and opened the windows to air the room out, she was starving.

"This is cattle country, right? So I should get filet mignon for dinner," she promised herself as she lugged the garbage bags out of the kitchen and shoved them into a huge dumpster on one side of the barn. "With new potatoes and baby asparagus. And a slice of chocolate cake."

But she couldn't eat until she bathed; she was that dirty. That meant dealing with the bathroom.

Neal cautiously looked around the door, and winced. It appeared the last time the facilities had been cleaned was sometime during the first Bush administration. Whatever male had used it since then— the old man?—had lousy aim, too.

"Two slices of chocolate cake. And a vanilla cappuccino."

Stoically she gathered her hair into a ponytail, armed herself with more disinfectant, and marched in.

"I can't believe I'm doing this," she muttered as she scrubbed. "This is the reason I never got married. This is the reason God invented cleaning services. And shotguns. And convents."

The porcelain tub's taps didn't work, but it was in slightly better shape. Doubtless because it had rarely been used. What that said about the old man made her shudder.

"Well, one thing's for sure," she said as she removed the final rings from the inside of the tub. "He'll probably bump into some soap one day, and die from an instant allergic reaction."

Only when the rest of the bathroom was thoroughly clean did she haul several buckets of water from the barn to dump into the tub for her bath. She found a reasonably clean supply of towels in one of the hall closets, and took two with her into the bath.

Her now-filthy T-shirt, shorts, and panties landed on top of her ruined dress. Neal eyed them as she stepped into the tub and sat down in the six inches of water.

Ice-cold water.

"Yiiiiiiiikes!" She jumped back up, then gingerly lowered herself, hissing in her breath. "Heavenly Father, what did I ever do to you?"

The Almighty didn't answer, which was a good thing. Neal was covered in goose bumps, shaking, and ready to go to hell just to get warmed up.

"No w-w-washing m-m-machine or d-d-dryer." Her teeth chattered as she put the bar of hand-milled French soap she'd retrieved from her case to swift use. "H-H-How do th-th-they expect m-m-me to do m-m-my laundry? On a r-r-rock in the r-r-r-river?"

The makeshift bath was frigid, but did a lot to make her feel better. She thoroughly rinsed out her hair, soaped herself, and scrubbed the hay scratches on her hands and arms. She stood and used the last bucket of water to rinse herself clean. She was too cold to talk, even to herself, until she dried off and dressed in her warmest clothes.

The reflection in the medicine cabinet's mirrored door didn't make her feel better, but at least she was clean and didn't smell like Elsie anymore. "Food. I need food."

Neal opened the windows in the kitchen before raiding the cabinets. They were completely empty, but while checking them she came across an odd sort of stone closet stocked with nonperishable provisions.

She scanned the available edibles, and groaned. "No steak?"

Neal found an ample amount of canned goods, mostly vegetables, more containers of oatmeal, and a few mason jars with handwritten labels. After she located a handheld opener, she grabbed a can of green beans and a jar of what appeared to be homemade pickles, and took her impromptu feast into her bedroom.

"I want filet mignon. I *deserve* filet mignon," she muttered as she sat on the clean floor beside the bed and dug a spoon into the cold beans. "They're going to be very sorry they did this to me. Soon as I get to a phone, I'm calling *Sixty Minutes,* then the *National Enquirer,* then Kenneth Starr."

Once she'd filled her stomach and cleaned up the remains of her meal, sore muscles and utter exhaustion drove her back to bed. As she dropped onto the stripped mattress, she pulled her coat over herself and fell into an immediate, dreamless sleep.

Wendy Lewis sat at her vanity, putting on a scant amount of makeup. As she did, she examined her reflection at the same time, looking for signs of a blemish.

There weren't any. There never were. But she still looked, every time, in every mirror.

She had her mother to thank for her flawless complexion and golden blond hair. Her grandmother had passed along her model-perfect body and light blue eyes. Jealous girls in school had sometimes called her Barbie, and although it infuriated Wendy, it was true—she looked almost exactly like the famous doll.

Her father certainly treated her like a doll, to be dressed up and posed and cherished. Only no one was allowed to play with her.

She occasionally wondered what her life would be like if she weren't so attractive. She certainly wouldn't have had it so easy in school. She suspected the judges at the various equestrian tourneys she entered might not have paid as much attention to her and Starlight if she were a plain girl. Her beauty had done a lot for her. It was going to take her places other girls only dreamed about.

She felt rather smug as she looked up at the long shelf of trophies and ribbons she'd won over the years. Most were for beauty contests and the contests she'd won riding Starlight. There was her favorite photograph, too—the one with her and Will and her father at last year's county rodeo. No, she was a very lucky girl, and truly couldn't wish for anything more.

She stared at the familiar, grinning face in the photograph, and sighed. *Well, maybe one thing.*

The door to her bedroom opened, and her father stepped in. "Honey? You done primping yet? Our dinner reservations are for five."

"Yes, Daddy." Feeling guilty for keeping him waiting, she rose and made a small twirl. The skirt of the pastel silk dress she wore flared out, revealing her shapely legs. "How do I look?"

"Sheer perfection, as always." Short, stocky, and graying, Dean Lewis still carried himself with the confidence of a young man. He came over and pressed a kiss on her brow. "Pink's definitely your color. I swear, you put your momma's prize tulips to shame."

Later, as they drove into town, Dean Lewis patted her hand. "You have time to come work at the office tomorrow?"

"Sure, Daddy. My next competition isn't for a week." Wendy checked the condition of her lipstick in the visor mirror. "Is Will going to be stopping by?"

"He made an appointment for eleven." Her father winked when she glanced at him. "I bet he'd be delighted to take you out to lunch after."

She flipped the visor up. "Maybe he'll be too busy. Evan said they've got a lot of new heifers at the calving shed this year."

"That's why Will has hired hands," her father chided her. "Man in his position has to oversee the operation, baby, not run it by himself."

Wendy suspected Will *liked* working the ranch and would never give it up, but her father didn't like her contradicting him. "Daddy, do you really think Will Ryder is going to propose to me?"

"No doubt in my mind at all, honey bunch." Her father reached over and stroked his palm over her golden hair. It was as fine and straight as it had been the day Wendy was born. "You're the prettiest girl in the state of Montana. When you and Will get married, we'll combine our ranches and run the biggest cattle operation in the region."

She automatically smoothed her hair back into place. Her father always talked about joining the two ranches, never about what her life would be like. "But what if Will doesn't want that? What if he doesn't want me? He's already been married once, and look how that turned out."

Dean's face grew stern. "Now, Wendy, you know that wasn't Will's fault. He made a mistake in judgment, is all. That woman was an outsider, an adulteress, and a drug addict. Thank the good Lord she had the sense to kill herself when she did."

"Maybe he'll think marrying me is a mistake."

Her father clamped both hands back on the steering wheel until his knuckles whitened. "I can't abide hearing that kind of talk, girl. Will Ryder has been like a son to me. He needs a good wife, one who can run his home and give him plenty of children. And that's you. You've got *my* blood in your veins."

"Yes, Daddy." Her father had never quite forgiven her mother for dying when Wendy was a baby, or for the fact that she had never produced a son for him. She went back to staring out the window. She shouldn't sulk, really. It would have been ten times worse on her if she'd been born a boy.

"Don't mope now, honey bunch." He stretched out his arm and gave her a half hug. "It'll all fall into place real soon, and you'll be the happiest woman in the world." He pulled into the restaurant parking lot and parked. Wendy waited as her father got out and went around to open her door. "Here we go. Where's my best girl's smile?"

Wendy smiled for him, even though it made her eyes sting and her cheeks hurt. "Right here, Daddy."

"That's my princess."

Later that night, Wendy gave her hair its nightly one hundred strokes, then put her brush down and reached up to her shelf. She took down the photograph and stared at it. Will wasn't smiling—he rarely smiled—but her father looked ready to burst with pleasure. She looked at the man standing off to one side, holding the reins of one of Will's prizewinning Morgans. With a fingertip, she slowly traced a heart-shaped circle around the man's face.

As if he'd been listening to her traitorous thoughts, Dean's harsh voice rang in her mind: *Will Ryder has been like a son to me.*

Slowly Wendy placed the photograph back on the shelf and went back to finishing her nightly routine. Cold cream to remove her makeup, toner to keep her pores invisible, and a gel mask she'd sleep with on her face to prevent wrinkles and dark circles under her eyes.

It was a woman's duty to look her best. It was one of the first things her father had taught her.

Before she went to bed, she practiced a serenely gracious smile to use on people when Will announced their engagement. How would she introduce herself after they were married? "Hello, I'm Wendy Ryder." She paused, then inclined her head the way royalty would. "How do you do? I'm Mrs. Will Ryder. Why, thank you. Yes, I'm the happiest woman in the world."

Hiring replacements for the two fired hands, arranging the sale of his yearlings, and consulting with the town vet on a minor outbreak of scours among the new calves took most of Will's day. He didn't want to end it by dealing with Neala Delaney, but he couldn't dump the problem on anyone else. On his way to Sun Valley, he checked in with his foreman, Evan Gamble.

"I've got another errand to run; then I'll be in," Will said over the cell phone. "How's the drop going?"

"Another twenty went today," Evan said. "Had to pull eight; lost a pair of hiplocked twins." He paused. "Will, old man Tabbeck called. Said a few things to Beatrice I won't repeat about you firing his kid and his doing women's work. Bea said he quit."

Since the old man had complained about the driving conditions, Will had let Tabbeck stay at Sun Valley over the winter to mend fences. Yesterday he'd given him orders to clear his gear out and get the ranch house ready for Neala. "Did he finish up at Sun Valley?"

"From what Bea told me, I doubt it. You planning to sell?" His foreman sounded curious.

Will would have bulldozed the place into the ground if he could have forgotten the past. But Sun Valley was a reminder, a symbol of all his past mistakes. That and half the land still belonged to his stepbrother. "No."

"Good thing, then, because I know Tabbeck's a slob. Bea offered to go over in the morning, fix it up proper."

Will's foot punched the accelerator. "No need for that just yet."

"Better get the electricity and the phone turned back on if you do put it on the market, or the agent can only show it during the day."

Will cursed inwardly. He'd been in such a hurry to rid himself of Neala Delaney, he'd forgotten about the power. The phone, however, would have to remain disconnected. "I'll go have a look, Evan. Thanks."

His foreman must have been drinking something, because he choked, then gasped, "Beg pardon?"

"You heard me." Will spotted the turnoff road and slowed down. "Keep an eye on the drop; make sure you've got a good night man working the shed. I'll be back in a couple of hours."

Neala's going to be madder than a hornet under glass, Will thought as he pulled up to the gate and put the truck in park. The condition of the fence made him frown. He hadn't noticed how bad it looked before. Tabbeck had probably sat around all winter watching television.

By the time he'd reached the ranch house, the extent of neglect made Will grim. Former rich pastureland lay brown and useless. Broken-down equipment had been left outside to rust away. The formerly lush flower beds had disappeared, and the wide lawns were a tangle of overgrown weeds. The empty barn loomed like a gray specter behind the shabby-looking house.

He'd grown up on this land. Ridden over every inch of it. His father had initially purchased the property for the additional pasture space, then later had the house built as part of his wedding gift for Will.

"You and Trish need your own place, son," his dad had said when he'd made the deed for half of the land over to Will. "And your mother and I aren't ready to give up High Point just yet."

Trish had hated Sun Valley at first sight. She'd wanted to move to Helena, where they'd have the many advantages of city life and the kind of busy, hectic social whirl she craved.

"What is there to do out here, besides watch the alfalfa grow?" she'd said after their second week at Sun Valley. "Can't we at least get an apartment in town?"

He'd assumed Trish had understood that marrying him meant living away from the comforts of the city. It took some time and patience, but gradually he'd convinced his wife to give ranch life a chance.

She'd promised him a year, but she hadn't lasted two months.

Trish's bitter complaints about the isolation and endless housework increased daily. He'd hired a housekeeper and made a point of taking Trish into town with him more often. He'd tried to get her involved in the business of running Sun Valley, and when that bored her, talked to her about starting a family. She refused to help him or have his children in what she called "this godforsaken emptiness."

"I can't stand it anymore! This place is killing me!" she'd shriek at him, then dissolve into tears. "You're killing me. . . ."

Will shoved away the unhappy memories as he got out of the truck and headed for the ranch house. He'd take care of this city girl, keep her safe, and maybe in some small way that would make up for Trish.

Beautiful, pitiful Trish, who had left him, then returned to Sun Valley to fulfill her own prediction.

Neal slept uneasily, her dreams filled with broken glass and bloodied knives. Waking up wasn't much of a relief. She sat up slowly, and groaned when she realized where she was.

"Oh. Right. The Ranch from Hell."

She shrugged off her coat and dragged her tired body off the mattress. Spring hadn't arrived during her nap, and if anything it was colder. Through the window she saw the last, fading rays of the sun sifting over the peaks of the mountain range. Shivering, she pulled on her coat and stumbled toward the kitchen.

"I should be at the Hilton. The Marriott. Motel Six, even. I bet they never did this to that guy who testified against Gotti."

Night would be here soon, and there'd been no sign of Ryder. He'd lied about taking her to a bus stop, so it was entirely possible he wouldn't be coming back tonight. She'd need more water, and to figure out how to use the wood-burning stove, or face imminent death by semistarvation and caffeine withdrawal.

"The jury will award me a million dollars for every hour I've suffered," she promised herself as she retrieved the bucket from the bathroom, slipped on her sneakers, and headed for the barn. "And order the director of the FBI to make a public apology. And make Ryder ship me free steaks for the rest of my natural life."

Elsie's head appeared over the stall door as soon as Neal entered the barn. Her subsequent impatient bellow seemed to indicate she'd run out of food, water, or both.

"Keep your horns on; I'm coming." Neal's arms

ached as she pumped more water into the bucket, then lugged it over to the stall. "Well, if you want more to drink, you'd better get out of the way."

The cow backed up enough for Neal to ease in, then went straight for the bucket, knocking it out of her hands. A wave of water sailed into the air, and landed on Neal.

"Hey!"

An unconcerned Elsie began lapping at the growing puddle around her sneakers.

"Nice work, cow. I can see why they'd want to turn you into steaks." Neal bent over to grab the now-empty bucket and repeat the process, when she heard someone shout, and straightened. "Is that—"

She ran to the barn door and saw a familiar black pickup parked in front of the ranch house.

He came back.

"Ryder?" she shouted, and saw a big silhouette move on the porch. She waved. "Over here! I'm in the barn! Don't go!" Shuffling sounds behind her made Neal swivel around in time to see the big animal push open the unlatched door and walk out of the stall. "Damn it, Elsie, can't you stay put?"

The cow lowered her head and gave Neal a distinctly malevolent glare before she bellowed again.

"Don't look at me like that. Did I knock over the bucket? No. *You* knocked over the bucket." As Elsie shuffled forward, Neal blocked the door to the barn with her body, and made shooing gestures with her hands. "Stay. Heel. Down, girl." Her eyes widened as the big animal rushed at her. She was caught between Elsie and the huge bales of hay blocking the door. "Oh, God, Ryder!"

The sound of Neala screaming his name sent Will into a flat run for the barn. His hat sailed off as he clambered over the hay bales blocking the open doors and grabbed Neal just before a black-and-white-spotted steer inside collided with her.

Neala Delaney practically climbed up him to get away from the disgruntled animal, then stared down as the steer abruptly settled down and began to work on the hay bale.

"Oh, Jesus. Oh, God." She was trembling and clutching at him with frantic hands. "Thank you, thank you."

"Never get between hungry cattle and hay," he told her as he set her down and eased her fists out of where she'd curled them into his work shirt.

"The hay?" Dazed dark eyes looked up at him, then down at the steer. "She just wanted the *hay*?"

Of all the positions he'd imagined Neala Delaney in over the past eight hours, tangling with a stray steer in his barn had not been one of them. Will blinked. Then he cleared his throat.

"That's it. So." He carefully looked at a spot just over her head. "Finding your way around the ranch all right, Ms. Delaney?"

"Don't you dare snicker at me, you—you—*bumpkin*!" She tried to thrust herself away, but her heels skidded on a patch of slushy mud and down she went.

Will tried, but her expression, combined with the sound of her backside landing in the mud puddle, was more than a mortal man could be expected to handle. He began laughing harder than he had in years.

"Cows and hay. Mary, Mother of God." Incredibly, she was grinning. "Yeah, okay, okay. It's hilarious. I'll never live it down." She held out her hand. "Fun's over, Ryder. Quit giving yourself a hernia and help me up, will you?"

He took her by the arms and gently helped her to her feet. "Don't you think you've gotten into enough trouble for one day, Calamity? Stealing cars is one thing, cattle is another."

"Oh, you're a real comedian." Neal went to wipe a trickle of sweat from her face, then saw the condition of her hands and thought better of it. "And my name is Neal."

"What are you doing out here?"

She pointed toward the steer. "I was *trying* to help that nasty-tempered witch."

He noted the brand on the steer's shoulder, and checked the ear tag. "This one belongs to Dean Lewis. Must be a stray, rooting around in the jug bins for leftovers."

"The jug bins?"

"In here. Come on." He climbed over the bale and helped Neal down into the barn. "Young cattle are used to being fed in the jugs—the stalls—so strays turn up here now and again."

"But I fed her before in there, this morning. See?" She pointed to a spot beside his feet.

He bent down to pick up the container. "Oatmeal? You fed it *oatmeal*?"

"Oats, oatmeal, what's the difference? Elsie seemed to like it." She frowned at his incredulous expression and looked back at the animal. "It won't hurt her, will it?"

"No." He cleared his throat. "And that's a steer, not a heifer."

"A what?"

"A steer. A bull minus his . . ." He made an appropriate gesture.

"Oh. Okay." Neal examined herself and groaned. "God, this is going to take forever to clean up. Can I go to a hotel now?"

"That's not up to me. Come on." He led her over to a huge sink and turned on the taps. When no water came out, he swore. "What's the matter with the pumps?"

"Excuse me, this part I know how to do." She turned and went to the front jug, then reemerged with a tin pail and placed it under the old hand pump in the center of the barn.

Will watched in amazement as the spoiled city girl worked the handle and washed the mud from her hands, then retrieved the bucket and started to fill it.

"Okay, lady, you've made your point. Go up to the house and get cleaned up," he told her.

"With what?" she asked, and gave him a snide look. "There's no running water over there, either." She stripped off her stained coat, then paused. "Could you do something about that?"

The outline of her lacy bra showing through the damp T-shirt she wore distracted him for a moment. "I'll go look at the pumps."

"My hero." Neal gave him an artless smile. "Make sure you turn on the one with the hot water, if you would?"

Will went around to the utility shed behind the barn, and found all four well pumps had been shut down. After he switched them on, he went back to the barn.

"Water's back up. The hot-water heater's up at the house," he said as he walked in. "I'll have to take a look at it and . . ."

Neala was kneeling beside the pump, sluicing her slim, bare arms with handfuls of water. Her T-shirt was soaked, and she was shivering. For a moment he watched the last rays of sunlight shining in through the lower clerestory windows play over her. She had the kind of body a centerfold would kill for, but it was her face, scrubbed clean of the cosmetics, that hypnotized him.

Her flawless skin glowed with health as tiny beads of water studded the tips of her dark lashes. Natural color flushed her full, soft lips and cheeks. Beneath the goop, Neala Delaney was even more beautiful than anyone had imagined.

"The pumps were shut down," he told her, his voice as tight as his jaw. "As soon as I get the hot-water heater going, you can take a hot shower."

Neal rose and slung her filthy coat over her arm as she headed for the door. "You really *are* my hero." She patted his arm as she passed him. "Thanks."

Chapter 4

She could feel him watching her as she made her way up to the house, and wondered how much leeway her wet T-shirt had bought her. Will Ryder evidently knew something about her situation. Obviously he'd had some contact with the government, or he wouldn't have invented the bus-stop story and left her at Sun Valley.

So how do I convince him to get me out of here?

She bypassed the back of the house so she could take a look inside his pickup. No keys in the ignition, and the cell phone charger was empty.

"Rats." She climbed up the porch to the front door. "I knew I should have picked his pocket while I had the chance."

After she stripped out of her sodden, muddy clothes in the bathroom, Neal turned on the sink taps and let them run until the cold, rust-colored water turned clear. Getting the mud off chilled her to the bone, so she swiftly pulled on dry jeans and another oversize T-shirt. At the rate she was using up clothes and towels, she'd soon have to find that rock and river.

She wrapped the last dry towel around her hair, and went out to find Ryder standing by the stove. A huge pot sat on top, and the smell of smoke filled the air.

"What are you burning?" She wandered over to have a look. "Boiling water?"

"Electricity's out." He took off his hat and tossed

it on the table before crouching to check the front of the stove. "I'm heating some water for you to wash with."

"Make me a pot of tea instead, and I'll be your slave for life."

He turned his head. "I'm not here to wait on you hand and foot, city girl. I've got work to do. You can make it yourself."

"I'd love to." She removed the towel from her damp curls and draped it around her neck. "Mind telling me how?"

He stared at her hair, then abruptly gestured toward the old tin pot on the stove. "Use that."

"Oh, I'd use that if I knew how—which I don't— but there's another tiny problem. No tea bags. No food, either, unless you're into canned goods and Aunt Martha's green tomato pickle." She tugged on the ends of the towel. "Tell you what—how about you run me over to the supermarket and let me do a little shopping?"

He collected his hand tools. "Pack up your stuff. You can stay up at my place."

And have him watching over her, listening to every word she said, counting every breath she took? She'd never get anything accomplished. "I don't think that's advisable."

"Why not?" He left the window. The room was growing darker, and shadows masked everything but his eyes. "You can't stay here."

"I can go back to Denver." Since honesty seemed to impress him, she decided to go for broke. "I have family there who can help me—my sister and my uncle—"

"This guy you're testifying against jumped bail. If you go back, you'll only be putting your family in danger."

So he did know everything. "You don't understand; my uncle is the one who got me into this mess. He works for the government. He's an agent."

"Sure he is." Ryder's teeth flashed. "When it's time for the trial, they'll come back to pick you up. Until then, Calamity, you're not going anywhere."

Neal willed her anger away. "I know it sounds crazy, but I'm telling you the truth. Call the army CID; they'll verify everything. His name is Colonel Sean Delaney. I have to talk to him." When he didn't blink, she stamped her foot. "At least take me to a phone and let me make one call. Just one measly phone call won't hurt anything!"

"Selbrook said no phone calls." He was only a few inches away from her now, and the proximity made her take a step back. "Get your stuff together and let's go."

Will Ryder was turning out to be the classic obstinate, inflexible alpha male, and a prime example of what too much testosterone could do to someone who might otherwise be a reasonable person.

What he didn't know was, she could be just as tenacious and mule-headed as any hormonally challenged guy. But he was about to get lesson number one.

"No." She braced herself back against the counter and folded her arms. "If I can't go back to Denver, or make a phone call, I'm staying right here."

He reached out, making her recoil. "Hold still." He plucked at one of her curls and showed her a piece of straw before dropping it to the floor. Then he touched her hair in the same spot again, with just the tips of his fingers. "I'll bet you reel them in like bass in a thunderstorm."

She couldn't see his expression clearly, but the way his voice had gone low and deep made an odd, answering vibration resonate through her limbs. "What?"

"Those rich old boys you sing for every night back in Denver." He propped an arm beside her and bent his head. "They must want to drape you in diamonds and satin."

"No." The touch of his breath on her skin made

her face feel hot. "I don't do . . . I mean, I just sing. That's all."

"A woman like you gets used to twisting men around her little finger." He picked up her hand and held it between them, rubbing his thumb around the base of her smallest digit. "You trying to wind me around this one, Calamity?"

"I don't think you'd, um, fit."

"I won't." He dropped her hand. "Remember that and we'll get along just fine."

She sidestepped him, and rubbed her damp palms against the sides of her jeans. "So they told you about Senator Colfax."

"I know you're the only one who can put his killer in jail."

Guilt and anger fought, and anger won. "Did they mention that's because those idiots *lost* the only other evidence they had against him?"

"Which is why in sixty days you're going to appear before that judge in Denver." Ryder picked up his hat and went to the back door. "Give up whatever crazy ideas you have about getting out of this, Calamity. You're staying here, or coming to High Point with me." He opened the door, then paused. "Take your pick."

He was making the whole situation into a dare. Of course she didn't want to stay in this wretched place. But if she went with him to his ranch, she might never get another chance to contact her uncle before the trial.

"Thanks for the very generous offer, but I'll stay here."

He didn't like that. "Fine." Not at all, judging by the way he yanked open the door. "See you tomorrow."

"Ah, before you go"—Neal smiled as he turned around—"you'd better make a list."

He eyed her. "A list. For what?"

"A few things I need. This is your ranch, right?"
She waited for the nod. "Then you can get the electricity turned back on. Send someone over in the
morning to clean the house and fix the refrigerator. A
washer and dryer would be nice. So would a television,
a radio, blankets, and some clean linens." She made
an airy gesture. "Send the bill for everything to the
FBI."

He snorted as he put his hat on and took out his
car keys. "Anything else?"

"Food would be convenient, if it's not too much
trouble. So would two pounds of tea and a kettle. The
whistling kind." She thought for a minute. Eight
weeks, three cups of tea a day . . . "Make that five
pounds of tea. I drink English tea, not American, but
I'll make do with Irish, if I must."

"I suppose you want bottled water, too?" he asked,
heavy on the sarcasm.

"That would be lovely." She smiled. "I prefer
Evian, in half-liter bottles. Ten gallons should see me
through to next week."

As his car sped along the interstate, J. R. Martin
sat in the back and listened to his attorney babble.

"We've got real trouble with this new judge." His
attorney sounded nervous. "I did the best I could for
you, but he ruled against my motion to dismiss and
issued the bench warrant for your arrest. The D.A.
refuses to drop the charges."

"The security tape is history." He fingered the head
of his cane. "The only evidence they have left is the
girl's testimony, and she's disappeared. So what's the
problem?"

"The D.A. says she's going to testify. They've got
her squirreled away somewhere, J. R."

He sat straight up. "When did they find her?"

"Seems they've had her all along. Let the missing-
persons report stand while they moved her out of the

state." The lawyer made a bleating sound as he cleared his throat. "Uh, J. R., she was in the suite when the senator was killed. You saw the papers."

"That photograph proves nothing. It's her word against mine."

"They're going to listen to her, J. R." His attorney's voice went from bleat to whine. "The best thing you can do right now is turn yourself in and talk a deal. I can probably get you man one—"

"I didn't kill the greedy bastard!" he shouted into the phone. Several moments passed as he composed himself. "Sorry, I'm a little on edge. You understand. Now, where are they keeping the girl?"

"The feds aren't going to tell me that," the lawyer said.

"Don't do anything else until I contact you."

J. R. ended the call and tossed the phone down on the seat beside him. He should have been back in Denver, making up for lost time. Maintaining control over his extensive operation required both visible presence and careful supervision.

Once this is over, I'll still be in charge. I'm still the boss.

He'd spent years amassing his Denver operation, slowly infiltrating and taking over various illegal enterprises. Chop shops. Prostitution rings. Fencing operations. Protection rackets. After five years, he'd gained enough wealth and power to run virtually all the organized crime in Denver.

Still, it wasn't enough. The Chinese kept their own stranglehold on certain lucrative areas, like drug smuggling and distribution. J. R. knew better than to start a war for supremacy with the tong. Instead he'd made contact with Shandian, and offered his services.

It would be interesting to see how far the Chinese would take him. They'd certainly been happy to offer to run things for him while he straightened out this Colfax situation. And perhaps they could assist him in taking care of this one, final complication.

He picked up the phone and dialed another number. The dry, cold voice that answered warmed a few degrees when he identified himself.

"It is good to hear from you, Mr. Martin." T'ang Yin was as formal and polite as his predecessor, but then, all the Chinese were like that. "I have been expecting your call."

"I imagine you have." J. R. smiled faintly.

"I gather Neala Delaney is the reason you have contacted me?"

"If your boys can find out where she is, T'ang, I'll take care of her myself."

"We have already determined Ms. Delaney's current location. However, there is a price for this information, Mr. Martin."

He ground the end of his cane into the plush carpet beneath his feet. "What do you want?"

"Negligence and poor management decisions have done considerable damage to Shandian's North American interests. Now that I am in charge, I intend to remedy this situation by forming a cooperative triad with On Leong in New York and Hip Sing in San Francisco."

J. R. knew both tongs by reputation—they were the largest and most successful of the five Chinese organized-crime groups operating in the United States. Forming a triad with them would guarantee T'ang Yin virtually unlimited power, resources, and near-absolute control of the Midwest.

"I suggest your own interests have nearly outgrown your current area of operation, Mr. Martin. Combining your efforts and resources with the triad will enable us both to explore a wide variety of opportunities in territorial expansion."

If he said no, he'd be a walking dead man. "All right. I'm in. Where is she?"

"She was moved to a town in south-central Montana."

J. R. listened as T'ang Yin related the balance of

his information. For a moment he was too stunned to comment. Then he became furious.

There's only one reason she'd be in Lone Creek. The bitch is setting me up for the feds.

He reached for the decanter of scotch on the mini-bar and poured himself a healthy shot. "Nothing to worry about, T'ang. I'll take good care of Ms. Delaney. I'll be in touch soon."

To do what he needed to do, he'd have to go in alone. He told his driver to take him to the nearest car dealership, then made a third call. "This is J. R. Tell the Irishman I want to talk to him. We've got business to discuss."

"Hello, Sean. Odd place for you to be taking your sick leave. Where are your crutches?"

As the Irishman stared, Kalen Grady checked the empty stalls, then stepped up to the urinal beside his.

Sean zipped up his pants, cursed lightly, and looked out at the rest-stop parking lot. From the time he'd left Washington, he'd been uneasy. Now the itch on the back of his neck made sense. "I thought I felt a tail. Who'd you put on me? Jennings?"

"Hessler. You're getting careless, old man." Grady smiled as he finished and flushed the urinal. He went to the sinks and calmly washed his hands. "Now tell me why I'm pissing in the middle of Helena, Montana, when you're supposed to be recovering in Washington."

If Sean told him everything, he'd end up in handcuffs in the back of Grady's car, being driven to the nearest military stockade. "I got the call from China. Jian-Shan's disappeared, left the country. You can have him instead of Martin. Get Neal out of there."

"Not possible. Shan's made promises and let us down before."

"He wouldn't have left the country if he wasn't ready to come over to our side."

"He's unreliable, Irish. It could be months before he surfaces, and I don't have that kind of time to waste. It has to be J. R."

Sean told him what he thought of that, startling a man walking in enough to send him straight back out to the parking lot.

"Settle down." Grady folded his arms. "We need her where she is. She's in no danger."

"The same way Laney was in no danger with Tremayne on Nightmare Ridge." Sean checked his reflection and walked back out to the parking lot. A nervous man dashed past him and Kalen into the rest room. "Damned fool nearly got her killed. No, I've got to take Neal out."

Kalen stopped beside Sean's car. "J. R. called our man. Seems he has a disposal job for you."

Sean dropped his keys and stared at his boss. "He knows where she is?" Grady nodded. "You let it leak, didn't you?"

"All part of the plan, Irish. We're not going to settle for one or two of them this time. They're all going down." The general glanced at his watch. "It should take you a couple of hours to reach Lone Creek. I'll expect a report by twenty-one-hundred hours tonight."

Sean unlocked the driver's-side door and yanked it open. "So you're going to let me go in."

"Of course. Your cover wouldn't have survived the Dream Mountain operation if Matt Pagent hadn't turned up working the op for the Bureau. The Chinese still have their doubts, but obviously they haven't passed them along to Martin. As long as Neal stays where she is, and you don't let her know you're in town, I have no objections to you providing backup."

"She needs to know—"

"Nothing. If she knows you're posing as a hit man, she might let something slip and blow the entire deal. You keep out of sight, or you spend your medical leave in the stockade." Grady handed him a slip of paper with a phone number on it. "Let J. R. know where she is as soon as you get there."

"I see. And if Neal ends up dead?"

Grady smiled. "You're the killer J. R. is hiring to get rid of her. All you have to do is make sure you don't do your job."

Spending a cold night in the dark made Neal curse her decision to stay at Sun Valley several times. She huddled on the bed, trying to keep warm and ignore the utter silence. Unlike her apartment in the city, which overlooked a busy metropolitan street, the empty house seemed to magnify even the tiniest sound. In the early hours near dawn, she finally dozed off into a thin sleep, only to be awakened by a hammering noise.

The sound wrenched Neal out of a dead sleep, and she sat up with a shriek. "Ahhhh!"

She was on the floor, not the bed. How had she ended up there? And who had hit her over the head with a two-by-four? Every muscle in her body screeched as she hoisted herself up by clutching the side of the mattress.

"Tea."

She staggered into the kitchen. Through bleary eyes, she spotted the battered tin coffeepot sitting on the back of the stove, remembered the lack of water and provisions, and wailed. "No. Don't do this to me. No tea?" She kicked a wall and promptly bruised her bare toes. As she hopped around the kitchen, holding her foot, she yelled, "That does it! Everybody gets sued! *Everybody!*"

A door opened. "You awake in there?" a deep, familiar voice called from the front room.

"Go away!" she yelled back, and limped over to a chair by the kitchen table. "Unless you have tea; then you can come in." She rubbed her sore foot, then looked up as Ryder walked in.

He looked at her hair, her face, then her toes. "Ready to go to High Point now?"

"Ha. Ha. Ha." She examined her toes and winced at sight of the forming bruises. "No."

Ryder flipped on the wall switch, and the overhead light came on at once. "You should have some hot water now."

"Thank God." She shuffled off toward the bathroom to drown herself in a warm bath.

"Come out to the kitchen when you're done. We need to talk."

"The man has no sense of self-preservation," she muttered as she gazed at her pale reflection in the bathroom mirror. It felt good to kick the door shut with her good foot. "None whatsoever."

Neal did feel better after she discovered that, along with the electricity, the hot-water supply had been restored. While she cleaned her face and teeth, she decided her first priority after getting rid of Ryder would be to indulge in a long, luxurious shower.

However, as soon as she walked into the kitchen and saw the bags and boxes of groceries waiting on the table, her empty stomach lurched.

"Food!" Neal eagerly sorted through the bags, delighted to find an abundance of fresh fruit and vegetables. "What else have we got here? Chicken and fish and . . . oh, yes. *Yes.*" She removed a jumbo-sized box of authentic English breakfast tea bags and caressed it with reverent hands before hugging it to her chest. "You remembered!"

Ryder came in carrying yet another large box and three plastic grocery bags. "This is the last of it. You can use the other stove now that the electric's back on. Teakettle's over there," he said, and nodded toward a carton on the floor. He eyed the box she cradled. "You've got it that bad, huh?"

"Worse. My pulse stops at four P.M. every day, and this is the only thing that jump-starts it." She put down the tea and attacked the box on the floor.

Maybe she was being a little too grateful. "Loose is better, of course, but I can manage." She took the kettle over to the sink, shoved some dirty dishes aside, and began to fill it. "Fancy a cuppa, cowboy?"

"I've had coffee already, thanks." He went to the door. "If I missed anything, make me a list. I'll stop in next week."

A week? She couldn't wait a whole week to talk to her uncle. *Don't panic, Neal. Think of a reason to make him come back sooner.*

"Hold it, Ryder. I don't see a television. Or a washer and a dryer. Or my Evian." She felt his gaze follow her as she put the kettle on the electric stove and switched it on. "How am I supposed to live without *The Young and the Restless,* clean clothes, and mountain springwater?"

"This isn't a hotel, lady."

"Tell me about it. No extra towels, no heat lamp, no cute little bottles of shampoo and conditioner . . ." Neal washed out a cup and opened the box of tea bags. "If you expect me to survive out here in the wilderness, I'm going need a few more things."

"Such as?"

"In addition to the missing items, a hair dryer, curling iron, emery boards, salon-quality shampoo and conditioner, liquid moisturizing bath soap, nail polish remover, and a poufie."

When she paused for breath, he asked, "A *poufie?*"

"It's what you put the liquid bath soap on. Exfoliates dead skin cells. Which reminds me, I'll need a good-quality skin lotion, too. And— Shouldn't you be writing this down?"

He sighed, took a small notebook and pen from his shirt pocket, then made a rolling gesture with his hand.

Neal recited all the beauty products she could think of, until the teakettle's whistle interrupted her.

"That's all the basic necessities, I think." She poured the boiling water into her cup and began dunking the tea bag up and down. "Oh, wait, I forgot, I definitely need cuticle remover, and—"

"Enough. I won't have any room left in the back of the truck." He pocketed the notepad and pen. "You really need all this glop to look good?"

"No, I really need all this glop to keep from losing my sanity out here in the wilderness." She discarded the tea bag and sipped gingerly from her cup. "You don't want to see me with ragged cuticles, Ryder. It's not pretty. What about the house?"

He looked around. "You planning on redecorating, too?"

"No, silly. If you hadn't noticed, your previous tenant was a total slob." She nudged a box of cleaning supplies with her foot. "I'll need a vacuum cleaner, some floor cleaner, and a decent mop."

"You? Clean?" He laughed.

She planted her fists on her hips. "I can clean."

"When? Between manicures?" He tugged his hat down and opened the door. "I'll be back later."

"Later as in when? This afternoon, I hope?" As he left, she hurried to the door and caught it before it closed. "Make it today, Ryder," she called after him. "I really need that cuticle remover. I'm not kidding. We're talking violation of my basic human rights here!"

He was still shaking his head as he started the engine and drove away.

Neal shut the door quickly and leaned back against it. "So much for Plan B. Now, how do I get out of here when he comes back? Assuming he comes back." She reached for her tea and nearly tripped over the box of cleaning supplies. Slowly she bent down and removed a can of oven cleaner. "Between manicures, yeah, real funny."

Neal had never been interested in the domestic arts, which was why the most time she'd ever spent in the kitchen was to make tea or microwave popcorn. Back in Denver, she had her own cleaning lady come in three mornings a week to handle everything else. Before that, Laney had done everything.

Still, the fact that Ryder assumed she was totally useless stung her pride.

"I'm a woman. I have estrogen. I can do this." Slowly she straightened and surveyed the mess around her. Maybe she'd never actually cleaned a kitchen by herself before, but she certainly had enough experience taking care of other people's messes. "How hard could it be, anyway?"

Neal spent the rest of the morning proving she wasn't helpless. Washing dishes and scrubbing the counters proved rather satisfying, as long as she didn't look at what the hot water was doing to her nails. It helped to pretend every dirty plate and patch of grease she tackled was Ryder's face, too.

"This isn't so tough." She began drying the dishes with one of the new hand towels she'd found among the supplies. A plate slipped from her hands and smashed all over the floor. "Okay, God, I promise, no more housewife jokes during my act."

The stove was a particular challenge, as it apparently hadn't been cleaned for years. Three applications of oven cleaner and an hour and a half of straight scrubbing finally rendered it sparkling clean. When she scoured the last of the stuck-on food from the interior, Neal's hands felt as if they'd been skinned.

"I am never using you," she told the stove. "I'll become a vegetarian. I'll eat my food raw. I'll *grill*."

It cost her eight nails and put a permanent crick in her back, but by noon the kitchen gleamed.

"I can't believe I scrubbed the whole thing," she said, looking around her with weary pride at her accomplishment. "Wonder what the cowboy will say when he comes back and sees this?"

The shadows behind the house seemed to stretch a little longer as a niggling, sly voice in her head piped up: *If he comes back.*

*   *   *

"One of your steers wandered onto Sun Valley, Dean. Got it penned up in the old barn. Do what now?"

Will listened as his neighbor offered to send a man over to collect the stray. The suggestion was tempting, but if one of Lewis's hands caught a glimpse of Neala, it'd be all over the county by the next day.

"No, that's all right. I'm headed down that way to-morrow. Yeah." He rubbed his tired eyes with one hand. "I'll drive it back and take a look at the fence while I'm there. No trouble at all. You too. 'Bye."

He hung up the phone and sorted through the day's mail. Dealing with the city girl and Sun Valley was his personal headache for the next two months, no matter how he felt whenever he set foot on the place. Unless he could convince Neala she'd be better off at High Point.

And what would I do with her if I did?

He pushed the stack of envelopes aside. Over the years he'd been tempted to call Jeb and buy him out, just so he could have the house razed to the ground. But he hadn't spoken to his stepbrother since Trish had left him, and no amount of annoyance would goad him to do otherwise.

Half of Sun Valley is mine, big brother. So is your wife. Do yourself a favor and stay off my land and out of my life.

And he had, until the call from Grady. Now he had no choice but to use the ranch to keep Neala Delaney safe until her trial date came around. After that, she'd go.

But I wouldn't mind having a taste of her before she does. His muscles clenched as the image of her kneeling by the pump splashing water over herself loomed up in his mind.

Keep thinking that way and you'll never get anything done.

He finished his paperwork and took a cold shower, then dropped onto his bed. An hour later he was up pacing the floor.

All right, so she was beautiful. He'd had his share of beautiful women. Trish had been a knockout, and he'd slept with other women since his divorce. He enjoyed sex, and had no interest in becoming a celibate. Avoiding commitment wasn't a problem, as long as he kept his affairs brief and outside of town.

It had been a couple of weeks since Barbara had broken it off with him. A vet from Billings, she'd enjoyed his frank, sensual lovemaking without wanting commitment. She'd also been honest when she'd met another man who'd interested her on other levels.

"You're a terrific lover, Will, but there's no future in this for us. Eventually I want to get married, have kids, the whole shooting match. And I know how you feel about that." She'd kissed him, and even cried a little. "I'm sorry."

He was, too. If he'd had another woman to go to, he could have relieved some of this nagging frustration. It might not have been right, or fair to Barbara, but it might have helped clear his head of Neala Delaney.

As it was, all he could do was wonder. Wonder what it would be like with her. She wouldn't be an easy woman to bed. Not with that temper. The challenge tempted him. Taking Neala would be as exhilarating as gentling a jittery mare. *Woman like her needed a firm hand, and plenty of attention.*

Still, it wasn't just the tug of lust that drew him. She pulled at him, got to him in ways he didn't understand. One minute he wanted to stretch her out and bury himself in her, the next he wanted to take her in his arms and cradle her like a baby. She acted tough, but he'd seen something in her eyes. She was afraid. He could feel it, and even more surprising, he felt his own, ever-increasing need to protect her.

She's not mine to protect. And she should be scared, considering what she's gotten herself mixed up in.

He went back to bed, but sleep eluded him. Only the image of Neala Delaney stayed with him through the night.

Chapter 5

Scrolls of thin frost trimmed the glass storefronts and windows of Lone Creek. One solitary, restless shadow passed by them, casting distorted reflections of an unremarkable figure. Anyone looking out might have questioned the presence of the ordinary person on the streets at that time of night, but the hardworking, early-rising townspeople had taken refuge in their warm beds hours ago.

Besides, the present danger was not in being discovered.

Maintaining an inconspicuous appearance was only one of the operative's many talents, but it was probably the most important—second only to the ability to wait patiently until opportunity presented itself. The time to act had arrived, but the ability to do so still hung tantalizingly out of reach.

Where is she?

Finding the woman T'ang Yin wanted should have been uncomplicated. The operative had been sent to Lone Creek for long-term surveillance, to settle down, blend in, and become a part of the community, to wait for the day when the call for more serious work came in. Given the operative's extensive knowledge of the area, the ridiculously small population, and limited number of places a stranger could be secluded, locating Neala Delaney should have taken only a few hours.

Instead, two days had passed with no results.

I have to find her tomorrow.

Midnight's cold silence provided clarity as the operative walked along the dark streets of the town and weighed the likelihood of potential disaster. If she had been moved out of the area, it would have to be confirmed. Yet even the source within the Federal Witness Protection Program had been unable to discover the woman's whereabouts. Neala Delaney's confidential records had been completely purged from the national database.

They must know we have a man inside.

If the American government had become aware of the informant among them, then there was little hope that further data would be coming out of Washington. At the same time, the operative was well aware that Shandian's new director would not accept further excuses or delay.

Find her. Interrogate her. Kill her.

It was the very lack of information that proved the most frustrating. With equal amounts of suspicion and curiosity, the townspeople invariably gossiped about the arrival of strangers—yet no one seemed to know what had happened to the beautiful, outrageously dressed woman who'd arrived at a nearby airport. By all accounts, she had shown up only to vanish moments later. A carefully worded call to the ticket agent confirmed that her two male escorts had flown back to Denver the same day—without her.

Where could such a conspicuous woman have hidden herself so quickly?

An anonymous package sat waiting on the doorstep as the operative arrived home. Inside, the contents were unpacked and examined. Everything that was needed to do the job—the medical supplies, coded instructions, and an untraceable weapon. The operative contemplated the dull gleam of the gunmetal, aware it could be used only as a last resort.

Make it look like an accident.

The supplies had to be hidden, and the packing materials destroyed, after which the new instructions had to be decoded. They detailed an unanticipated turn of recent events, and a new directive that, once carried out, would put a swift end to the entire operation in Lone Creek.

After I find her, it will be over.

The operative struck a match and lit the corner of the single sheet of paper that had been sent in the package. As the coded communiqué burned, the task of finding Neala Delaney dwindled into insignificance.

She would be found and dealt with, because failure was now entirely out of the question.

Will discovered the next morning that his restlessness hadn't gone unnoticed.

"I'm heading over to Sun Valley," he told his housekeeper.

"You got no time to eat, much less be chasing strays for Dean Lewis," Beatrice Knudson said, miffed that he'd refused breakfast. As his full-time housekeeper since the death of his wife, she had few qualms about airing her opinions. "Send Evan down instead."

Will pocketed his cell phone and pulled on his jacket. "Evan spent most of the night down in the calving shed."

"I'd say you didn't get much shut-eye, either." She turned and caught his expression, then sighed. "I know it's not my place to be telling you your business, Mr. Will."

He took his keys down from the wall rack. "That's never stopped you before, Bea."

"You've been doing the work of five men all winter, and I worry. Something's got to give soon."

"I'll be fine." The sound of a truck stopping outside the house made Will glance out the window. "I've got a delivery to load up before I go. Let Evan know I'm on the cell phone if he needs me."

As he helped transfer the boxes of supplies for

Neala Delaney from the back of the delivery truck, Will eyed the young heifers waiting in the big corral outside the calving shed. They still had another two hundred waiting there to drop their calves, and daily trips had to be made to check the older heifers and their new calves out on the range. Now that he was four hands short, his situation had gone from dire to critical.

"Mr. Ryder?" The delivery man held out a clipboard for Will to sign the invoice. "Sorry, we didn't have all what you ordered in stock. Manager's called it in to our warehouse; back order should be here by Monday."

"Thanks." Will signed off on the invoice and handed it back. When the other man hesitated, he asked, "Something else?"

"No, sir. Well, my sister Vicky, she owns the beauty parlor in town. I could check with her if you need that, uh, fingernail stuff before next week, see if she has some to spare."

The man was making such a heroic effort *not* to look at Will's hands that he had to bite back a laugh. "I appreciate the offer, but it can wait until Monday."

"Yes, sir." The delivery man beat a hasty retreat.

As he drove down the mountain, Will noted new signs that early spring had arrived. The blankets of snow that had covered the surrounding country had all but disappeared. Meltwater had begun to fill the ditches, and new green covered the fields. He made a mental note to send a crew out to check the condition of the west alfalfa fields; too much drainage there would ruin the soil for the rest of the year.

Will's father maintained that cattle ranching was a never-ending struggle with nature, and spring always brought with it the usual battles: calving out the herd, irrigating fields, mending fences, branding new calves, making hay to get the cattle through the next winter. Not all the battles could be won, and even in good years the price of beef sometimes dropped so low that it made all the effort seem futile. A lesser man might have been intimidated by the prospect of so much labor with scant guarantee of return, but Will had inherited his father's respect for hard work and love for the land.

Nothing worthwhile ever came easily. He glanced in the rearview mirror at the boxes in the back of the truck, and his hand tightened on the steering wheel. That was something a pampered city girl like Neala Delaney would never understand.

Neal had spent her second afternoon at Sun Valley waiting for Ryder to show up, and carefully plotting how to relieve him of his truck keys. When he didn't show by nightfall, she indulged in a rare fit of sulking before making herself dinner in the sparkling-clean kitchen. After that, she searched every inch of the house, but found nothing to help her in her quest for freedom.

She did find some other interesting items that indicated she was not the first woman to stay at Sun Valley: clothes, a beautifully warm crocheted afghan embroidered with the initials *PLR,* some abandoned toiletries, and a brush that still had a few long, golden hairs tangled in it.

So who's the blonde? PLR?

Brooding over the mystery woman and Ryder's no-show while soaking in a hot bath didn't make Neal feel any more relaxed, and the headache that gave her made her lie awake most of the night. Finally she couldn't keep her dry, gritty eyes open another second, and fell asleep.

It seemed like only a minute passed before someone started hammering on a door. Her *bedroom* door.

Neal groaned and pressed a hand over her aching brow as she peered over the edge of the afghan. "What?"

Ryder appeared beside the bed. "Come on, Calamity." He tugged the afghan away. "Rise and shine."

Neal covered her eyes. "I have a gun."

"No, you don't."

She sat up and pushed the hair out of her face. "I'll buy one. A big one. With lots of bullets."

"I'll alert the sheriff." He stood back as she crawled off the bed. "Let's go, I haven't got all day."

"Yeah, yeah. Hold your horses." Neal shrugged into her ugly bathrobe and belted the edges down before hobbling to the door. "I don't suppose you'd put the kettle on, would you?"

"You're not crippled. Get a move on."

She glanced at him over her shoulder. "Be nice to me until I wake up, Ryder. Or I won't be responsible for the fractures I inflict." She sighed and headed for the kitchen.

"What's wrong with you?" He followed her, looming behind her as she made her way into the kitchen. "Were you out messing with that steer again?"

"No." She went to the sink and filled the teakettle. Water splashed on her raw hands, making her grimace. "I'm just badly in need of a manicure, an electric blanket, and a large-caliber weapon. Not necessarily in that order."

When Ryder didn't respond to her joke, she turned around. He stood in the center of the kitchen, looking around with an expression of sheer amazement. He hadn't seen what she'd done, Neala recalled, and allowed herself a small smirk as she set the kettle on the stove.

"Looks nice, doesn't it?"

He gave her the once-over. "You did all this yourself?"

"No, the house was burglarized overnight by a criminal with a neatness fetish. Of course I did it." And she had the sores to prove it. She might try whining a little about them—it was better if Ryder kept thinking she was a wimp—but for now, her life depended on immediately drinking her tea. "I've decided to charge eighty dollars an hour for my labor. You do have a checkbook with you, right?'' The kettle whistled. ''Excuse me.''

''No wonder you can't sleep.'' He watched her prepare her mug. ''You drink too much of that English stuff.''

Neal was too busy scalding her mouth with the first gulp to present her opinion that the English stuff was the only thing that kept her from lapsing into a coma on a daily basis. She added a spoonful of sugar, then took another sip and moaned with sheer pleasure. ''Oh, God, this is worth insomnia.''

Ryder folded his arms. ''If you say so.''

''Speaking of stuff, did you bring mine?''

''Yeah. Most of it.'' Without another word, Ryder walked out, then returned carrying more boxes.

Neala didn't offer to help, but sat and watched as he brought in the supplies. She was too tired to poke around and see what he'd managed to find, but summoned a lazy smile of thanks when he came in with the last of it.

''You're so good to me, thanks.'' She set her tea aside, rose, and went to him, keeping her movements slow and her expression serene. ''Keep this up and I'll be your slave for life.''

Ryder's blue eyes narrowed, and a muscle twitched along the side of his jaw. ''Seems to me Lincoln freed the slaves a while back.''

''Lincoln never had to go two days without a beauty treatment.'' She lifted a hand and rested it against the front of his jacket. From the location of the jingle when he moved, his keys were in his right front pocket. She had to distract him long enough to slip them out. ''I really am very grateful for all that you've done.''

''Are you?''

Up close, he seemed even bigger than she remembered. Suppressing an urge to turn and run, she trailed a finger around the edge of one of his steel buttons, lifting her other hand in readiness. ''Uh-huh.''

He caught her wrist in one hand, and stepped away before she could slip the other into his pocket. "Save it, Calamity. It won't get you anywhere with me."

She frowned. This was going to be harder than she'd anticipated. "Why do you keep calling me that?"

"You remind me of Martha Jane Burk."

"Martha Jane Burk." Neal gave up on getting the keys for the moment and went back to the stove. "And she is . . . ?"

"Was. Her daddy was a Mormon lay preacher; brought his whole family up here from Missouri during the gold rush."

"Let me guess. Martha hated it here."

"She loved it. Even lived in Lone Creek for a spell, before she joined Buffalo Bill's Wild West show. They've got pictures of her at the town hall."

Buffalo Bill? "Calamity . . . Martha Jane . . ." Neal groaned. "You're talking about Calamity Jane."

"That's her."

Well, he could call her worse things, Neal supposed. "Why did they call her that, anyway? Was she a klutz?"

"No, just a wild, hard-drinking woman. Could have been from all the hard times she lived through, or the fact she liked to help folks who were in trouble. Or because she could shoot like a real gunslinger."

"Well, I don't drink, I avoid hard times, and I haven't shot anyone. Yet." Neal felt rather indignant. "What else did she do?"

"What most women like her did. Started out as a saloon prostitute. Later on she got into scouting and prospecting. In the end, she ended up dressing and drinking and acting just like a man. Died from the liquor, if I remember correctly."

"I see." Neal's face burned. So that was what he thought of her. "Guess I really impress the hell out of you, don't I?"

"If the shoe fits."

Suddenly the idea of stealing Ryder's truck was as appealing as her new nickname.

Okay, so I'll stay.

She went over to the boxes and began rummaging through them. The bottles of water made her suppress a grin. "You forgot the cuticle remover, Ryder. But thanks for the skin lotion. Oh, and I should mention that I have this monthly problem that I'll need some supplies for. It's just another one of those girl things."

He came over, grabbed her by the wrists, and examined her hands on both sides. "What's this from?"

She wasn't going to volunteer the specifics. "This place was a pigsty. Do the math."

"If you have any sense, you put on some rubber gloves before you use oven cleaner. Bathroom cleaner, too. Says so on the labels. Otherwise it eats your skin right off."

"Right. Labels. I never read labels."

"Have you put something on them?" She shook her head, and he let her go. "I don't need you to clean this place up."

"Who else is going to do it?" She made an airy wave. "At eighty dollars an hour, I'm a bargain."

He stomped out, but kept going past the truck and into the barn. A minute later he came back and slapped a round, flat tin in her hand. "Put this on."

She dutifully read the torn label. "Hag Balm? Is this a cure, or a preventive measure?"

"*Bag* Balm." He unscrewed the top, scooped out the white salve inside, and rubbed it into the palm of her hand. "Keep them clean, and put it on three times a day until they're healed."

It felt good on her sore hands. So did his incredibly soothing touch. How did he manage that, as hard and rough as his own hands were?" Can I smear some under my eyes? I think I feel Samsonite forming."

One side of his mouth hitched up. "No. Just your hands. And make sure you wash them first."

"How about under your eyes? You don't look like you've been sleeping too well, either."

He glared at her as if it were her fault he looked so tired. "Never mind about my eyes."

"Okay." She curled her fingers around his. "Thanks."

Something odd happened. Time slowed down. The air around them seemed to buzz. Every one of Neal's senses sharpened, while her skin grew heavy and hot. *Not this again.*

It was his fault, of course. He was standing too close, crowding her. She looked up to tell him to back off, then stopped. His eyes weren't so glacial now. They were darker, hotter. Maybe it was the shadow from the rim of his hat. It moved over her face, blocking out the setting sun completely.

"You're welcome." He lifted his hand and ran the back of it down her cheek.

That single caress made something stir deep inside her—something simple and primordial. It made her feel more feminine than she'd ever felt in her life. Why? Because he was big and tough and strong, and yet being so gentle? No, it was her, something she'd spent years denying: the basic need for a man. Ryder touched her, and made her see him as a potential mate.

Potential, my butt. I want him.

His jacket smelled like hay and horses, but Neal didn't mind. It was a good smell, a guy smell. The men she'd known had always showered and doused themselves with aftershave before touching her. Despite that, she decided she'd take Ryder's scent over designer cologne any day.

He'd gone as still as a statue, only his eyes moving as he stared at her mouth. "I have to move that steer."

His voice had altered, too. It sounded more like a low, deep growl. Whatever had stirred abruptly woke up and demanded a few things—namely her hands on him, his hands on her.

"Uh-huh." His shirt felt damp beneath her reddened palm. She had no idea how her hand got under his jacket. She was too busy deciding where to touch him next. His throat, where his shirt was unbuttoned? The heavy line of his jaw? Up into that sun-bleached mane of his? "Move it, then come back. I don't have anywhere to go."

He had no problem choosing his spot. His hand slid around the back of her neck and held her there. "I'll be back tomorrow."

"Tomorrow?" She tilted her face up, letting her hair slide over his arm. He tightened his grip, and she nearly closed her eyes and purred, it felt so good. She inched her hand up and traced his mouth with her fingertip. "That long?"

"Yeah." He muttered something, then abruptly pulled away from her. "Okay, you can turn it off now."

What?

Ryder turned and walked away, leaving her standing there, alone and aching with longings she'd never wanted in the first place. She could have cheerfully killed him at that moment.

You can turn it off now.

As if she'd been the one to turn it on. Damn him, how could he do this to her? Clamping down on her temper, Neal squinted against the setting sun to watch him lead the steer from the barn and load it into the back of the trailer hitched to his pickup.

She still needed to speak to her uncle and find out if he'd gotten the call from overseas. If she got up early, dressed warmly, and walked down the highway, surely someone would give her a ride.

And wouldn't Ryder be surprised when he came back and found her gone?

The sound of the trailer doors slamming made her frown. *Ah, but you're not going to go without having one more look, are you?*

"Ryder."

Neal waited until he turned his head and she had his attention. *Here's what you're going to dream about tonight.*

She licked the finger she'd used to touch his mouth, from the base all the way to the tip. Slowly. Sensuously. As if it wasn't a finger at all.

He watched.

This is you, Ryder. Can you imagine what it would feel like? My mouth on you, just like this?

Neal wanted to give him a little more to think about. She eased the tip of her finger between her lips. She swirled her tongue over her fingertip. She caressed it with her lips. She used her teeth to nibble on it. She made it playful and explicit.

Ryder didn't move. Didn't blink. Didn't breathe.

That's right. Don't take your eyes off me. Here comes the big finale.

She finished with her last, graphic tease: sucking her finger into her mouth, slowly, inch by inch, then letting it slide back out. When the tip emerged, the suction caused a low pop.

Like that, my man? I bet your Calamity Jane never put on that kind of show for old Buffalo Bill.

He clenched his fists at his sides, then took an involuntary step toward her.

"Ah-ah-ah." She smiled, the waggled no-no with her wet finger. "You had your chance. See you tomorrow."

Revenge, she decided, was an excellent thing. Without another word she turned her back on him and went into the house, kicking the door shut behind her.

"You got any experience working short order, Mr."—Molly Hatcher checked the application in her hand—"Harvey?"

"Couple of years, on and off. It's all there." He wasn't worried about her checking.

"These jobs you've listed for the last two years are all over the country—New York, Los Angeles, Denver." She set down the form and gave him her full attention, the same way a drill sergeant would to a smart-ass recruit. "You're a real traveling man, Mr. Harvey."

Suspecting no amount of charm would make a dent in her armor, he gave her a shy smile instead. "Never found the right place to settle, until I got here. And please, call me George."

"Okay, George. I'll be honest, I'm short two cooks and I can't afford to be picky. You can start today, and if you haven't killed anyone by closing, you're hired."

He wondered what she would think if she knew he'd paid both cooks to quit on her and take an extended vacation out of town. "I really appreciate the job. Thanks, Miss Hatcher—"

"Molly. Everybody calls me Molly. Come on." She pushed her dark glasses up on her nose and slid out from the booth. "I'll show you the kitchen setup, and go over the food prep."

Slipping back into his role as a cook was no problem; he'd often used it as cover. An hour later he stood dressed in borrowed whites, flipping burgers at the grill with one hand and shaking a full fry basket with the other. After showing him the basics, Molly had left him alone, and the mindless task of cooking let him plan what he had to do that night.

"Hey, George!" Molly stood, one hand on her hip, peering in through the order window.

"Ma'am?"

She held up a plate of his meat loaf special, and smiled. "You do nice work."

He smiled and turned back to the grill. That he did.

Neal spent the rest of the day preparing for the trip, and planning what she'd do when she got to Lone Creek.

"Jeans, T-shirt, and sneakers." Neal laid everything she intended to wear out on her bed. "Water, a couple of granola bars, and sunscreen." She got that from the kitchen and packed them in her purse. "Something to cover my head." She looked through her case and pulled out a silk scarf. "It'll have to do."

Once she got to town, she'd contact her uncle and get an update on the situation in Denver. Ryder would probably think she was trying to run. Well, she'd show him. She'd wait until the trial. She'd find something to do on the ranch for the next two months, until they sent for her. Then it would be over. Finally, irrefutably over.

The next morning, Neal got up before dawn, got dressed, and headed out. The first couple of miles were easy—she was rested and determined. Then the sun rose, and the temperature started to climb.

"I bet they lied to me," she told a cow standing by the fence that ran down both sides of the road. "This isn't Montana. It's the Mojave Desert. Those mountains are just big cardboard cutouts. I'll bet you're really a camel, dressed in a cow costume."

The cow didn't deny it as it shuffled off.

She pulled out her bottle of Evian and drank half without stopping. After she parked herself under the shade of an elm tree, she pulled the scarf from her head and blotted her face with one end.

"I must be halfway there by now." The sound of an approaching car made her lean over to get a look at it. No, not a car—a truck. Ryder's black truck. "Oh, great, here comes the truant officer. I'll have to do a week of detention."

The truck came to a stop as soon as she got to her feet. *Might as well face the music.* Hauling her purse onto her shoulder, she walked up to the road—and stopped when she saw the man behind the wheel.

He wore a cowboy hat like Ryder's, but the blunt features beneath it were decidedly friendlier. "Hi, need a lift?"

"Yeah." Cautiously she approached the truck. A pile of feed sacks filled the back of the bed. "I do."

"Hop in."

"Thanks." Neal hurried around the truck and climbed in. "I really appreciate this."

"No big deal." The man put the truck into gear and started on down the road. "I'm Evan Gamble. I work up at High Point," he said, and held out his hand.

Neal took it. Like Ryder's, it was tanned and paved with calluses. "Neala Delaney. I'm staying at Sun Valley for a few weeks."

That made him stare. "You are?"

"A little vacation, courtesy of Will Ryder." She hoped he'd settle for that.

Evan grinned. "So you're the reason the boss has been running out every morning."

"That's me. I love to see men run. So, Evan Gamble, where are you headed?"

He pulled back onto the road. "Lone Creek Grain and Tool. Will's got a shipment of mineral supplement waiting for pickup." He glanced sideways. "You?"

"I don't know. New York? Boston? Acapulco? What do you suggest?"

"Acapulco is pretty crowded this time of year. I hate driving in Boston. Never been to New York." He rolled his shoulders and adjusted the tilt of his hat. "I can take you as far as Lone Creek."

He was being so nice that Neal felt guilty. "Listen, I appreciate this, but I should probably get out and keep walking. Ryder might not like you giving me a ride."

"Will won't mind." He shrugged. "Besides, no woman should be out here on her own. It's not safe."

"It looks pretty safe to me." She stared out the window at the fenced-off pastureland. There were miles of it, dotted with cattle, in every direction. Her uncle would love it here. He was getting too old for the game; it was time he retired.

If I let him live after I get back to Denver, that is.

She looked at Evan, who was humming along to the country music playing on the radio. "So what do you cowboys do around here for fun? Besides watch the hay grow?"

"Let me think." He pushed his hat back in a gesture Neal was starting to mentally tag as cowboy-thoughtful. "There's four rivers around here, plenty of good trout fishing. In a few weeks we'll have the Cutting Horse Show in Big Timber. And when we really get bored, there's always the pig races."

"You race *pigs*?"

"Yes, ma'am." He gave her a sideways smile. "Won twenty bucks last week myself, betting on a speedy little Chester White."

"Really." Neal couldn't decide if he was pulling her leg or not. "Does all this land belong to your boss?"

"Most of it. A couple of ranchers have grazing leases on some tracks to the south, but we use the rest." Evan went on to tell her about the High Point operation. The huge herds of cattle had to be moved regularly, for grazing and to market; there was an extensive dairy operation; and Ryder also bred Morgan stock horses for ranch use and cutting competitions.

"High Point's breeding program is so successful at producing quality Morgans that Will's usually got more offers than he has horses to go around."

"What's so special about these Morgans?"

"They're hardy, intelligent, strong, and have cow sense—that's not just important in this country, but necessary. You can't run a cattle operation without dependable stock horses."

"How many horses does he have?"

"We keep a regular stable of about seventy-five horses. A few of the stallions are kept for breeding and put out for stud, but most are gelded for ranch work."

Neal knew what *gelding* meant. "Ouch."

"So what are you going to do while you're staying at Sun Valley?"

"I might work on my tan, if the sun ever stays out longer than ten minutes."

"There's a nice plot out back of the property," Evan said. "Why don't you put in something?"

"Like what?" Neal thought of the big, open area behind the ranch house that was mostly mud. "A racing pigsty?"

"I wouldn't recommend it." He chuckled. "How about a garden?"

"Now, there's a serious fantasy. When I was a kid, I wanted to live on a farm and grow my own corn." Neal shook her head at the memory. "Probably came from watching too many episodes of *Green Acres*. You know, I wouldn't mind planting some stuff. Can you grow corn out here? And watermelons? I love cold watermelon."

"I wouldn't try growing them together," Evan said, evidently trying not to laugh.

Which reminded Neal how much she knew about gardening—absolutely zero. And if she tried, and made a mess of it? Evan might laugh, but Ryder would never let her live it down.

"Who am I kidding?" She studied the horrible condition of her nails. "All I've ever done was buy houseplants for my apartment, and even they keep dying on me. Besides, I'm not going to be here that long."

"Most vegetables take only a few weeks to grow. The soil's so rich around here they practically spring up overnight."

Neal gave him a suspicious look. "You really think someone like me could do it?"

"You won't know until you try."

The more she thought about it, the more Neal liked the idea. "Has anyone planted a garden there before?"

"I think Will's mom started one for him when he got married, but Trish never did anything with it."

Somehow the bottom fell out of the world. "I didn't know he was married," she said slowly.

"That was a long time ago, but"—he shook his

head—"let's just say the story didn't have a happy ending."

Her relief was instantaneous—and startling. "So he's divorced."

Evan gave her a measuring look. "She didn't much like living out here. Will tried to work it out with her, but she ended up running off with his stepbrother. Cleaned him out in the process—nearly cost him the ranch."

"No wonder he doesn't like women."

"Trish did a number on him. After the divorce, she got into some drugs, some other trouble. Died from an overdose a couple of years ago."

Neal felt a little sick. "Then I guess he has the right to be bitter."

"He's never had much time for women since then. Especially the good-looking kind."

"Don't tell me." She covered her eyes. "I look just like her, right?"

"Trish? No, she was a little blonde."

What had he called her, besides Calamity? *City girl.* "Where was she from?"

"Some big city down south. Not sure which state—"

"I'd put my money on Colorado, if I were you." Neal dug her fingers into the edge of her seat. Why did it hurt to think of Will married? Being dumped? Suffering? She couldn't care less. "No wonder he hates the sight of me."

Evan didn't catch on for a moment, then he groaned. "You're from the city, too?"

"Born and raised." She rubbed a hand over her eyes.

"Now I'm confused." He pushed back his hat to rub a thumb over his right brow. "You say Will can't stand the sight of you, but he's got you staying at Sun Valley. You think he'd be upset about me giving you a ride, but he's been out to see you every day himself. Maybe you could draw me a picture here, lady, 'cause I sure can't figure out what's going on."

"It's a really long story." By that time they'd reached the outskirts of town. "Let's just say Ryder and I rub each other the wrong way."

Evan shrugged. "Okay by me."

Like most small towns, Lone Creek had a wide main street, two rows of business establishments, and several side streets leading off to private homes. The buildings weren't new, and some needed a coat of paint, but even the shabbiest looked appropriate, given the setting.

The sense of a small, secure community was everywhere—in the flowers in the window boxes, doors left open, and people gathered in twos and threes, chatting and doing business. It tugged at Neal, and made her wistful for a moment.

What am I doing? I don't like little towns. I like cities filled with skyscrapers.

She spotted a pay phone. "Would you let me off here? I need to make some calls."

"Why don't you have lunch with me first?" He pointed to a restaurant with a blinking blue neon sign that read MOLLY'S DINER. "Best food in town."

She *was* hungry, and Evan Gamble seemed pretty harmless. "Okay, Evan. Lunch it is."

Chapter 6

"I'm going riding this afternoon, Daddy. See you at the house." Wendy hung up the telephone and looked at Will. "Daddy said to apologize for him, he didn't mean to miss your appointment. He's got to stay over in Billings tonight."

"No problem. I'll stop by the house when he gets back."

"So." She covered her typewriter and got up from her desk. "Did you hear about the woman who disappeared?"

Will looked up from the applications he'd been reading. Wendy Lewis sat down beside him on the office sofa and crossed her legs, showing off her shapely calves.

He eyed the silky green dress she wore. It was expensive, tailored, and made her look even younger than she was. He wouldn't tell her that. Wendy was twenty, heading with determination for forty. "You're going riding this afternoon like that?"

"No, silly, I'm going to change before I go." She tilted her head, letting the polished length of her fair hair brush against one shoulder. It was a beguiling gesture, one she'd probably practiced in front of a mirror. "But did you hear about that woman?"

"What woman?"

"The brunette. You know, the one who vanished into thin air?"

"No." Will set the applications aside and gave the girl his full attention. "Where did you hear about this?"

She gave him an exasperated frown. "Lord, Will, this town doesn't get any smaller. Everybody's heard about her. They say she was dressed like a street-walker, came into the truck stop with two strange men. Molly said you talked with them in town." Wendy leaned forward and dropped her voice to a whisper. "Who were they? Maybe they did something to her."

"I doubt it." He put the applications away and handed the file back to her. "Tell your dad to send the men over in the morning. I'll interview them myself." He got up and headed for the door.

Wendy beat him to it. "Do you have to go back right away?"

He thought of Neala, and the erotic little tease she'd given him the night before. "I've got things to do."

"Surely they can wait another hour." The young woman put her slim hand on his arm and squeezed. "Why don't you take me out to lunch?"

He wasn't hungry. "Another time, honey."

"But Will, we haven't spent any time together all winter." She gave him a pretty, little-girl pout. "I've missed you."

"Wendy—"

Her fingers tightened. "Please? Daddy wanted me to talk to you about putting Starlight out to stud this summer."

Dean bred all his mares at High Point, so that wasn't unusual. Wendy was particularly attached to her prizewinning stallion, too. "All right."

He waited until she collected her purse, then escorted her over to Molly's Diner. Along the way, Wendy passed along some of the wild rumors flying around town about the mysterious woman in red.

"Vicky over at the beauty parlor thinks she's a prostitute, and the sheriff had to run her out of town."

Will wouldn't mind seeing Neal run out of town. He wouldn't mind having splinters hammered under his nails one by one, either. "Lone Creek doesn't have a big draw for prostitutes, Wendy."

Wendy nodded to a pair of women passing by. "Mrs. Logan at the post office thinks she's hiding out from the police somewhere. Were those two men working undercover?"

"No."

Grady had called him last night and argued against moving her to High Point. "Keep here under wraps, Will. And yeah, this makes us even." Will had told him the way he saw it, Grady owed him. "She must be as bad as Selbrook said, then."

Which only made Will wonder how good she'd be. For hours.

"She could be a criminal, you know. Old man Tabbeck swears a woman dressed in red tried to steal his truck from him," Wendy said.

Will rubbed a hand over the headache pounding behind his forehead. "She didn't try to steal Tabbeck's truck."

"Aha!" Wendy smirked. "So you *do* know something about her."

"No, I don't." He pulled open the door to Molly's Diner. "And don't go spreading gossip that I do."

"I never spread gossip, you know that. I can't help hearing it, though." Wendy walked in, then came to a dead stop. "Well, now. Look who's here."

Will saw his stock manager sitting in a booth across from Neala Delaney, and swore softly before steering his companion in the opposite direction. Or he tried to. Wendy shook off his hand and headed straight for the unlikely couple.

"Evan, what a surprise." Wendy gave him her haughtiest smile, then turned to look down her nose at Neal. "Hello, I'm Wendy Lewis."

"Hi, Wendy Lewis." She picked up her soda and drank some through the straw. Next to the golden girl's smooth perfection, Neal appeared somewhat disheveled, but her dark eyes were amused, and her tawny skin practically glowed.

Windburn, he decided. Certainly not embarrassment at being caught by him.

Wendy's mouth got tight before she spoke to Will's foreman again. "Evan, I was just saying to Daddy the other day, we don't get to see too much of you anymore."

Evan nodded. "We've been pretty busy over the winter."

"I haven't seen your friend around here before." The girl sat down beside the foreman and leaned across the table to get Neal's attention. "What's your name?"

She set her glass down. "Neal."

"Neal." Wendy forced a laugh out. "*Really?* But that's a boy's name."

Dark eyes flashed up and sent a blatantly flirtatious message toward Will. "No one's mistaken me for one so far."

A man would have to be blind and nerve-dead from the neck down to do that, he thought as he watched her face. Even dressed in a T-shirt and loose jeans, she gave off a disturbing aura of feminine confidence and undiluted sensuality that made Wendy seem like an overdressed preteen in comparison.

"Neal's staying out at Sun Valley," Evan put in.

Will suppressed a groan as the blond girl's jaw dropped and her voice went shrill. "She is?"

"Uh-huh." Neal avoided Will's gaze by examining the floral pattern of Molly's wallpaper. "It's a nice place. Very, uh, rustic and peaceful."

Wendy's hands clenched as she looked up at him. "Seems like *someone* might have mentioned your visit before this."

No one responded to that. Obviously frustrated, Wendy studied Neal's rumpled clothes and windblown hair. "You know, you really ought to clean up before you come to town, dear. People will get the wrong impression."

"Will they?" Neal studied the other girl's immaculate dress. "I bet you never have that problem."

Aware her attack was being expertly countered, Wendy went on the defensive. "It's a woman's duty to look her best."

"For who? Him?" Neal switched her gaze to Will, and a suggestive gleam flickered in her eyes. "He doesn't think much of women who dress to aggravate men, do you, Ryder?"

Evan choked on the ice water he was trying to drink.

"I don't know where you come from, but around here people show Will respect." Wendy looked ready to grab Neal by the throat and shake her teeth out. "As his guest, maybe you should do the same, Neal."

"His guest." Neal snorted. "Is *that* what he's calling me?"

Will decided it was time to put an end to the hostilities, before the younger of the two felines resorted to using some claws. He took Wendy's arm and urged her out of the booth.

"Would you mind getting us a place to sit, honey? Thank you." He pushed her in the direction of some empty tables and waited until she had stomped off before addressing his foreman. "You've been busy this morning, Evan."

The younger man cleared his throat. "Neal needed a ride into town, boss. I brought her along and asked her to have lunch with me."

"For which I will be eternally grateful." Neal half rose from the booth. "Now if you two will excuse me—"

"Oh, no." Will clamped a hand on her shoulder and pushed her back down on the seat. "You're not leaving just yet."

"You're not *my* boss, Ryder."

"As far as you're concerned, I am for the next eight

weeks." He sat down next to her, compelling her to slide over to avoid contact. Which was fine with him; he didn't want to touch her. "Stay put. Evan, excuse us."

"Evan, don't leave. Much as I admire your diplomacy, Ryder, as well as your strong-arm tactics against women, there isn't a thing you can do to stop me—if I *wanted* to leave, that is." Neal turned to Evan and gave him a brilliant smile. "This place is really starting to grow on me."

Will saw his foreman's momentary confusion, but it didn't make the surge of anger inside him recede. On the contrary, it just took another direction. "Don't waste your time, lady. He works for me."

Neal let out a low, sexy laugh, which drew the instantaneous attention of every male sitting in the diner.

"But he's taking his lunch break with me." She reached across the table and linked her hand with Evan's, threading her slim fingers through his. "Now, if you don't mind, we were having a private conversation."

She thought she could dismiss him. Just like that.

Molly came over. "Good morning, Will. You going to order something? My new cook's got an omelet everyone's raving about."

"No, thanks," he said, staring at Neal's mouth. The instant memory of what he'd seen her do with it the last time they'd clashed made him go hard. He wasn't going anywhere for a few minutes, so he decided to even the score. He slid his arm up along the back of the booth, just behind Neal's shoulders, and smiled as she stiffened.

He wasn't the only one feeling hot and bothered.

"I'd suggest you get over there and calm Wendy down," Molly was saying. "Right now she looks ready to throw a hissy fit. And you know how I attached I am to my glassware."

"Ask her to order for both of us." Neal's nearly

black eyes had more than amusement glowing in them now, and he liked watching the heat flare. Once Molly had gone to placate Wendy, he asked, "How long did you walk before Evan picked you up?"

"Not long." She moved her shoulders, discreetly inching away. "Maybe a mile or two."

He closed the gap between them by bending his head to murmur near her ear, "Why didn't you put on the red dress?"

"Oh, I never wear the same outfit twice." Neal slanted a look around him. "That girl seems pretty young to be cutting her teeth on you. Do you have a thing for teenagers?"

Evan cleared his throat again.

"Drag your mind out of the gutter, city girl," Will told her. "Wendy's a neighbor, and the daughter of a friend of mine."

"The girl next door." Neal rubbed her thumb over the back of Evan's hand, making little affectionate circles. "How sweet."

His foreman shifted uneasily. "Will, I'll give Neal a ride back to the ranch. Neal, we'd better go."

They both ignored him.

"I've known Wendy since the day she was born." Will moved his hand until it rested against the back of her neck. "Leave her alone, Neala. She's not in your league."

She gave him an ironic look. "I don't pick on children."

"So what am I going to do with you now?" He moved his own thumb over the delicate skin of her nape.

Her eyes narrowed. "I have some suggestions."

"You've got a mouth on you, woman," Will said. "Keep running it and see where it gets you."

"I know where you'd like to get me." She batted her eyelashes at him. "Maybe we could work something out."

The fact that she was plainly willing to barter herself

frayed the last threads of his equilibrium. "Can't you go a week without crawling into someone's pants?"

"Gee, I don't know." A slow, insulting smile appeared. "Are you *that* horny?"

He wanted to slap her. Kiss her. Drag her kicking and screaming back to his ranch. To his room. To his bed. But he'd be damned if he'd let her know it. He turned to his foreman. "Got a quarter? The lady needs to make up her mind."

Evan looked appalled. Neala went white.

Molly instantly appeared. "Will, why don't you come on over here?"

His foreman let go of her hand, grabbed his hat, and put it on. "Neal, let's go. Now."

"Sit down, Evan. Or you're fired."

Molly hit the table with a menu. "Will! That is enough!"

It wasn't enough. Not by a long shot. He looked at his gaping foreman, then back at the lovely face that had haunted him for days. "Tell you what, honey. You want to tangle with me, forget the quarter. Just say the word."

Molly gave up trying to distract Will and turned toward the kitchen. "George, I need you out here."

Neal let go of Evan's hand and scooted over, getting close enough to bump Will's nose with hers. "Ryder, I have *four* words for you: Don't hold your breath."

He could feel her shaking. "I won't have to, will I?" He cupped a hand around her neck, watched her nostrils flare, and saw the rage in her eyes change to something else. She was as wild and hungry as he was. "Pretty soon you'll be begging me for it."

"George!" Molly yelled, then stamped her foot. "Where *is* that damn man when I need him? Got to do everything myself." She turned back to the table and hit Ryder with a menu. "All right, Will. Turn that girl loose and get on over there with Wendy, now. *Now,* or I'm calling Caleb."

He slowly released her and rose to his feet. Neal

reached for her empty soda glass and played with the straw, refusing to look at him. Which was fine with him. Another second of this and he would throw her over his shoulder and carry her off into the woods. "Evan, when you're done here, take the lady back to Sun Valley."

Will put his hat on and headed for the entrance. A moment later, Wendy hurried after him, pausing long enough to give Neal a sneer before she went out the door.

Molly's dark-tinted glasses slipped down her nose as she leaned over to put a gentle hand on Neal's arm. "You all right, honey?"

"Yes." Pushing her plate away and wiping her damp hands with her napkin gave her something to do. She definitely felt like she'd been hit by a truck this time. One that had turned around and backed over her for good measure. "Sorry about that."

"I don't know what's bugging Will Ryder, but I've never seen him act like that before. Oh, well. I'm Molly Hatcher, by the way." She gave Neal a strained smile, then looked across the table. "I'd run her home now, Evan, if I were you."

The foreman stopped staring at the front door and shook his head. "The lady has some phone calls to make first, I believe."

Molly glanced at the wall. "I'd offer mine for you to use, but I'm not going to risk riling Will."

"I will," Evan said. "There are plenty of pay phones on Main Street."

Neal touched his arm. "Evan, I don't want to get you fired—"

"I don't know what your situation is, but Will's got no right to keep you from making phone calls."

She shook her head. "You don't know the whole story."

"That's true enough, but it's still a free country." He got up and paid for their lunch. "Come on, Neal."

"Don't let Will see her making them," was Molly's advice.

Evan led Neal out to the nearest pay phone, and stood sentinel a few feet away as she picked up the receiver and went to put a coin in. When it wouldn't fit, she stared at John Kennedy's profile and swore.

Idiot. Pay attention, will you?

She scrounged in the bottom of her purse for smaller change, and found enough to make her calls. Or try to. The overseas number she'd memorized rang endlessly, with no answer. Her uncle Sean's phone had been disconnected. Laney had left a message on her answering machine saying she was on her *honeymoon*. The only person she could reach was her neighbor, Beth.

"Laney came around a few weeks ago, Neal. I haven't seen your uncle since before Christmas. Excuse me for a minute." Beth yelled at her kids to stop fighting. "Sorry. They're trying to brain each other again. Bobby, put that down. Do *not* hit your sister with that baseball bat."

She waited until there was a lull in the shrieks. "Bethie, if you see my uncle, will you tell him I'm in Lone Creek, Montana? A place called Sun Valley. Ask him to get in touch with me as soon as he can. It's really important that I talk to him."

"Sure, sweetie."

"Thanks, Beth."

"Oh, wait, I forgot. Some guy came by last week to see you."

"What did he look like?"

"Tall, dark, and handsome. Nice suit. Carried a funny-looking cane. I passed him knocking at your door in the hallway, and told him you haven't been around for the last couple of weeks. What are you doing in Montana, anyway?"

J. R. had been to her apartment.

"Just hanging around with the cows."

There was an ear-piercing scream, then the sound

of sobbing. "Whoops, now Bobby just got brained. I have to go, Neal."

"Okay. I'll talk to you when I get back. 'Bye." She hung up the phone. "Evan, I need to take a walk and do some thinking. I know you're already probably in deep, hot water with Ryder, but would that be okay?"

"Sure. I'll meet you back here in an hour. You all right, Neal?"

"Yes." No, she wasn't. "Thanks."

She wandered aimlessly for some time, processing what Beth had told her, and what it meant.

Her uncle was gone, the FBI had dumped her off in the middle of nowhere, and J. R. was actively looking for her. She didn't have a phone, neighbors, or agents protecting her. She'd been virtually a prisoner at the ranch, unable to leave or communicate with the outside world. Suddenly it came together.

She was the bait.

It wouldn't have upset her so much if they'd told her they wanted to use her to get J. R. But the ominous fact remained—they hadn't. Why? They didn't know what had happened in the senator's suite. If they had, they certainly wouldn't be using her like this.

But why leave her at Sun Valley? Why not keep her in Denver? It made absolutely no sense.

She stood and stared at an antique window display for so long, eventually the owner came out to see what was the matter.

"Excuse me, dear?"

"Huh?" The gentle touch on her arm dragged her back to reality. "Oh, sorry."

The elderly woman smiled. "Are you window-shopping, my dear, or looking for something specific?"

"Um, neither, really. I was just passing by."

"Why don't you come inside? All my books are fifty percent off this week."

She liked to read, and it would give her something to do while she was stuck out at the ranch. "Okay."

Neal followed her into the small shop, which was

filled with an eclectic assortment of furnishings, knick-knacks, and clothes. One card table was stacked with a collection of antique books; another had more recent editions, most written about the region.

"Do you have a particular subject matter you enjoy?"

"History." Knowing how little money she had left in her wallet, Neal went to the newer books. "Do you have anything about Calamity Jane?"

"I believe she's mentioned in *High Border Country*. There's more in Connelley's biography of Wild Bill Hickok."

Wild Bill. Neal's mouth quirked. "Was he really her boyfriend?"

"Her husband, if you believed her stories. Calamity claimed they'd gotten married secretly, though most historians didn't believe her. It's my understanding that woman told some real whoppers."

She's not the only one.

The shopkeeper came over to the table and started sorting through the books. "Still, she maintained it was the truth to the very end—even got herself buried next to Wild Bill. Here." She pulled out a slim edition. "This was published locally, by a town historian back in the thirties."

"Wild and Wonderful, a history of Martha Jane Burk," Neal read the title out loud, then read the first paragraph. "It looks interesting. How much?"

The shopkeeper named a reasonable sum, and Neal paid for the book. She took the bag and frowned when she heard a faint rattle. Inside were several packets of seed, bundled together. "What's this?"

"Just a little spring gift I give my customers," said the older woman. "Everyone forgets how nice it is to plant a garden."

Neal read the directions on the back and recalled what Evan had said. "Isn't it too early to start one now?"

"Not at all. The ground has been thawed for weeks."

"Sounds like a plan, then." She grinned at the shop-keeper as she pocketed the seeds. "If this works, I'll have to bring you some salad."

"Just leave out the zucchini, my dear." The woman winked. "It gives me terrible gas."

A few minutes later, she met Evan in front of Molly's Diner.

"Everything go okay?"

"Not really. Everyone back in Denver is gone. My uncle. My sister, too. She went and got married, for God's sake." She tried to sound nonchalant, but her heart was aching. *Laney got married and they never told me.* "That pretty much takes care of anyone who can get me out of here. I guess I'm stuck depending on Ryder for the duration."

"I've got some money put away. I can float you a loan, if you want."

His generosity touched her. So did his willingness to lose his job. "No, Evan, but thanks for the offer."

He argued with her for a few minutes, then gave in. "All right, you little mule. Come on, I'll take you home."

Evan drove her back to Sun Valley, and politely pretended not to notice how her attention drifted from their conversation. When they arrived, he walked up to the house with her. "Home, sweet home. You need anything else?"

"A phone. A Doberman. An Uzi."

"Can't help you with any of that, sorry. How about I stop by in a couple days, see how you're doing?"

"That would be nice. I can burn some lunch for you." She gave him a faintly guilty look. "Thanks for everything. Especially letting me do that thing in the diner. You know. With the hands and all."

He faked a horrified look. "You mean you're not head over heels in love with me?"

She laughed. "No, but I could use a friend."

"You've got one." He tipped his hat. "Nice meeting you, Neal. See you soon."

She felt even more alone when Evan left, then re-membered the seed packets in her pocket, and took them out. "So what have we got to plant? Tomatoes, cucumbers, lettuce . . . and the dreaded zucchini." She shook the packets and listened to the seeds rattle. "Time to plant a salad."

Molly found her new short-order cook leaning up against a wall outside the delivery entrance.

"There you are. I thought I'd have to drag Ryder out of the place by myself." She looked around. "What are you doing out here? Watching the grass grow?"

George crushed a cigarette out under his shoe. "Just taking a break, Molly."

"Your break's over. I've got ten orders waiting for you. And don't think you can get on my good side by batting those pretty dark eyes at me."

"Yes, ma'am." He followed her back into the kitchen and glanced through the pickup window. Neal was still out there, sitting with the cowboy she'd come in with. He'd have to keep out of sight for now. "What's the problem with this fellow Ryder?"

"Will's a cattleman, owns most of the land around here. He's got some girl staying out at his old place, Sun Valley. They had a run-in a few minutes ago." Molly shook her head. "I never saw Will blow his top like that before. That girl's really got him steaming."

He didn't like hearing that. At all. "Sorry I missed it."

Molly gave him an odd look, and he quickly con-trolled his expression.

"It was something to see, that's for sure." She joined him at the grill and started laying out rows of hamburger patties. "Got some compliments on that special omelet of yours. The customers really like it."

"Glad to hear it." He flipped over a couple of grilled cheeses and checked the potato fryer.

"Don't talk much, do you, George?"

He smiled. "Don't have much to say, ma'am."

George wouldn't have been grinning if he'd heard the phone call Molly Hatcher made as soon as he left the diner that afternoon.

"Molly, I think your imagination is working overtime." Sheriff Caleb Walton said. "I did the background check, just like you asked me to. George Harvey is just who he says he is."

"He asks a lot of questions. And the minute that girl Ryder has out at Sun Valley showed up, he disappeared on me."

"Maybe he needed a break, like he told you."

"Maybe he didn't want her to have a look at him. Have you found anything out about her?"

Caleb had, thanks to a phone call from the Denver district attorney, but he couldn't pass on what he'd told him to Molly. "She's a friend of Will's. Like George, she's got a clean record. Stop reading all those detective novels, Molly. They're giving you too many wild ideas about folks."

"Something is going on here, Sheriff," Molly said. "And I mean to get to the bottom of it."

"No call for that. I'll have one of my deputies check into Harvey a bit more. Will that satisfy you?"

"For now."

Will silently checked the new mineral supplement Evan brought back to High Point, then helped his foreman unload the fifty-pound bags into the storage shed.

After they'd stowed the last sack, Evan dusted off his hands and regarded his boss. "You intend to tell me what's going on with that gal, or should I collect my gear and find myself another job?"

"I'm not going to fire you," Will said, disgusted with himself for even considering it. "She's staying at Sun Valley for the next two months. I'm looking after her for a friend."

"She's the one who came in with those government

boys." Evan resettled his hat. "In a world of trouble, too, isn't she?"

"It doesn't help that everyone in town got a look at her and knows where she is." He opened the door to the pickup. "You find her on the road again, you take her back to Sun Valley and leave her there."

"I hope you know what you're doing, boss."

Will's eyes went cold. "Steer clear of this, Evan. She's my problem, not yours." He climbed in and started the engine. "Tell Bea not to worry about dinner for me. See you later."

As he drove down the road to the valley, Will replayed the entire scene in Molly's Diner once more. He should have grabbed the city girl and marched her out of there the moment he'd seen her. Instead he'd let her upset the daughter of a good friend and provoke him into losing control. Plus it had nearly cost him the best employee he had.

It was time for Neala Delaney to stop playing games.

He didn't bother to knock this time as he went to the front door. "Neala?"

Her voice sounded faint. "Back here."

He walked through the house, saw the remains of a small meal on the kitchen table, and heard a strange shuffling sound outside the back door. When he opened it, he found her standing in the middle of the yard, using a shovel to dig what appeared to be a crooked, shallow trench.

"Burying something?"

"Not yet." She stuck the blade of the shovel in the ground and propped herself against the handle. "Still mad about what happened in town today?"

"We need to talk."

"Okay." She abandoned the shovel and brushed past him to get into the kitchen. Her expression was completely serene as she washed the mud from her hands at the sink. "Can I offer you something to drink? Coffee? Ice water? English stuff?"

"No, thanks." He tossed his hat on the counter and leaned back against the wall. If he kept his hands in his jacket pockets, maybe they'd be able to settle this without fireworks. "Did you make your phone calls?"

"Tried to. Not much luck in that department." She gave him a little smile as she began clearing the dishes from the table. "Have you had dinner? I've got some desiccated chicken breast and overcooked broccoli spears left over from mine, if you're interested."

"I'll pass." He watched her run a sink of hot water to immerse the dishes in, then felt something inside him snap. A moment later he had her turned around and backed up against the counter. "I said we need to talk."

She kept her chin up and her expression bland, but he could feel the tension vibrating beneath the hands he'd latched around her upper arms. It matched the urgency knotting up his own muscles. "Feel free."

If he took another step, he'd be all over her. He tightened his grip, hoping that would preserve the space between them. "What you did today could get you killed."

She scoffed. "The food at Molly's wasn't that bad. I sort of liked it—though I have to say, my sister is a much better cook."

He gave her a small shake. "You pull a stunt like this again, you'll be eating your meals vertical for a week."

"You're into spanking?" Neal's eyes widened with mocking astonishment. "My, my. You country boys certainly are more, um, unconventional than I thought. You know, personally, I've never tried it—is it as erotic as they say it is?"

"You're playing with the wrong man, Calamity."

"Oh, but I'm not really *playing* with you, Ryder." She tilted her head back and gave him an adorable smile. "Believe me, when I do, you won't be asking me to quit. Now, let go of me."

He might have resisted the taunting and the smile,

but the way her voice purred out those last four words reminded him of what she'd said at the diner: *Don't hold your breath.*

She must have realized she'd pushed him too far, because as he moved in she tried to dodge to one side. A moment later he had her body trapped between him and the hard edge of the counter, and it required only a quick jerk to position her so that his thighs straddled hers. He clamped one arm around her waist, and caught her chin with his other hand.

"Ryder, don't—"

He didn't let her utter another syllable, but took her open mouth with his.

The kiss didn't start out very well. Ryder was angry, his mouth bruising. He kept her clamped against him with one arm, and took a handful of her hair to hold her still. The smell of sweat and horses and temper rolled off him as he forced her lips apart with one brutal thrust of his tongue.

She'd wondered more than once how it would feel to kiss him. Hot and deep and more than a little cruel was how. She groaned, but he swallowed the sound and took more.

Just when she thought she'd have to whack him on the side of the head with the teakettle, something inside her unfolded and welcomed the near-violent invasion.

Oh, boy. I'm in trouble.

All her life she'd handled men with minimal effort. A little innocuous flirting, combined with some careful manipulation, had always brought even the most determined males to heel. Now, here, held captive in Ryder's arms, she felt her self-imposed constraints collapsing. For once she was not in complete control of the situation, and it was frightening and paralyzing and absolutely marvelous.

Because deep inside Neal suddenly understood that Will Ryder couldn't ever be handled.

The long-dormant feminine side of her nature came forth with a vengeance. At last, she could let it all go. Show him what lay beneath the facade. Her hands crept up as she held on, clinging bonelessly to him, letting him take what he wanted, giving him her softness and heat in return.

As she responded, the kiss changed. Savage demand became confident possession. The thrust of his tongue inside her mouth slowed, savoring and stroking hers in an intrinsic imitation of sex. His hand swept down her back and spread over the curve of one hip, pulling her away from the counter and into him.

So good. How does he make me feel so good, so wild, so fast?

He lifted his head and tugged hers back by the curls in his hand. His eyes became piercing slits as he pressed her closer, her breasts against his chest. "Tell me what you want, Neala."

She loved the way he said her name; it sent a thrill through her that made her skin tingle and her pulse race. "Kiss me again."

"That's all?" His breath warmed her lips as his mouth hovered. "Don't you want more?"

She wanted a lot more, and tried to press her lips to his. He turned his face and buried it in her hair. "Ryder, *please*."

"Tell me, Neala." His voice suddenly went low and lethal. "What's your price? Another trip to town? More phone calls? A plane ticket out of here?"

Neal went still as his hand settled over her breast. "What?"

"A woman like you doesn't give it away for free." He swept his thumb back and forth over the rigid peak of her nipple. "What's this going to cost me?"

Her breast swelled under his hand, even as disgust made her stomach clench. "I'm not for sale." She shoved at him, but a concrete wall would have been easier to move. "Get off."

Slowly he let his hand slide away and stepped back,

making it clear it was his choice to do so. "So it's all a tease, is it?"

"You're the one putting on the performance here, Ryder. Not me." Neal jumped down from the counter and prayed her knees would hold. After one alarming quiver, they did. "Are we through, or do you want to yell at me again?"

"We're done." He headed for the door.

"Wait. You didn't fire Evan, did you?"

"Evan Gamble is the best foreman in the entire state," he said, abruptly turning away. "He's also my friend."

"He's a good man." She wrapped her arms around her abdomen as the deep, unrelieved ache within her intensified. "I didn't intend to get him in trouble with you."

"Then do both of us a favor, and don't hitch any more rides with him." He opened the door. "Or anyone else."

"You can't seriously expect me to sit here and do nothing until the trial."

"You'll do exactly what I tell you to do, Neala." Now he looked at her. "Or a spanking will be the least of your worries."

Chapter 7

A long shadow separated from the darkness surrounding the barn and started stretching toward the ranch house. Lights still burned in the kitchen, but the rest of the rooms were pitch-black and silent.

Ryder had left hours ago, but Neala Delaney had spent half the night digging up the backyard. The operative had waited patiently, watching as Neala Delaney shoveled a series of narrow trenches that eventually formed a rectangular grid in the soft, loamy soil. She stopped infrequently to lean against the shovel handle and utter a few soft curses.

Most were directed against Ryder, which wasn't surprising, given the passionate scene inside the kitchen earlier that evening. The operative was aware of the danger posed by the cattle rancher, and his obvious infatuation with Neala. His frequent presence at Sun Valley was yet another unnecessary complication, requiring that the work be done swiftly and in the middle of the night.

Finally Neala finished digging her trenches, placed the shovel beside the back door, and went inside.

An hour had passed since then, and the intruder judged the time was right. Noiselessly the figure left the shadows and moved toward the bedroom window. Once satisfied Neala was asleep, the operative took only a minute to pick the lock on the back door and slip inside the house.

The outline of the sleeping woman in the bedroom

proved tempting, but the intruder kept to the plan and began a silent, methodical search. Only when it became apparent the item was not in plain sight did the shadow stretch over the woman again.

At the same time, Neal dreamed of something creeping over her, and shuddered in her sleep.

Spiders.

She hated spiders, had hated them since childhood. There had always been webs in the corners of the bedroom she'd shared with Laney. Bridget had never been big on housecleaning, and Laney had always been too busy messing around at the stove. When Neal had complained about them, her mother had only laughed.

"Spiders are lucky, Neal. They eat all the other bugs, and they're cute. Leave them the hell alone, will you?"

Neal didn't think spiders were lucky, or useful, or cute. She thought they were bloodsucking little monsters, just waiting to crawl down and bite little girls while they were sleeping.

Later, when she'd gone into foster care, she'd actually been bitten by one. That had happened when one of her "parents" had locked her in the cellar overnight as punishment for disobedience. Even after her uncle had found her and brought her home to live with him and Laney, she usually stayed up half the night, covers clutched tightly around her neck, watching for them.

In her mind, a huge spider dangled just above her. It had slanted black eyes and a sinister smile. She tried to cringe, but she was paralyzed as it moved closer, whispering her name. The dream became an authentic nightmare as it pinned her arm, and stung her.

Even then, it wasn't finished. It began talking to her. *Neala . . . tell me about my crocus, Neala. . . .*

"Leave me alone." Somehow Neal pulled her pillow over her head and huddled under the sheets. The pillow muffled her voice as she said, "I don't have your crocus. I'll plant one tomorrow. Just go away!"

If she had been conscious, Neal would have seen the operative beside her bed, carefully replacing the syringe in the case on the nightstand. However, the injection of flunitrazepam raced through Neal's bloodstream, and went to work at once on her nervous system.

The drug enabled the operative to ease the pillow away and pull the covers back without fear of waking the drugged woman. A subsequent impersonal search turned up nothing. "Neala. Tell me where the microdisk is. Did you bury it outside? Is that why you were digging?"

Trapped in her nightmare, Neal felt the spider's cold touch wandering down her body, but she was too terrified of being bitten again to move or open her eyes.

The spider didn't bite her, but its voice got nasty. *I'm waiting, Neala . . . tell me where you put it . . . where you put my crocus. . . .*

She tried to swipe at it, but something was holding her down, and she was too groggy to fight it. If she could just wake up. . . . "No. Get lost. Go spin a web or eat a bug or something."

Searching the house proved useless for the operative. She must have hidden it somewhere, but where? Then the thought occurred—perhaps the microdisk was encased in an ordinary object. One she could have left sitting out in plain view.

The operative confiscated every item that could have been disassembled, then put back together to hide the item. It was tempting to think of retrieving hand tools from the storage shed behind the house and doing the work here, but it was getting close to dawn now.

After taking care to make the house appear to have been ransacked by an eager burglar, the operative went back to have one last look at the woman. She was lying on her side now, her cheek resting against her hand.

Such innocence in sleep. Such a scorpion when awake.

Dawn crept up from behind the mountains, making the stars fade. The operative eyed the horizon, and swiftly recalled what facts had been included in the woman's profile. Abuse had required intervention and removal from one foster home, and the child's resulting severe arachnophobia had been noted. So Neala had not outgrown her fear of spiders. That could prove extremely useful.

"If you don't tell me where it is, Neala, I will lock you back in the cellar."

The huge head bent closer, and Neal saw something gleam. Fangs. It was going to drag her back down into the dark. Bite her. Poison her. She shrieked and twisted out of the spider's grip.

"Don't hurt me!"

She stumbled out of bed and ran. Instinct led her through the house and out the back door. Something hit her from behind, causing an explosion of pain. Darkness dragged her down, and with a grateful sigh Neal tumbled into that endless pit, oddly confident the spider couldn't follow after her.

The operative bent to check the woman's pulse, which was slow, but steady. Apparently five milligrams was not enough to keep her docile. Unfortunately, the blow to the back of the head meant Neala Delaney wouldn't be able to answer any more questions—for now.

After dragging the unconscious woman and propping her under a tree, the operative returned to the house for a second, more thorough search.

Failure was not a concern. Should the items taken prove to be worthless, the final order would be carried out.

The tong must be protected. If you cannot retrieve the microdisk, ensure that it is destroyed. Along with the woman.

The house was old. Neal Delaney spent much of her time alone. All the equation needed was a tragic accident that would obliterate all traces of the woman and the item.

A fire would do nicely.

"Neal."

She turned over and mumbled something.

"Neal, you're getting a pink nose."

She swatted at the sound. "Go away."

Firm hands shook her out of her sleep, and she opened her eyes, completely disoriented. Then she spit a piece of grass out of her mouth and squinted up at the woman standing over her. "Molly?"

"Here, grab my hand." Molly helped her up. "Do you always sleep out in the yard?"

"Not as a rule. Ugh." Neal brushed at the dried mud and grass clinging to her clothes. "I must have been sleepwalking." When she stood, she yelped and grabbed her head. "Or aliens tried to abduct me."

"Maybe you should check where Wendy was last night."

"Wendy's an alien?"

Molly huffed out a laugh. "She's too pretty. I keep wanting to check behind her ears for surgical scars."

Neal managed a grin in spite of the throbbing pain behind her eyes. "So what are you doing here? Did we forget to pay the bill yesterday or something?"

"I didn't much care for what Will Ryder did yesterday at my place. Thought I'd stop in, see how you're getting along."

"That scene was partly my fault, too."

"With a man like Ryder, a woman's got to stand up for herself." Molly pushed her glasses up on her nose and looked down at her sensible shoes. "I have to admit, I also felt bad about not letting you use my phone. Lone Creek's a small town, and we usually do try to look out for each other."

"I'm not exactly a permanent resident."

"Even more reason I should have helped you out." Molly took Neal's hand between hers. "I'm real sorry about that, Neal. Next time you're in town, your meal's on the house, okay? And if you need anything in the meantime, all you have to do is holler."

Without a phone, she might have to do just that. "If you steer me toward the house, we'll call it even."

"Sure." The older woman chuckled and put an arm around Neal's waist. "Let's get you inside, girl."

Neal stumbled along, leaning heavily against the other woman. "So am I the scarlet woman of Lone Creek now?"

"You've certainly become the number one topic of conversation with my customers." Molly opened the back door, then came to a halt. "Neal? You get rambunctious when you sleepwalk?"

"I don't think so."

"It looks like someone else did last night."

The kitchen had been completely trashed: drawers pulled out, cabinets emptied, refrigerator door hanging open. Food was strewn from one end of the room to the other.

"I just *cleaned* this kitchen, damn it!" Neal stalked out into the living room, and shrieked with outrage when she saw what had been done there. She would have gone to the bedroom, but Molly grabbed her by the arm and pulled her out through the front door.

"Someone might still be inside," the older woman said. "Stay out here and let me get to my car phone. I'll call the sheriff."

Neal paced back and forth in front of the house while Molly made the call. "I can't believe this. Who would do this to me? Why? I'm going to buy a gun. A huge gun. An elephant gun. I swear to God. And when I find out who trashed my house, I'm going to shoot him right in the—"

Molly interrupted her tirade with, "Sheriff's on the way. He said you and I had better head up to the front gate and wait there for him."

                    *   *   *

Sheriff Caleb Walton was a big man who did not
like being dragged out of his office early on a Sunday
morning. Especially for a burglary that could have easily been prevented. After he thoroughly checked the
house and found no signs of a forced entry, he told
Neal as much.

"You can't expect to safeguard your possessions if
you go leaving the house unlocked all night, Miss
Delaney."

"I thought you people in the country never locked
your doors."

The sheriff rolled his eyes. "This ain't Mayberry,
ma'am. I'll go check the barn and the utility shed
now."

As Caleb Walton searched the other buildings, Neal
sat on the front steps and rubbed the back of her
head. Beneath her fingers, her scalp felt sore. She must
have rapped it on the tree when she was sleepwalking
last night.

But I've never done that. Not even when I was a kid.

It scared her to think she'd lain unconscious in the
yard while someone had vandalized the house. Although perhaps it had saved her from being raped,
or . . .

*Or whoever did this hit me over the head and
dragged me out there.*

For a moment, the image of J. R.'s cruel, thin face
swam before her eyes, then she shook it off. It
couldn't be him, he would have never left her alive.
Who else could it be? No one knew where she was,
except the government, and they had no reason to
knock her out and search the house. Then she recalled
something Molly had said.

*You've certainly become the number one topic of
conversation with my customers.*

Of course. After her run-in with Will, by now everyone in town knew she was staying at Sun Valley.

"Ms. Delaney," the sheriff said behind her, startling

her. "Would you walk through the house now, see if anything is missing?"

"Sure."

Neal went from room to room, but despite the mess evidently nothing had been taken. "I think everything's still here, Sheriff."

"Could have been a couple of kids, looking for money." He didn't sound convinced by his own theory.

Neal frowned. Vandals wouldn't search a house so thoroughly; it had to be someone looking for something specific. She had no money and nothing worth being pawned. Unless . . .

. . . *tell me where you put it* . . . What had the spider called it? *My crocus.*

Which sounded a lot like *microdisk.*

"I think you'd better talk to Will Ryder about a security system," the sheriff was saying.

If the Chinese knew where she was, knew she had it, why had they left her alive? "I don't have one," she said absently.

"Which is why he should put one in. I'll write up the report and send him a copy. That's about it, then."

They couldn't kill her. Not until they got their hands on the microdisk. And she couldn't give it to anyone until she spoke to Karen. She stared blankly at Caleb Walton. "That's it?"

"Give me a call if you see anyone hanging around the property. Sometimes they like to come back." The sheriff touched the rim of his hat. "Ladies." He started for his car.

"Excuse me, Sheriff Walton." Neal came after him, stunned that he meant to leave. She had to know if the Chinese were responsible, but she couldn't exactly explain that to him. "I'd sleep a lot better if I knew who did this."

"So would I."

"Maybe you could investigate a little further."

"What else would you like me to do, ma'am?"

"I'm not sure. Isn't there some way to identify who broke in?" She gestured around her. "You know, dust everything for fingerprints or something?"

"Well, now." He pushed his hat back. "I can put a call in to the county coroner's office. Doc Sutter could probably head on out here and dust the place, say by next Tuesday. Of course, you won't be able to touch or move anything until after he's done. You got somewhere else to stay in the interim?"

Neal thought of Will's offer. No, she couldn't go to High Point now. She had to stay where she was and find out if the Chinese had indeed tracked her down. Then she had to find her uncle. "Skip the fingerprints. What else can we do?"

Caleb looked at Molly. "You see anything, Miss Hatcher?" Molly shook her head. "And you already said you slept through the whole thing, Miss Delaney. Seems to me you two are the only witnesses."

"Maybe the FBI could help you out."

He met her gaze steadily. "Oh, I plan to put in a call to Denver, ma'am. Soon as I get back to the office."

So he knew something about her situation. Perhaps a report would convince the feds to move her again. "Thanks. I'd appreciate that."

"Have a good day, now." Out he went.

Neal pressed the heels of her hands to her temples. "Not without a bottle of aspirin."

"It's not as bad as it looks." Molly patted her shoulder. "I'll stay and help you clean up."

Molly did more than that. After they had restored the house to fundamental order, she sent Neal to take a hot shower and made breakfast for both of them.

"Can I use your phone, Molly?" Neal asked when she emerged from the bathroom. "I need to talk to Ryder about this."

"Already put in a call to High Point myself. He's out on the range, but Bea promised to give him the message as soon as he rides in."

A truck pulled up in front of the house, but it was Will's foreman who strode up to the door.

"Bea told me what happened." Evan made a disgusted sound when he saw the disarray, then followed Neal into the kitchen. "Are you okay?"

"She's fine. Pull up a chair." Molly set a place for him.

As Neal toyed with her food, Molly filled Evan in on the burglary.

"I'll ask Will about an alarm system." Evan finished his coffee. "Though I don't think he's going to be too happy to hear about this break-in."

"It's my fault," Neal said automatically. "I forgot to lock the doors." She looked at the foreman. "When will he be back?"

"Probably around noon. Don't worry; he'll take care of it, Neal."

She smiled at the foreman, and nodded. It didn't really matter what they did—if the Chinese knew about the microdisk, they'd be paying her another visit.

Ryder had to let her go now.

Molly left Sun Valley to open up the diner, and Evan reluctantly took his leave as well.

"Tell Ryder I really need to speak with him, Evan. Today."

"I will, Neal. Keep your doors locked up in the meantime."

He liked Neal, and thought Will Ryder had her pegged all wrong. Sure, she was beautiful to look at, but she also had a great sense of humor, a good heart, and plenty of determination.

Not at all like the other beautiful woman he knew, he thought as Wendy Lewis cornered him at the hardware store in town a few minutes after he arrived.

"You're not doing yourself any favors hanging around that woman, Evan Gamble." Wendy brushed

Gena Hale

an invisible speck off the sleeve of her immaculate red riding jacket. "If you're not careful, she'll get you fired."

"For what?" He handed the purchase order to the clerk. As usual, her snobby attitude put a dent in his good humor. "She's just a nice woman, Wendy."

"Evan, I don't know much about her, but she's certainly not *nice*. She's appallingly rude, for one thing. And a schemer—you can tell that a mile away. I bet she tries to make a play for Will before the month is out."

He exchanged a look with the clerk, who was busy memorizing every word of the conversation. "Well, maybe then you'd better warn him. Or are you too occupied with trying to get his ring on your finger?"

Wendy's jaw clenched. "I don't need a ring. Will Ryder is in love with me."

Evan chuckled. "Honey, you are putting your money in the wrong bank."

Her cheeks turned pink. "Don't you laugh at me."

"Then stop acting like a silly kid, Wendy. Will's fond of you but he's not going to marry you." He signed the charge receipt for his order, then saw the pain he'd inflicted. "I'm sorry if that hurts your feelings, honey, but it's the truth. It's time you faced it."

"You're just jealous of him." She stalked out of the store.

Well, she'd gotten that much right.

Wendy pulled off her jacket and went down the hall toward her bedroom. As she passed her father's study and saw the door ajar, she tried not to make any noise.

It didn't work. "Princess, come in here for a moment, if you would."

Reluctantly she pushed open the door. Her father summoned her into his private den only when he was upset. Which he already was, judging by the pinched look around his mouth.

He motioned for her to sit in the chair before his

massive oak desk. She did, and folded her hands in her lap.

"I got a call from Jimmy Tate. Seems he was at Molly's yesterday and saw you make a scene. Is this true?"

For once she wished she didn't attract so much attention. "Daddy, I did *not* make a scene. You raised me better than that."

"I would hope that I have, princess. But Jimmy gave me plenty of details that disturb me, and I'd like to know exactly what happened."

Wendy knew she'd never leave the study until she told him everything, so in a faltering voice she did.

"I see." Her father got up and paced back and forth in front of the window behind his desk. "Appears to me you were just being friendly to this woman, and she's the one who made the fuss. And you say Will sent you over to another table, then sat and talked with her some?"

She hadn't paid much attention to what Will had been doing at the time. Her eyes had been locked on the slim hand touching Evan Gamble. Even now, she burned with fury, thinking of the way Neal had pawed Will's foreman. A sound from her father dragged her back to attention.

"I'm sorry, Daddy. I couldn't hear what he said, but I think he was angry with her." The same way she'd been furious, but of course she couldn't admit that. Her father didn't like women who lost control of their tempers.

Dean Lewis sighed heavily. "When a man acts that way around a woman, he's feeling more than angry."

It was bad enough that Neala Delaney had put her hands on Evan. But Will Ryder was going to be her husband. Wounded pride forced Wendy to her feet. "Are you saying Will has feelings for her? She's nothing but a stranger. She just got here."

"He's strayed the wrong way once before." Her father swiveled around and planted his hands on his desk. "Wendy, I expect better of you. You should have gotten Will away from her."

"But Daddy—"

"It's all right, honey. I understand you weren't prepared for this. I've arranged to have Will take you to the annual spring dance. I want you to promise me you'll keep him away from this Delaney woman."

He'd probably bullied Will into agreeing to take her, which didn't sit well with Wendy. "I'll try my best, Daddy, but—"

"You'll have to do better than try, Wendy. Now, I'm going over to Butte for two weeks, so you'll have the house all to yourself. Invite Will up here after the dance. Show him how much you love and respect him."

The prospect of being alone with Will made her heart sink. "Of course I respect him, Daddy, but I'm not sure I'm in love with Will."

"You can fall in love while you're engaged, Wendy. You just get him up here and give him what a man most wants from a woman. You do that, and I guarantee he'll measure up with an engagement ring within the week."

Her father was telling her to seduce Will Ryder. He was actually giving her permission to bring Will Ryder home and have sex with him. This was the way he wanted to make Will propose to her? By her giving herself up to him? Like some sacrificial lamb on the altar of matrimony? Wendy didn't know whether to laugh, cry, or shriek.

She realized how much her father wanted to join his ranch with Will's. But she had never known, until this moment, that he didn't care if she loved Will or not. It was getting a ring on her finger that was important, not her heart.

"Do you understand what I'm saying to you, girl?"

The way his face was turning red alarmed her. "Yes, Daddy."

"Good. Now you go get changed for dinner."

She went to the door.

"Honey bunch?"

She looked back.

"I know you can do this for me." He was smiling. "Trust me, you and Will are going to be very happy together."

That would be nice, Wendy thought in a numb daze as she continued on to her bedroom. And she deserved it, too. Because right now, she was probably the most miserable person in Montana.

Bea didn't wait for Will to come in from stabling Blue, but walked out to the barn to greet him with the bad news. "Sheriff Walton called, Mr. Will. There's been some trouble."

Riding the range all day normally cleared his head, but he'd been unable to shake the image of Neala Delaney as she looked up at him, her mouth open and inviting. Now this. "What happened?"

"Someone broke into the house down at Sun Valley."

He nearly dropped Blue's saddle as he swung around, then remembered his housekeeper knew nothing about Neala. "Anything taken?"

"Apparently not, but the woman staying there was a bit shaken up."

"Was she hurt?"

"No, just scared, according to Evan. He went by earlier, and left a couple of messages for you to head down there when you got back." His housekeeper held out his keys. "I expect you'll be skipping dinner again."

He put a hand on her thin shoulder. "It's a bit of a story, Bea. I'll tell you about it later."

She sniffed. "I've already gotten a dozen calls about this gal from folks in town, thank you kindly." Her expression softened a few degrees as she handed him a large brown bag. "I packed enough sandwiches for the both of you." With that she marched back up to the house.

Hoping Kalen was working late, Will put in a call to his office as he drove down to Sun Valley. The automated voice mail that answered frustrated him, and he ended the call without leaving a message. Then he called Caleb at home, and got the details on the break-in.

"Looked to me like the lady's made herself unpopular with someone, Will." The sheriff sounded wry. "Could be Dean Lewis's daughter. I hear she didn't take kindly to being set down in front of the entire town."

He frowned. "Wendy wouldn't do something like this."

"If you say so. I'll have one of my deputies do a drive-by tonight, but I can't do more than that."

Will thought of the two men he'd hired that morning. "You won't have to, Caleb. I'll put a couple of my hands out here to keep an eye on her."

"Given that I only have two men working the night shift, I'd appreciate it."

Neal jerked open the door as soon as he pulled up in front of the house, and met him at the truck. "Where have you been?"

"Working." In spite of what his housekeeper had said, he spent a moment looking her over for cuts and bruises. "Tell me what happened."

"Someone broke in last night and trashed the house. I need to get out of here." She sounded almost desperate.

He shook his head and pulled the keys out of the ignition. "Let's go inside."

"Someone knows I'm here. I have to talk to my uncle. I have to *go*."

"After we talk about what happened." He took her arm and guided her back toward the house.

"You don't understand." She pulled away from him

and paced around the front room. "This is serious. I can't stay here another night."

She had worked herself into a genuine panic. "I'll take you back to my place. You'll be safe there."

"No!" With visible effort, she collected herself. "Please, Ryder. Just let me go. I'll go back to Denver when it's time for the trial, I promise."

"Neala, you can't leave."

"If I stay here I'm going to end up dead."

"I'll protect you."

"How?" She jumped as another truck stopped outside the house, and hurried over to the window. "It's Evan. Before you get angry, I asked him to pick up more groceries for me."

Will watched the tension leave Neala's shoulders as she greeted his foreman at the door. Her happiness in seeing him seemed genuine, and did nothing to improve Will's mood.

Evan helped her put away the bags of groceries he'd brought, then sat down with her in the front room. "Any progress on finding who broke in yet?"

Will turned from the window as she gestured to him.

"I was just trying to convince your boss to let me slip out of town."

Evan stared. "What sort of trouble are you in?"

"I—" Will shook his head at her, and she glared before continuing. "I'm just a little nervous about staying out here all by myself."

Will studied her pale face and decided to push the issue. "You won't be alone if you stay at High Point."

"I'd rather take my chances here."

"Make up your mind, lady."

"She doesn't have to stay by herself, Will. Jake and Lou will be on spring break for a couple of weeks, we can spare them to watch the house. I'll take the first shift myself."

Neala put her hand on his foreman's arm. "Oh, would you, Evan? I'd feel a lot better knowing you're close by."

Will turned back to the window, and resisted the urge to ram his fist through it. "If that's what you want, fine."

Sean waited until the lights in the house went out before slipping out from the tree line. A minute later he climbed through the back bedroom window, and found himself about to be clobbered by a very angry young woman wielding a small table lamp.

"You son of a bitch. Now I've got you!" Neal swung hard.

He jerked out of the window just in time, and hit the ground. "Hold on, darlin'," he called to her, and groaned. "It's only me, your favorite relative."

She stuck her head out of the window, and stared at him in horror. *"Uncle Sean?"* The lamp crashed to the floor inside. "What are you doing here?"

"Trying to get to you. Mind getting out of my way?" He rubbed his abused backside as he got up, then climbed back in.

Neal pulled on her robe before she kicked him in the shin. "Ever think about knocking at the front door? I thought you were the burglar, you idiot!"

"I heard about that in town. Who was it?"

"If I knew that, he'd be in jail!" She tried to fold her arms, then hissed with pain. "When did you get here? More important, why *are* you here?"

"Have you been able to reach Karen?"

"On what?" She gestured around her. "There's no phone. I tried one day when I was in town, but there was no answer. Do you know if she's still in China?"

"No, I haven't been able to reach her. I was hoping you had."

She sat on the edge of the bed. "Damn. This is getting down to the wire." She looked at her uncle. "What are we going to do?"

"Give the microdisk to me. I'll explain things to Grady."

"And get them killed, and yourself thrown in Leavenworth? No, I don't think so."

He wanted to tell her no such thing would happen, but he couldn't guarantee it. Not with Grady. He sat down beside her. "Okay. So we go to Plan B. Give me the number Karen gave you." Neal recited it for him, and he memorized it. "I'll keep trying her. In the meantime, you sit tight and don't go anywhere."

"I couldn't, even if I wanted to." She filled him in on everything that had happened up to that point. "They're using me for bait, but they never told me. Why?"

"Grady wants it all—J. R. and Shandian. He didn't think you'd cooperate." Sean sat down on her bed. "To tell you the truth, darlin', neither did I."

"I don't get it. I've done everything you ever asked me to, Uncle Sean. Doesn't the general know that?"

He watched her closely. "It could have something to do with this Ryder fellow. Grady served with him during the Persian Gulf War."

"Maybe." She rubbed her upper arms. "But how is Ryder involved?"

Sean saw the condition of her hands and grabbed them. "What did you do?"

"Cleaned a kitchen, not that you can tell anymore." She eyed the window. "You'd better head back to town and start calling that number. Once you know Karen's safe, come back out and get me."

"You're going to do it then?"

She nodded. "Then I'll go back to Denver and tell them what really happened that night."

Chapter 8

Kalen called early the next morning. "Problem?"

"Yeah. Someone's after your witness." Will told him about the break-in. "You've got to move her out of here."

"Sounds like a routine burglary to me."

"On the same day she showed up in town? Unlikely."

"Look, I told you, Will. There's a leak on my end. Until I plug it, there's no point transporting her."

"She isn't going to be much of a witness dead."

"I'll send a couple of marshals in to watch the property. Just leave her at Sun Valley for now, Will. Things will be coming to a head shortly."

"Goddamn it, Kalen, this is her *life* you're screwing around with!"

"Park a couple of your men around her until the marshals get there." The general waited a beat. "Or if you're that worried, take care of the job yourself."

His grip on the phone tightened until his knuckles went white. "You owe me, Grady."

"Yeah." Kalen uttered a single laugh. "I'll be in touch. Keep her out of trouble."

Will knew the only solution was to move in with Neala at Sun Valley. Instantly the memory of his ex-wife loomed up, the way she'd looked the day he'd found her body. She'd been in the bathtub, arms hanging limply over the sides, the needle she'd used to inject herself with sitting on the toilet. He'd touched her face, felt the cold, stiff flesh, and made his last vow to her.

I'll never live in this house again.

He'd have to break that promise now, because there was no other way to protect Neala.

After calling the two college boys he regularly employed to do odd jobs, and arranging for them to meet him at the ranch, Will saddled his horse and went for a final ride around the property. Evan met him in the east field just as he was rounding up a dozen strays to drive them back to the main herd.

Silently they worked together to move the cattle, then rode around the herd to check the condition of older heifers who'd recently dropped their calves.

"Looks like we've got mostly cheat grass growing down in the south pasture," Evan said. "I thought we might reseed before the summer hits."

"I noticed some Russian thistle out that way, too. Have one of the men burn it over, and make a note to watch for it next spring." Will reined in Blue and regarded his foreman steadily. "Any more trouble last night?"

"No."

"I'm moving down to Sun Valley for the time being," Will said, astonishing his foreman. "Jake and Lou will take the night shifts. You'll have to manage things here while I'm gone."

"You haven't lived down there since Trish died."

"I haven't got a choice anymore." Blue reacted to his anger, and he had to tighten his grip on the reins. "Tell me now if you're involved with her."

"I'm not." Evan pushed his hat back. "Even if I was, she's not."

"Good. Keep it that way."

The sound of low voices drew Neala from the kitchen to the front window. On the porch, two young men in jeans and T-shirts sat watching the road.

She opened the door and stepped out. "Hi. Can I help you guys?"

Both boys jumped to their feet and removed their hats.

The older boy spoke first. "Morning, ma'am. I'm Lou Squire, and this is my brother, Jake. Will Ryder asked us to meet him here."

She pushed the door wider. "Would you like to come in?"

"No, thank you, ma'am." Lou looked at her the same way he would a sleeping rattlesnake he was about to step on, and caught Jake's arm when he would have started for the door. "We'll wait out here for him."

The younger boy glanced at her, blushed, then looked away.

"Okay." Neal fought a grin. "If you change your mind, the door's unlocked. I'll be out back."

Ryder arrived some time later, but Neala didn't notice until she saw Jake and Lou walking with him around the utility shed. As he pointed to different areas of the property, Will gave them instructions. Both boys listened and nodded, then left him to return to the front of the house.

Ryder spotted her, but turned and followed Jake and Lou.

Well, good morning to you, too.

Curiosity compelled her to trail after them, and she was stunned to see Ryder carrying a suitcase from his truck into the house. The boys were also hauling in more boxes of groceries and supplies. "What's all this for?"

"I'm moving in."

"Huh?" Her mouth dropped open. "You mean here? With me?"

"I'm not sleeping in the barn." He brushed past her, making her follow him into the house.

"Ryder, this isn't exactly what I had in mind." She

watched him put the suitcase in the bedroom across from hers, then met his bland gaze. "Besides, Evan said—"

"Evan is staying at High Point." He paused, looking down at her with undisguised impatience. "Anything else you want to complain about?"

"I'm not complaining, I just would like to—"

"Fine." He walked back out to the truck.

"—finish a complete sentence in your presence." She planted her hands on her hips. "Honestly."

Ryder drove off a few minutes later. Since he was making such an effort to ignore her existence, Neal decided to do the same and went to work on the garden. She attacked the newly sprouting rows, yanking weeds until her hands were streaked green and black.

"You'd think he would have said something about this last night." She tugged at a patch of dandelion and worked it free. "But no, I'm just supposed to sit back and let him move in with me, like it's nothing."

When she took a break to get a cold drink from the kitchen, she found the boys cleaning up the burglar's mess. "Would you guys like a drink?"

Lou nodded toward a small cooler on the floor beneath the kitchen table. "Thank you, ma'am, but we brought our own."

"What have you got in there?" She knelt down to take a peek, and grinned. "Root beer. I've got some Evian. Want to swap?"

"You can have mine," Jake said. "I'm not thirsty—"

"Shut up," his brother muttered, and gave him an elbow nudge. "Remember what the boss said." He wouldn't look at Neal. "Help yourself, ma'am."

Embarrassed, Jake went back to sweeping up spilled flour, while Lou unpacked a box of cleaning supplies.

"The boss get that for me?" Neal asked.

"No, ma'am. He said we should take care of the cleanup, seeing as you, uh . . . I mean . . ." The younger boy faltered, and his cheeks flushed.

"I get the picture." Neala sighed. "Well, if you're going to be my butlers, the least I can do is make some breakfast for you."

Jake eyed his brother, then shook his head. "No, that's okay, ma'am. We've already eaten."

"Then how about lunch?" Lou's expression made Neal's smile falter. "You can't accept a couple of sandwiches?"

"The boss will take care of that, ma'am." The older boy stepped between them, giving her a hard look. "We'll be getting back to work now. Come on, Jake."

She watched the boys retreat. "So Ryder thinks a couple of teenagers aren't safe around me now?" She made a tutting sound. "We'll just see about that."

Will needed ammunition for his rifle, but he had no intention of arming the boys with anything but a couple of radios. He bought everything at the hardware store, then stopped in at the auction house to speak to Dean Lewis.

Wendy must have been watching from the window, because she met him at the door. "Will! I just tried to call you."

"Wendy." He looked past her toward Dean's office, which was dark. "Dean's back at the house?"

"Daddy's gone out of town for a few weeks. Another of his buying trips." She fluttered around him, trying to draw him farther in. "I was counting on you coming over to have dinner with me one night, to keep me from feeling lonely."

"I can't, honey. Something's come up. If you hear from your dad, have him give me a call on my cell phone."

She frowned. "He can reach you at the ranch, can't he?"

"I'm not going to be there for a while." He tipped his hat and backed out of the doorway. "Take care now."

He picked up the lunches he'd ordered from Molly's

before heading back to Sun Valley. The diner owner handed the containers over along with a warning.

"I better not hear you're browbeating that little girl out there at Sun Valley, Will Ryder." Molly took his money and handed him the change. "She's been through enough."

"That 'little girl' could charm the collar off a Catholic priest," he said. "And make him think it was his idea in the first place."

"I imagine she could." The older woman grinned. "Maybe I should be worrying more about *you*."

He wasn't worried about leaving Neala alone with Jake and Lou—he'd given them strict instructions to steer clear of his houseguest. Which was why after he arrived back at Sun Valley, he found himself standing in the front room for a full minute, listening to Neala and the brothers laughing in the kitchen.

"I'm serious, Lou." Neala sounded anything but. "Next time I volunteer to do something like this, do me a favor—*refuse*."

"You're doing fine, Miss Neal." Lou chuckled again. "Just keep working it like that."

Neala began humming a sexy little tune under her breath.

"You've really never done this before?" That came from Jake.

"Only watched." Something thumped, and she groaned. "It's getting really stiff now."

"That's just how it should be," Lou told her. "Don't stop."

Will strode in, not knowing what to expect, and found his hired hands flanking Neala at the kitchen counter. She was covered with splotches of white powder, and wrestling with something on a wooden board. All three were so involved in what they were doing that no one noticed his presence.

"You have to try making Mom's potato-herb bread," Jake said. "It's really good, Miss Neal."

"Sounds yummy." Neal blew a piece of hair out of her eyes. "I've got potatoes, but what kind of herbs do I need?"

"Rosemary, thyme, and parsley." Lou nodded at the window overlooking the yard. "You could put in a row of herbs out there. My mother's already planted her kitchen garden; she could probably spare you some sprouts to get you started."

Will stared. Jake was as friendly as an oversize puppy, but he'd never heard Lou Squire ramble on like this. The taciturn boy tended to be remote around people he'd known all his life, and yet here he was, giving the city girl advice on gardening, of all things.

He must have made a sound, because Jake whirled around with wide eyes. "Mr. Ryder!"

Lou shuffled and cleared his throat. "Boss."

"Boys." Over Neala's shoulder, he inspected the mound of honey-colored dough she was kneading. "What's this?"

"Bread Making One-oh-one. Isn't it beautiful?" Neala held up the dough the same way she would a newborn baby. "It has to rise one more time"—she glanced at Lou to confirm this, and he nodded—"then I can bake it. It's Mrs. Squire's special honey-wheat recipe."

"Uh-huh." He looked around at the otherwise spotless kitchen. "You did a good job in here."

"Miss Neal helped us. We told her not to, but she insisted," Jake told him, eager to explain. "Then she wanted to make sandwiches, but she didn't have any bread."

Lou gave him an apologetic look. "We were finished, boss, and I didn't think you'd mind."

"I brought some sandwiches back from town." Will set Molly's containers on the table, and saw Neala stiffen. What the hell, he'd indulge her little experiment. "But I'd rather have homemade, myself. Especially if it's Martha's special recipe."

Both teenagers grinned with relief. Neala didn't look at him, but went back to kneading and humming.

"Lou, I've got a couple of handheld radios in the truck. Why don't you and Jake take them out by the front gate and test them for range?"

"Will do, boss." Lou touched Neala's arm. "Remember, let it rise again before you put it in."

When the teenagers had gone, he watched her carefully place the bread in the square, floured pan near the stove. "I never thought making bread could be racy until I heard you say it was getting stiff. Thought I'd have to run in here and pry you off both of them."

"You've got a corrupt mind, Ryder." She sniffed. "For your information, I don't debauch teenagers, as a general rule."

"How long did it take you to talk them into bread-making class?"

"Jake was a pushover." Neala wiped some flour from her cheek with the back of her hand. "Lou was tougher. He held out for almost a whole hour." She glanced at him. "They're good kids, don't yell at them."

He raised a brow. First Evan, now the Squire boys. For someone who made herself out to be nothing but a helpless good-time girl, Neala Delaney spent a lot of time defending her conquests. "I don't intend to."

"Good." She covered the bread pan with plastic wrap and pushed it to the back of the counter.

He liked seeing the flour on her skin. "Seems like you're getting pretty domesticated, Calamity."

"Who, me?" She patted floury fingers over a fake yawn. "I was just bored with doing my nails."

That made him catch her hand with his. The once long, polished nails were now naked, and neatly trimmed down. "Been a while, hasn't it?"

Her hand drew back. "I ran out of emery boards."

"And the garden?"

"Self-interest." She swiped at her face. "I'm considering becoming a vegetarian."

"I can't figure you out, lady." He reached up and wiped the last trace of flour from her cheek. "Just when I think I have, you do something else to baffle me."

Her dark lashes swept down. "It's only some bread, Ryder."

"But you've never made it before. I don't think you did much digging in the dirt back in Colorado, either." He moved his hand to her mouth. Under his thumb, her lips were soft as flower petals. Full enough to tempt any man to sink between them, first with his tongue, then with his— "Why now?"

"I can't exactly drive to the bakery," she said, sounding a little breathless.

Which reminded him of why he was there. Slowly he let his hand drop. "No, you can't."

He left her there, and went to find the other two males she'd seduced with her smile.

Near dawn, T'ang's operative paid another visit to Sun Valley. None of the stolen items from the house had yielded anything, and the time for caution and patience was over.

Getting past the two teens sitting in the back of the truck posted at the front gate presented little difficulty, but even the smallest risk of discovery was too great. To avoid detection, the operative bypassed the main highway and took an access road into the woods. After the car was concealed, a two-mile hike enabled an unseen approach from the back of the property.

The operative was astonished to see Will Ryder's black pickup parked outside the front of the house. His aversion for Sun Valley was common knowledge, and he'd certainly displayed nothing but dislike for his unwelcome houseguest. But a glance in the bedroom windows confirmed it—he had moved in.

How much did he know?

Neal Delaney didn't wake up as the operative slipped into her bedroom. Nor did she do more than twitch as the needle slipped into her vein. The operative waited, then took her pulse. With twice the original dose in her bloodstream, she would surely be more cooperative this time.

"Neal. Wake up."

The woman opened her eyes. They were glazed and dilated. "Hmmm?"

"Neal, tell me where the microdisk is."

"Your crocus? I didn't plant any crocus." She yawned. "Can't eat them."

"Where did you hide it, Neal?"

"Heads I win, tails you lose." She rolled over.

The operative tried to coax the information out of her, but all Neal did was mutter about how much she hated spiders and, oddly, President John F. Kennedy.

At last the operative gave up. She'd have to burn, along with Will Ryder and the contents of the house.

A trip to the kitchen produced the materials necessary to start the fire: oil, some dish towels, and some strategically placed wads of newspaper.

It would have to look like an accident, of course. Since the woman obviously couldn't boil water, the logical way would be to start the fire on the stove, and let it rage out of control.

Which was exactly what the operative did.

Neal dreamed she was back in the club, in J. R.'s office, finding out the reason she'd been hired.

"What am I paying you to serenade these drunks?" J. R. sat back in his big leather chair, watching her. He was lean and dark, and considered gorgeous by most of the waitresses. Neal personally thought his eyes were a little too close together. "Three bills a week?"

She wished. "Two-fifty, plus tips."

"With a body like yours, you could make ten times that." J. R.'s smile spread around the thin cigar he clamped between his teeth. "Interested?"

"Sure." *Nauseated* was more like it. "I need some details here, boss. What is it you want me to do? Exactly?"

He extended the cane he always carried and used the oddly shaped handle to caress her cheek. "I'll keep you for myself for a while. You can have a condo, credit cards, all the perks. Hell, you can even keep on singing here, if you want."

And all I have to do is crawl in bed with you whenever you want. "What about when you get tired of me?"

"Smart girl, always plan for the future." He lifted a curl of dark hair with the end of the cane, then let it fall back against her neck. "Some of my business associates like brunettes. They're Chinese, so you should be able to handle whatever they want."

He not only wanted her, he wanted to rent her out. Neal opened her mouth to tell him what she thought of that, then froze. J. R.'s head abruptly shrank, then turned black. Six more arms punched out of the sides of his Armani jacket. They were black, too. Horrified, she watched her boss turn slowly into a huge, hairy spider.

It's a nightmare, Neal. It isn't real.

He opened his mouth and showed her his fangs. "You got a problem with that?"

"Not at all. I'm very interested." Even if it was just an illusion, she was scared to death. "I'll need to end my current arrangement, of course." She named a prominent politician she'd only seen on television.

Suddenly he turned back into a normal man. "If he gives you any shit, let me know." He reached out and traced the outline of her lips with the gold handle of the cane. "I'll take care of him."

How? By biting him on the leg with your fangs?

It's just a dream. A little mental trip in the way-back machine. "Thanks, boss."

As she had before, Neal left him to do her second act. After she finished singing, she knew she would go home, pack, and get a visit from her uncle.

Too bad I can't really go back to that night. I'd change everything, and Colfax would still be alive.

She went back up onstage, the same way she had before. But when she took her place behind the microphone, the room became crowded with leering, cigar-smoking old men. They lit more cigars, holding four and five in each hand. The smoke became so thick she couldn't breathe.

Senator Colfax had smoked cigars. He did other things with them, too—

Terror jolted her out of sleep, and she rolled out of bed. Immediately she started coughing. Someone was smoking in her house? After she'd spent all those weeks getting rid of the stink from that nasty old man? She struggled to her feet. Someone was going to get a piece of her mind.

Only she couldn't see, and couldn't breathe. There was too much smoke. And it was the wrong color. It was black.

Black smoke? And the smell of something burning. What was happening? Something seemed to drain the energy from her limbs, and drove her to her knees. She looked around the room, dizzy and disoriented.

Fire? The cantina? No, no flames.

Although the dizziness made it impossible to get back up, Neal knew she had to get out. Even if the house wasn't on fire, the smoke would kill her. Remembering what she'd done in Mexico, she went down on all fours and started slowly crawling toward the window.

God, let me reach it before I pass out.

Chapter 9

Will had always been a light sleeper, and the faint smell of smoke woke him up almost at once.

"What the hell is she cooking now?" He rolled out of bed, took a breath, then coughed. Dark smoke was pouring into his room from the gap beneath the door. "Jesus Christ. Neala!"

He tested the doorknob with a quick touch, found it cool, and yanked it open. Smoke filled the hallway, and he automatically bent in a crouch and pulled his T-shirt up over his mouth and nose. He lunged across the hall and burst through her bedroom door.

No fire inside, but no sign of the city girl, either. "Neala! Answer me!"

"Will . . ."

That was when he saw her, lying on the floor near the window, coughing, struggling to get up.

She's alive.

"Thank God." He bent down, grabbed her, and felt her hands clutch at him. Confused, bloodshot eyes stared up at him. "Hang on to me."

He carried her straight out through the front door and set her down in the front yard, then started checking her for injuries. Smoke had left black streaks on her face and arms, and she was still coughing, but was otherwise unharmed.

She's not burned. She's okay.

He told himself the cold sweat inching down his

face and neck was from relief. Relief that whoever had tried to kill them hadn't succeeded, nothing more.

Carefully he stretched her out on the grass, then went back to make a circle around the house. By checking through the windows, he discovered the source of the smoke in the kitchen, where a sizable fire raged on the stove and had begun to migrate over the upper oak cabinets.

Breaking out the windows would only fan the flames. Covering his face again, Will shoved open the back door and went in. After he grabbed the extinguisher from the wall mount, he pulled the handle ring and put it to use. The foam doused the flames and revealed three blackened, smoldering pans, as if Neala had been cooking and forgotten about it. Evidently she left what looked like a couple of dish towels too close to the heating elements, too.

Making it look like an accident.

Once the fire was completely out, he staggered outside and filled his burning lungs with clean air. The sound of Jake's and Lou's frightened voices calling Neala's name made him run back to the front of the house.

The terrified boys were kneeling in the grass beside her. Lou looked up at Will, his face white.

"I phoned the sheriff, Mr. Ryder. Fire truck'll be here in a few minutes."

"Thanks, Lou. I got it out already, but we'll still need the house checked." Will went to them and bent over to check Neala with urgent hands. "Neala." He patted her cheek. "Come on, lady, open those pretty eyes and talk to me."

"She's going to be okay, isn't she?" Jake asked. He looked sick.

"Sure she will. Won't you, city girl?" Will kept speaking to her, until her eyelids lifted a centimeter and she began to cough. He smiled down at her. "Welcome back."

It hit him then, what a close thing it had been. She

could have been burned, maimed, killed. She could have choked to death on the smoke. Her life snuffed out in a few seconds. Easily. Irrevocably.

Rage collected inside him, dumping a stream of icy determination into his veins. *Whoever did this is mine.*

He sat down on the grass, pulled her onto his lap, and held her until she got her breath back. He let himself stroke the dark hair back from her face. His heart pounded as he settled the weight of her more firmly against him.

Neala lifted her grimy face as she focused on him for the first time. "Will." Her voice sounded odd, thick.

Had the smoke damaged her throat? "Don't try to talk."

"So . . . scared."

"You're safe now." He pulled her close again, and rested his chin on the top of her head. "We made it out alive, Calamity."

"Not calamity." She smacked him with a clumsy hand. "Didn't."

He pulled back. "Didn't what?"

"Didn't tell." She struggled out of his arms, got up, and took a couple of wobbly steps toward the house before grabbing onto the porch railing. At the same time, the Lone Creek Fire Department arrived. As Will went after Neala, the boys ran to meet the fire truck.

So much for keeping her presence concealed.

"Whoa, now." He caught her in his arms as she nearly collapsed. "You can't go back in there just yet." He waved a hand at the men pouring out of the truck. "It's all over," he shouted to them. "I got it out."

The men stared at Neal, and Will looked down to see what was so interesting. He swore as he tugged down the hem of the oversize T-shirt she wore. He'd forgotten she was practically naked.

One of the firemen took off his helmet. "We should still take a look inside, Will."

The eager way he grinned when he said that made Will want to snarl. So he did. "Then quit ogling her and do it."

Neala abruptly straightened and gave him an owlish look. "I'm fine." She coughed, then cleared her throat. "Really."

He hustled her off to the side, out of the way. "Stay here. I'll go in and find you some clothes."

"Stop that." She stamped her foot, and nearly fell over again. "What did I do now?"

Why was she slurring her words like that? Had the smoke affected her mind? He'd have to get her over to the hospital in Big Timber. "Neala—"

"Go ahead, leave." She waved her hand at him. "Everyone leaves me." She turned to the firemen. "Hey, you guys. Why don't you stay for a while?" She covered her mouth and coughed once more. "I'll make you some coffee. Or English stuff. Or root beer. We have root beer. Do you like root beer?"

The men stopped, exchanged glances. Several answered her with an enthusiastic "Yes, ma'am."

Will ran a hand through his hair. It was better than throttling her. "Lady, all you're going to do is head for the emergency room."

"No. I don't like hospitals. They always want to make me swallow pills and pee in a cup." She cocked her head as if bemused. "Damn, what's wrong with my voice?" Neal cleared her throat again, then sang a couple of lines from a blues song about a hard man to love, and loving a hard man. She squinted and looked around. "Am I back in Mexico?"

The firemen didn't move an inch. Didn't make a sound. Didn't bat an eyelash. No way were they going to miss this.

"You're in Montana." Will tried to steer her toward his truck. "Let's go over to the hospital now, get you checked out."

"Don't you like my voice, Ryder?" Neal smiled and stroked her fingers across his jawline. "I know it's not

as nice as my body, but I do pretty good singing. I
can dance, too." She stretched her arms out, and performed a classic bump-and-grind.

A couple of the firemen whistled. Two others el-
bowed each other.

Will grabbed her as she staggered and nearly fell.
"What's the matter with you?"

"Nothing. I'm fine. More than fine." She waggled
her eyebrows at him. "I like it when you look at me
that way—yeah, just like that, with your mouth all
hard and grim."

Then he did grab her. "You'd better sit down." He
tried to guide her toward the steps.

"I don't want to sit down." She locked her knees,
refusing to give way. "I want you to kiss me. I love
your mouth. You definitely have the best mouth I've
ever seen on a man. Even better than Hugh Jack-
man's—and you know they pay him millions just to
get his mouth on film. I read that in a magazine." She
cocked her head to one side. "Wonder what they'd
pay you, Ryder? Have you ever thought about taking
a screen test?"

"Could be from the smoke," one of the men said
in a helpful way, then ducked his head when Will
scowled at him. "Seen it before. Oxygen deprivation
does strange things to people."

"Okay, fun's over, boys." Will took her by the
shoulders and tried to maneuver her around the men.
"As for you, city girl, let's take a little walk. You need
some fresh air."

"What I really need is you, Ryder." Neal threw her
arms up around his neck, making the hem of her old
T-shirt rise to new, alarming heights. "Want to know
what I'd do if we were alone?" She wriggled her hips
against his. "What I'd really, *really* like to do?"

"You're taking a walk."

"Nope. Guess again."

"Right now." He tugged the edge of her shirt back

down over her panties, and tried to set her away, but she had a death grip on him. "Neala, let go."

She pouted as she slowly removed her arms, then gave the watching firemen a sloppy grin. "Do you guys know what I'd like to do to this big, gorgeous man here?"

Will tried to clamp his hand over her mouth, but she ducked under his arm and staggered over to one of the other men.

"I'd like to get him naked," she said to the fireman in an elaborate stage whisper. "The first time I saw him, I thought, I have to get his clothes off. I bet his body is *gorgeous*."

He gave up and simply clamped his arms around her. Instead of struggling, she made a throaty sound and tested his biceps with her hands. "Can you blame me? Look at how muscular he is. All hard and strong and smooth."

Several of the men were now trying so hard not to laugh that they dropped their equipment.

"Neala." He shook her. "Neala, cut it out!"

Unconcerned, she started plucking at the front of his shirt. "Unbutton this. I want to see your chest. Then I want to kiss it. And lick it. All of it. Slowly. Would you like that?"

He'd like that. But he was going to give her backside a walloping first. "Why are you acting like this?"

"I want you. Come on out to the barn with me, right now, and we'll get naked together. What do you say?" She didn't wait for an answer, but started tugging him in the general direction of the barn. "I don't want a roll in the hay, though. Who thought of that saying? Hay sucks. It's too sharp and it'll scratch up my backside for sure." She stopped halfway to the barn and looked up at him with a serious frown. "Have you got a blanket or something we can use? My butt is pretty sensitive."

Two of the firemen dropped onto the porch, rolling.

"Christ, woman, *will you shut up!*" Will hauled her up into his arms and glared once back at the men. "Get inside and make sure it's out; then hit the road."

He carried her the rest of the way to the barn, away from prying eyes. Along the way she began working on his neck with her lips. Then her tongue. Then her teeth.

"Um, you taste salty. I like that." She lifted her face up and gently blew in his ear. "Did you remember the blanket?"

He ducked in through the entrance and strode in to dump her next to the pump. "No blankets."

"Okay." She swayed a little. "I'll be on top."

This wasn't oxygen deprivation. She was acting like she was plastered—but there was no booze in the house. "If this is your idea of a joke, it's not funny."

"Funny?" She sputtered with laughter. "Yeah, well, I guess it can be pretty funny. I mean, Evan's in love with Wendy; go figure that one."

She was making no sense at all. "What's Evan got to do with this?"

"Nothing." She began wandering around him in an uneven circle, as if inspecting him. "I wonder if this is such a good idea. You're a lot bigger than Terry."

"Terry who?"

"Terry, my first. He dumped me for a poet wanna-be who could quote Shakespeare. Well, no great loss. Shakespeare is highly overrated. Just like Terry. You'll be gentle, won't you?"

"Neala—"

"Then there was Marc, my marine." She grabbed his waist from behind and wrapped her arms around him. "We were engaged for a month before he shipped out to Sarajevo. Now, Marc, he was a real sweetheart, you know? When they told me he was dead, it broke my heart."

He hauled her around, and was astonished to see tears shimmering in her eyes. Both pupils were dilated, and danced, as if she couldn't keep her focus.

He pulled out both of her arms, and saw the telltale needle mark on the inside of her elbow.

A terrible coldness clutched at his heart. *Not again. I'm not going through this again.* "What did you take?"

"What?"

"This." He yanked up her arm to show her the tiny wound. "What kind of filth are you shooting up?"

"You mean drugs? Are you nuts?" She sounded deeply offended. "I don't do drugs."

"You're acting like you're stoned."

"Spider bit me, is all." Her voice changed, became frightened. "You don't have to lock me in the cellar again. I'll be good."

No spider in creation left a mark like that. "Who locked you in a cellar?"

"My foster dad. He didn't like me talking back to him. Just like you." Neal tried to grab him, lost her balance, and ended up sprawled at his feet. "It's okay; I know exactly what I'm doing." When he hauled her back up, she ran her hands over his chest, and smiled blindly up at him. "Want to take off your shirt for me now?"

"You're going to get more than you're asking for, lady." He backed her up against the nearest surface, which happened to be a post beside an empty stall. "Who gave you the stuff?"

"Can't tell," she said, her expression turning crafty. "Unless you kiss me. I'd really like that."

"Yeah." He jerked her into his arms. "Me, too."

"Wait here for me."

Kuei-fei stepped inside the apartment door, then closed and locked it. T'ang's man had picked the locks for her, but with ill grace. He didn't like taking orders from a woman. No Chinese man did—except T'ang, of course.

Pliable fool that he was.

When the operative reported in earlier that morning, T'ang felt satisfied that nothing more needed to be done.

"The witness is dead, and the microdisk destroyed." He gazed fondly at his wife. "My uncle will be pleased."

"Have you sent someone to search the woman's home, to be certain she did not hide it there before she left the city?" As her husband's smile slipped, Kuei-fei rose. "Permit me to see to this for you personally, husband."

The air inside Neala Delaney's apartment was stale, but someone had been watering the houseplants. Posters lined the walls, all portraits of famous women performers. There were a few framed playbills of Neala's own performances. And in the center of the room, one Andrew Wyeth print of a woman reclining in a deserted field.

Kuei-fei could understand the allure of the stark scene. She often dreamed of the day she could free herself from the claws of the tong and escape to someplace silent and uninhabited.

A place where no one can touch me.

She performed a methodical search, learning much about the other woman as she did. Neala Delaney was sentimental, rather untidy, and collected jars of condiments, judging by the assortment in her refrigerator. She'd tacked a dozen photos of a smiling redhead on the wall beside the phone. Her crumpled receipts filled a shopping bag. Costume jewelry lay scattered everywhere.

Neala had her obsessions, as well. A four-drawer cabinet revealed a veritable library of sheet music. Hundreds of songs, all perfectly arranged and indexed by composer and performer. Behind the doors of another cabinet were stacks of video and cassette tapes. All had been labeled with dates and club names.

Kuei-fei chose a cassette tape at random and put it on the expensive stereo system. The voice that poured out of the speakers was so rich and powerful she had to immediately adjust the volume.

I've waited forever for you,
stayed up every night praying for you,
but you won't come home, and it's giving me
*   the blues. . . .*

The blues. That was an odd term for suffering abuse at the hands of a man. Perhaps it referred to the color of bruises. She'd endured her share of those, and more, over the years.

Before she'd discovered T'ang's fatal weakness, Kuei-fei had been forced to do whatever the tong leaders demanded. They'd taken her freedom, her body, and even her only child.

Jian-Shan. I will have my day.

Thanks to T'ang, that day was at hand.

She shut off the song and put the tape in her pocket. Once she felt confident the singer had not left the microdisk behind, she let herself back out into the corridor. It was a tragedy Neala Delaney had to die; she was quite beautiful, and her voice was simply magnificent.

"Did you find what you were looking for, Lady T'ang?"

"No." She looked up and down the hall. Every apartment was occupied, according to the building superintendent. "Come back here tonight, and make sure the fire appears accidental."

"It is an old structure," her husband's hireling said. "The flames will spread quickly."

A baby in a nearby apartment began crying.

Kuei-fei listened for a moment. None of what she felt showed in her voice when she said, "Then see to it that you do not linger once the fire starts."

Breathing in the smoke and trying to get to the window had left Neala weak and dizzy. She'd been so glad to see Ryder. Everything had gone fuzzy after that, but when she'd woken up in the yard, something was wrong. Her head felt dense and weighty. A funny cloud seemed to press in around her, making it hard to figure out where she was, or what was going on. But all that took a backseat the moment Ryder came back to her.

We made it out alive, Calamity.

She was very, very happy to be alive, and proceeded to show him that. On some deep level she knew he'd never forgive her for her rotten behavior, but she couldn't seem to help herself. All her normal inhibitions had somehow vanished, and it only seemed natural to fling herself at him and declare her innermost desires.

Desires that Ryder definitely shared, judging by the way he was kissing her now. The smells of hay and manure receded as his masculine scent filled her head. Greedy for more, she accepted the hard thrust of his tongue, reveling in the way his mouth virtually devoured hers from the moment she parted her lips. With deliberate provocation, she used her own tongue to glide and tease, then wrenched her mouth away.

Her head was spinning. She wasn't quite sure which way was up. He'd have to deal with that. But the last time, he'd left her aching and alone, and she wasn't going to fall for that again. "You aren't going to walk out on me, are you?"

That was all it took. She could almost hear his control snap as he flattened her against the post and sank into her mouth.

Their tongues mated as the kiss went from desire to demand. She held nothing back. Neala's need matched his as she arched into him and dug her nails into his back. A sound came from him as she raked her hands down, then pulled his hips into hers. A deep, wild rumble of need that was as hard and urgent as the thick bulge pressing into her belly. Almost as hard as the unforgiving wood biting into her back.

"Neala," he muttered against her lips.

She rocked her hips up and down, caressing him and tormenting herself. "I'm right here, my man."

Her feet left the ground as his big hands dragged her up the post. As he held her suspended, she rested her cheek against his shoulder, glad he was strong enough for both of them.

"I'm hot. Are you?" She found his hair with her fingers, and combed them through it. She could feel the dampness of his sweat, felt the iron tightness clenching his muscles. Gently she blew on his neck. "It's so hot in here."

He swore under his breath, then said, "Hold on to me."

She locked her hands behind his neck as he reached down and lifted the hem of her nightshirt. A moment later he drew it up over her head and tossed it away. She emerged, shook out her curls, and smiled as the cool air washed over her bare skin.

He stared down at her breasts, and cradled one in his big hand. "You're too damn beautiful."

She slapped a hand on his chest. "Your turn."

But Ryder wasn't interested in playing fair. He bent his head and put his mouth to the curve of her shoulder. When she felt the edge of his teeth, she yelped, and the odd fog clouding her head start to thin.

"Ryder?" She shook her head, trying to clear it.

He didn't respond, but only lifted her higher, sliding her up until he could get at her breasts. Automatically she curled her legs around his hips, tucking her feet between the backs of his thighs. "That's it. God, you feel good on me."

Her beaded nipples hardened even more as his breath touched them. "Ryder, I don't think—"

He opened his mouth over her breast, sweeping the tip of his tongue around the jutting peak. The fierce ache at once became pleasure, so immediate and intense that she shuddered. Adrenaline poured into her veins as her body stiffened, and the last of the puzzling confusion disappeared.

Now aware something was terribly wrong, Neala brought up her hands and covered her breasts. He didn't stop her, but started sucking on her right through her fingers. "Let me see you, Neala."

"See me?" Everything became suddenly, shockingly clear. "Where . . . ?"

She turned her head and for the first time realized they were in the barn. Everything else blanked out for a moment. Then she gazed down at Will's mouth, which had nudged aside her hand and fastened over her breast.

Okay. How did I get here? Why am I letting him do that?

"Ryder. Um, Ryder." Distracted by the fantastic things he was doing with his tongue, she patted his cheek awkwardly. "Hold on there. Wait a minute."

He kept right on sucking her nipple, as if he'd gone deaf.

"Ryder. *Ryder!*" Only when she grabbed his hair and yanked hard did he lift his head. "Stop this. Turn me loose."

He didn't move an inch. "Why? We both want this. Let's get it over with."

Let's get it over with? Like she was some kind of flu shot?

Slowly she unwound her legs and slid her knee between her and Will. She rested it against his erection, applying just enough pressure to gain his undivided attention.

When he met her gaze, she gave him a careful smile. "Put me down. Nice and easy. Right now."

He set her down so quickly her teeth clicked from the jolt. "What's your problem now?"

"We're not going to have sex in this barn, so just cool down."

"Think again." He reached for her.

She put several splinters in her back by sliding to one side, and swore softly before grabbing her shirt up from the ground. "Ryder. No. I mean it."

He saw that she did, and clenched his fists. "I should have known it was just another tease. Proud of yourself, Calamity?"

"Proud? No. Confused? Big-time." She gestured around herself. "How did I get in here? What did you do to me?"

"You don't remember?" He snorted. "You *wanted* this. Hell, if I had let you, you'd have stripped me down and screwed me right there on the porch in front of the entire volunteer fire department."

Neal felt her knees give way as everything she'd done and said just minutes before flooded back into memory. She put a hand on the post for support. "The fire?"

"I put it out." He strode a few feet away from her and looked out. "They're gone. Jake and Lou are waiting at the front gate. It's just you and me here now."

"I'll be fine." She gestured vaguely toward his truck. "You can go."

"You'd like me to, wouldn't you?" He didn't go. He came right back at her, stopping a scant inch from touching her again. "This time, you offered. I'm taking."

"I'm not sure what I just did."

He put his hand over her breast, and stroked her nipple with his thumb. "This is what I'm talking about. This is what I'm taking. Along with the rest of you, Neala. Today."

She thrust aside the confusion and fixed him with her best steely gaze as she pushed his hand away. "Ryder, considering the house nearly burned down with us in it, and the way I just made a total fool out of myself in front of all those firemen, the very last thing I want to do is get naked with you now. Sorry."

"That why your heart is beating so fast?"

She didn't have to look down to know what he said was true. "Listen. I don't like you; you don't like me. Maybe I'm weird, but I have to at least *appreciate* •

someone before I jump into bed with him. So make no sex with you my standing preference for, oh, say, the next forty years."

"That's some speech, Calamity." He bent closer, letting his breath warm her lips.

"Thanks, now back off, Wild Bill."

He smiled. "I could kiss you right now and make a liar out of you."

She wasn't stupid—of course he could. Still, she didn't twitch a muscle. "I could knee you in the groin and make you into a temporary soprano." When his mouth nearly touched hers, she found she couldn't go through with her threat, and turned her head. "Please. Don't."

"Need another fix?"

"Another what?"

He took her arm and extended it to display the needle mark. "I don't know what you took, but get rid of it. All of it."

"But I didn't—"

"All of it, Neala. Or I'll make you wish I'd locked you in the cellar."

Neala watched him stalk out of the barn, and waited until she heard his truck roar down the drive before she let herself sag to the dirt floor.

"God." She propped her head in her hands. "I can't believe I actually told him I wanted to lick his chest. In front of the entire fire department."

It took a little time to gather herself together and head back to the house. The firemen had opened all the windows, but the smell of smoke eventually drove her back out. She worked in the yard for a couple of hours, yanking at anything that even vaguely resembled a weed and wishing she had a deer rifle—to use on herself.

Molly stopped by late that afternoon, with a cooler full of frozen homemade meals and a small microwave.

"Will asked me to deliver this for you. What's all this about a fire?"

Neal helped her carry everything in and pointed to the stove. "My latest disaster."

"Oh, honey." Behind the tinted lenses, Molly's eyes went wide. "What did you do?"

"I don't know how the fire got started. I know I turned the stove off before I went to bed." At least, she was fairly sure she had. The triumph of making her own bread had been so intoxicating that Neala had gone on and made three more loaves. She sadly contemplated the three charred mounds sitting on the back of the scorched stove. "I guess that's why he ordered the nuke-it food. He's afraid he'll have to eat dinner with a fire extinguisher next to him."

"Why are you cooking for him?"

"He's living here now." At Molly's glance, Neala rolled her eyes. "I know what you're thinking, but believe me, it's separate bedrooms and sustained hostility, all the way."

"Now that's a real shame." Molly opened the cooler and started unloading the cardboard trays. "He's quite a man."

"He's a Neanderthal."

"True, but honey, even cavemen have their uses." She transferred the first stack of meals into the freezer. "And before you start putting up a big fuss, I saw the way you looked at him when he walked into my place."

Neala brought over the next stack. "Am I that obvious?"

"He's got it just as bad. Lord, there was so much heat simmering between the two of you at that table I thought you'd set off *my* smoke alarm."

"I know he wants me. But he doesn't want to want me." Neala took the ruined loaves of bread and dumped them into the garbage. "I wish it could be different, but my life is a mess, and Ryder thinks I'm useless."

Molly eyed the streaks smoke had left on her skin. "You ought to go have a nice, long bath and relax. And don't worry about Will. He'll come around."

"I doubt it." She looked down at her arm. "As of this morning, he even accused me of being a drug addict."

"Why did he do that?" Molly closed the freezer.

"Beats me. He just went ballistic over this bug bite." She showed the older woman her arm. "Me, on drugs. I can't even swallow pills unless I crush them up and mix them in something first."

Molly placed the lid back on the cooler, then studied her arm carefully. "Well, I'm no doctor, but that sure looks like the kind of hole I get when I donate blood at the Red Cross."

Neal stared at the tiny puncture wound in the center of the small bruise. She'd given blood herself a few times. "You're right; it does." She rubbed at the mark, then shuddered. "I swear to God, Molly, I don't use drugs."

"I'll take your word for it." Molly went to say more, then pressed her lips together.

"What?"

"It's just . . . odd, you having this mark on your arm with Will here and all." At Neal's blank look, she shrugged. "Neal, Will's ex-wife died of a heroin overdose."

"What does that have to do with this?"

"Everybody knew Trish Ryder took drugs—she popped pills and snorted coke and smoked marijuana. But for some reason, she was terrified of needles. I know because of one time the Red Cross lady tried to talk her into giving blood. She wouldn't have anything to do with it. Turned green at the thought. Then she died, shooting up heroin—one year to the day she left Will."

Chapter 10

Wendy decided it was time she talked to Neal Delaney herself, before the dance. That way, there would be no misunderstandings, nothing would go wrong, and she and Will could get on with their life together.

Hearing the news about the fire at Sun Valley gave her the perfect excuse. Wendy could pay a visit to see how she was, take her a nice casserole, and put things straight at the same time.

Her father wouldn't approve of Wendy going by herself—appearances needed to be kept up—so she asked Vicky if she wanted to go with her.

"Are you kidding? I'm dying to meet her," the hairdresser said. "Let's go."

Armed with sympathy casseroles and avid curiosity, the women drove out to Sun Valley. Jake and Lou stopped them at the gate, and Vicky had to explain why they'd come before they allowed them to pass.

"Those are Martha Squire's boys." Vicky looked back, her mouth a scarlet O. "What are they doing out here?"

"I bet they're guarding her—making sure she doesn't leave the county," Wendy said with a smug smile. "She's been on the run from the law, you know."

"For what?"

"I don't know exactly, but with the way she

looks . . ." Wendy rolled her shoulders. "Could be anything."

"Oh, my." Vicky parked her SUV in front of the house and peered through the windshield. "Just look at the smoke damage around the windows. That poor girl could have been killed."

Wendy suppressed a sigh of regret. "Terrible, isn't it?"

Neal answered the front door on the second knock. She was dressed in a robe and carrying a cup of tea, which made Wendy exchange a significant look with Vicky. It was past noon.

"Hello . . . Winifred, is it?"

"Wendy." Behind her smile, she gritted her teeth. "We heard about the fire and wanted to stop in and see how you were doing. Here." She held out the casserole. "This is just a little something to tide you over until you feel better."

Neal didn't take it. "I'm fine, thanks."

"Hi, there, dear. I'm Vicky Blake; I own the hair salon in town. We're real sorry to hear about your troubles. Might we come in and visit for a spell?" The hairdresser was a combat veteran at barging in where she wasn't wanted, so she stepped forward and leaned against the door. "I imagine you'd be glad to have the company, wouldn't you?"

Neal reluctantly opened the door. "Sure, come on in."

She led them to the kitchen, and showed them where to put the casserole in her refrigerator. It was already packed with other dishes, some Vicky recognized by the china pattern.

"Well, looks like you've had some other visitors."

"Seven, to be exact." Neal sat down at the kitchen table. She hadn't put any makeup on yet, and still looked darkly beautiful. "You two make eight and nine. I won't have to cook for another month."

Wendy sat down beside Neal and put on her best

supportive expression. "It must have been a terrible experience."

"I managed to survive," Neal said in a dry tone. "Though Ryder gets the credit for dragging me out of here."

"He saved your life? That is so *incredible*." Vicky finished poking through the refrigerator and had the sense to look a little uncomfortable. "I mean, how frightening for you."

"He was incredible. I was unconscious."

Wendy leaned forward. It was time to establish her territory. "You know, Will is so generous and kind. And he's always helping out someone down on their luck." She paused, and put a hand on Neal's arm. "But don't mistake that for something else, dear. I know him *very* well. He's just trying to be neighborly."

"Neighborly." Neal nodded thoughtfully. "That's one way to put it."

"Are you going to the spring dance in town on Saturday, Ms. Delaney?" Vicky asked.

Before Neal could answer, Wendy said, "Oh, I don't think that would be a good idea. You probably need time to recover from this horrible ordeal, don't you, Neal? I mean, it's such a shock for a woman your age."

"Oh, I don't know. If I take some extra vitamins, and put on my support hose, I should be able to hobble a couple of times around the dance floor."

Wendy controlled the urge to slap the smile from her face. "It's just a little to-do for the local people," she said, feeling her temper rise. "A cosmopolitan woman like you would be totally bored."

"She'll love it." Evan stepped into the kitchen, carrying a portable CB radio, which he put on the counter. "I've asked Neal to go with me."

Evan was here. With *her*. While the awful woman was still in her *robe*.

"You did." Wendy didn't move. So Evan was her

target, not Will. Or did she want both of them? Wendy wouldn't put it past her to be angling for two men at the same time. Carefully she controlled her tone. "Will already asked me to go with him, so I guess we'll see you there."

Neal sipped her tea. "That will be nice."

"Evan, I didn't know you two were dating," Vicky said, her gaze bouncing between him and Neala like a rubber ball. "I'm sorry, but I thought you were only staying here for a few weeks."

"That's right. I'm dating Evan. And I'm leaving in a couple of weeks."

"Well, you two have a nice time." Wendy wished for a moment that the fire had spread a little faster. "And if you need anything, feel free to call me. I'll leave you my number." She took a notepad out of her purse, wrote it down, and handed Neal the paper.

"Thanks." Neal got up and carelessly shoved the note into her robe pocket. "And thanks for the food."

On the way back to town, Vicky kept gushing about how pretty Neal was and how scandalous it was to be lounging around in a robe after the sun was fully up.

"And she's seeing that Evan Gamble. I'd never have put those two together. Why, he's at least four years younger than her."

Wendy stared blindly at the mountains. "Evan's twenty-five. I doubt she's much older."

"But he seems so young, while she's . . . well, so sophisticated and, you know, voluptuous." Vicky shook her head. "More Will's type than Evan's."

"Will is not interested in that woman, Vicky." Wendy pulled down the visor and checked her image in the little square mirror. She was younger and prettier; how could Evan even look at Neal Delaney?

"I don't know, Wendy. She's awful good-looking."

"She's just plain *awful*!" she snapped, then shoved the visor back up. "I don't want to talk about it anymore."

"No," Vicky said with a rueful glance. "I can see you don't."

Back at Sun Valley, Evan finished hooking up the CB radio and showed Neal how to use it to call for help. He was still on edge from Wendy's unexpected visit, and Neal convinced him to sit with her on the porch for a few minutes before he went back to High Point.

She handed him a glass of iced tea. "Why do I get the feeling Wendy was hoping to see my hair had burned off?"

"I'm sorry about that." He sat down and propped his boots on the railing. "She's got a bug up her nose about you. I hope you didn't eat whatever she brought you."

"Do I look stupid?" Neal laughed. "That casserole is going right in the garbage."

"Smart lady." He frowned. "I don't know why she's acting like this with you. Doesn't make sense."

"It does, when you think you're God's gift to men, and then find out you're not the only one they want to unwrap. What's her problem with you?"

"I don't know," he admitted. "I never knew a girl so determined to run everybody's life. And the way she goes about it is all wrong. Look at her—she's so pretty, she could have everyone eating out of her hand, if she wanted. Smart enough to do anything she wants, too. If she'd just grow up and realize she can't have everyone sitting at her feet, adoring every word that comes out of her mouth."

"How long have you been in love with her?"

Evan gave her a quick, startled look, then flushed. "About four years. Ever since I came to work at High Point."

"She would have been about, what? Sixteen?" Neal sat back and looked down the drive. "You've never told her, have you?"

"No. She's still just a kid."

"You're a patient man, Evan."

"With her, I have to be." He drank the rest of his tea. "She'll call Will and probably tell him some nonsense about me being over here. He won't be happy."

"Why's that?"

Evan smiled. "Because where you're concerned, Will's got a whole wasp's nest up his nose."

What had Evan said to her about this stupid dance? *It'll be fun, Neal. You'll see.*

She stood in front of the bathroom mirror and scowled at herself. *Fun. Right.* Why had she let him talk her into going to this hick-town shindig? She didn't have anything to wear. She had things to do. She didn't want to go.

Neal, you've been spending way too much time with the little green sprouts.

She laughed in spite of her mood. Living at Sun Valley might be the equivalent of joining a convent, but working in the garden had certainly made up for it. Just that morning she had solved a budding problem with aphids by using a variation of her organic insect repellent—diluted with garlic juice.

"Aphids. God almighty."

She went to her closet and surveyed the pitiful collection of what clothes she had. There were the bag-lady outfits, or shorts. She'd already tried to salvage her red dress, but it was history. Then she noticed a dusty garment bag hanging at the very back of the closet, and pulled it out.

"What's this?"

It held a wedding dress, two formal gowns, and one dress with a matching jacket. When Neal pulled out the last, she whistled.

"Wow." She felt the black material. "Real silk. They must have paid someone to smuggle this over the state lines."

It wouldn't fit her, of course. She couldn't be that

lucky. She kept telling herself that as she tried the dress on, saw how it looked in the mirror, and found her luck had finally changed.

Oh, boy. Did it fit her.

She put on the beaded bolero jacket. Once that was buttoned up, she looked everything elegant and proper from the waist up. The skirt was a bit short, but she had the legs to go with it.

As far as what was beneath the buttons, well, Will was bringing his little girlfriend to the dance instead of her.

He kisses me like that and then still wants to play with Barbie, does he?

"That settles it. I have got to wear this."

After she dried her hair, Neal piled it on top of her head and let a couple of dark curls dangle around her face and neck. The effect was elegant and sexy.

"Perfect."

She grabbed her makeup bag and started working on her face. She had a light tan now, so liquid base and concealer were unnecessary. Not that she had really needed them before, but putting on the full war paint always made her feel better. Well, she'd just put a little more effort into her eyes.

A skillful application of dusky shadow made her dark eyes look enormous. An extra coat of mascara made her own thick, dark lashes seem to lengthen into forever. A whisk of rose blush made her high cheekbones stand out, while the crimson gloss she stroked over her lips screamed *sex*.

"Want to dance with me, cowboy?" she said, and made a sulky, sultry face at herself. "Ha. Barbie hasn't got a chance."

The FBI still had most of her jewelry, so she made do with pearl earrings and a silver chain bracelet. She slid her toes into the stiletto-heeled black pumps she usually wore for a performance. They made her almost six feet tall, but it didn't bother her anymore, not since high school. Back then she'd been the tallest kid in her class, and often wondered if God was making her pay for not getting pimples.

Is this really a good idea?

Evan had threatened to pick her up by seven, and she checked her watch. Five minutes to go. No time to chicken out now. She sprayed herself with White Linen perfume, then turned a full three-sixty in front of the mirror. Yes, she definitely did *not* resemble a farm girl.

Let Little Miss Prom Queen try to outshine me tonight. Ryder will be so busy staring at me—

She swore and thrust her cosmetics back into the bag. She'd made a vow not to think about him, or what had happened after the fire. Bad enough she'd made a total fool of herself. But the memory of how it felt to be in his arms always hovered, just off to one side, like a storm cloud waiting to pour down over everything.

Then there was Will, who hadn't spoken more than three words to her since the morning of the fire. Well, no, that wasn't true—he'd had the decency to tell her she hadn't started it, but that it had been deliberately set to look that way. Beyond that one terse conversation, he'd spent all his time working on repairing the smoke damage to the house and ignoring her. It was as if she'd become invisible.

The little warning visit from his girlfriend had iced the cake. She'd show him just how visible she could be. And he could drool all he wanted while she danced with Evan. Hopefully some of the drool would land on the Prom Queen's head.

Someone knocked at the front door.

"Showtime."

When she opened the door, Evan looked at her with very complimentary shock. "Holy mackerel!"

Neal had missed seeing awed male appreciation. "Thank you."

"You're welcome." Evan swallowed as she walked by him and he got a whiff of her perfume. "I think."

She grinned, thinking of what was—or wasn't—under her jacket. "I think we're going to have a real good time tonight."

Will was bored.

Dean had pestered him for days until he'd agreed to escort Wendy to Lone Creek's annual spring dance. Now he regretted it. He could have spent the time dealing with some of the endless paperwork he'd brought down from High Point. Instead, he was stuck for the next two hours, sipping spiked punch and watching the townspeople slaughter the two-step.

He noticed Martha Squire had both Jake and Lou manning the refreshments table, so he walked over to talk to them about their night shift. Lou assured him they'd be back on duty as soon as the dance was over.

He asked for two cups of punch. "Have either of you seen Evan?"

"Over there." Lou pointed toward one corner. Will turned, spotted his foreman, and raised a hand to catch his attention.

Who was that standing beside him?

The tall woman had her back toward Will, and was chatting with a couple of hands from Dean Lewis's ranch. Whatever she said made all three men laugh. Evan handed her a glass of punch, and she took a sip before slowly turning around to scan the room. Her dark chocolate eyes met Will's.

Neala?

"Will?" Wendy appeared at his side, and he absently handed her one of the cups of punch. "Would you like to dance with me?"

The question barely registered. He couldn't take his eyes off Neal. She handed her drink back to Evan, then lifted her slim hands. Slowly she unbuttoned the front of the short jacket she wore over her dress. Will was spellbound. So was Evan, both of his friends, and everyone else within fifty feet. At last, her shoulders moved to shrug off the garment.

Next to him, Wendy followed his gaze, then gave a strangled gasp.

Luscious yards of naked skin gleamed, revealed by the strapless, backless, and nearly frontless black sheath. Two skimpy triangles covering her breasts challenged gravity every time she took a breath.

Dear God. Will's jaw clenched against the urge to growl. It wasn't a dress. It was a *napkin.* Then he recognized it, and nearly crushed the cup in his hand.

Neal draped her jacket over the back of a chair. Smoothed the line of her skirt. Sauntered across the dance floor. Couples seemed to scurry out of her way.

Why didn't I notice before how long her legs were?

Wendy began muttering a long string of surprisingly vile words under her breath.

"Hello, Ryder." Neal halted directly in front of him, smiling, holding out one hand. Absently he took it, and her fingers curled around his briefly. "I hope you don't mind me coming with Evan tonight."

She wasn't going to do a damn thing with Evan tonight. Not with her nipples all but popping out of that damn dress. Heat pumped into his veins as he focused on her face. Her mouth was red and wet, the stuff of dreams. "This your idea of a joke?"

"You mean this?" She tugged at a fold of her dress. "It's just a dress, Ryder."

Just a dress. Like a tornado was just a little wind.

Wendy chose that moment to step directly into the line of fire. "My God, don't you have an ounce of modesty?"

His houseguest folded her hands like a demure schoolgirl. "Fresh out. Can I borrow some of yours?" While Wendy sputtered, she turned the adorable smile on him. "When do we bob for apples?"

Will wasn't letting her bend over for the rest of the night. Before he could tell her that, Molly Hatcher came over and gave Neal a hug. "Good to see you here, honey. You look positively ravishing tonight."

"Thanks, Molly. About that lasagna you made—I'll

never be able to eat the store-bought kind again. You've ruined me for life." She patted her flat stomach, and Will saw that her short nails had not only been manicured, but she'd painted them with that glossy scarlet polish again. "I wish you could meet my sister, Laney. She owns a diner, too, back in Denver."

Molly was surprised. "Your sister does? And you can't cook?"

"No point, she could." She made an artless gesture. "My talents lay in other areas."

"I can just bet what you're good at," Wendy muttered.

"Me, too." Molly chuckled, and touched Will's arm. He tore his attention away from Neal, but it took effort. "We could use a hand bringing in the rest of the party platters, Will. Can I steal you away from these young ladies for a few minutes?"

He wasn't leaving Neala. Not for a second.

Evan chose that moment to join them. "Why don't Wendy and I help you, Miss Hatcher?"

"Why, sure, Evan. Thank you."

Wendy didn't take the hint. "I'll catch up with you in a minute."

Once they left, Neal tasted her punch and made a face. "Whew, this stuff is pretty powerful. Are you supposed to drink it or strip something with it?"

"Don't say strip," Will heard himself snap at her. "Not in that dress."

"She's making a spectacle out of herself, Will." Wendy refused to look at Neal. "For goodness' sake, make her leave."

Black curls danced as Neal leaned forward to murmur, "That shade of green isn't very flattering, Wanda."

"My *name* is *Wendy*." The younger girl frowned at her own dress, which was elegant, tasteful, and next to Neal made her look about twelve. "What are you, color-blind? This isn't green."

"I wasn't talking about your dress."

Will saw his neighbor's daughter clench her fists, and decided it was time to split these two up, before hair started flying. He took his houseguest by the hand. "Wendy, you'd better go help Molly. Come on, Ms. Delaney."

He hauled Neal around the banquet table and onto the dance floor.

Neal saw the golden girl's face crumple as Ryder dragged her away, and felt a twinge of remorse. *I've got to stop playing with Barbie.*

Several couples edged away as Will pulled her onto the dance floor. The band's energetic swing segued to a slow, romantic beat. Without ceremony, he took her in his arms.

Exactly as she'd planned.

A soft sound left Neal's throat before she could stop it. Something knotted deep inside her abdomen and started crawling through her limbs, making her flush.

Okay, maybe she could have planned this part a little better.

This close, the differences between her body and his were very apparent. His shoulders were like roof beams under her palms. Her narrow torso barely spanned half the width of his concrete-wall chest. She could feel the steely muscles cording his thighs—no doubt from spending hours every day riding. One of his strong hands flattened against her back, covering her entire shoulder blade. If he wanted to, Ryder could snap her spine in half with minimal effort.

That should have worried her—but it didn't. She actually *liked* him being bigger, stronger, tougher.

The faint stubble on his chin brushed her temple, rasping against her skin. Whatever cologne he wore smelled crisp and clean. When he moved, she could feel the powerful play of sinew and muscle under his shirt. Even the sound of him breathing made her thighs feel weak.

Things were starting to get a little out of hand.

Neal blamed it on a number of things. Getting up close and personal with Will Ryder was stupid, considering how attracted to him she was. He was a good dancer, too. Neal had always been a sucker for a man who was light on his feet.

No, she was in way over her head.

Maybe it would help to get some breathing room. She pulled against the cradle of his arms, tripping over her own toes for a moment. He allowed her to create a small amount of space between their bodies.

Only that didn't help much. She could still feel the heat. It was time to find a nice quiet corner where she could sit down and stuff her brains back in her ears.

"Satisfied with yourself, Calamity?"

Just like a caveman to keep swinging his club when he'd already dragged her around by the hair. "I'm working on it."

"I bet you are." He tugged her closer. This time both of his hands splayed along her spine, and didn't allow her an inch of breathing space. His voice got rough. "Dressing to aggravate men again?"

"You figure it out." She tried to push him off. That was when he moved one down to rest just above her buttocks. Outraged, she stiffened. He only stroked the bare skin there. "Keep doing that and the sheriff is going to haul us both out of here."

"Caleb's not here." He sounded tired now. "You shouldn't be here, Neala. You're supposed to be staying out of sight."

"Yeah, well, the big secret is pretty much history, so what's the use?"

"It's not safe." His hand clenched. "Whoever set the fire at Sun Valley could be here."

"Good. He owes me three loaves of homemade bread."

"Where did you find this dress?"

"In the back of a closet." She shimmied her hips, making the short skirt twirl. "Like it?"

Something ugly flared in his eyes. "It's not yours."

Neal decided she'd had enough fun. "No, it's not, but I didn't have anything else to wear. I'm tired of looking like a homeless person." Honesty compelled her to add, "And your little Prom Queen needed a wake-up call."

"That wake-up call belonged to my ex-wife."

Oh, great. "I'm sure she wouldn't have minded my borrowing it, under the circumstances."

"Trish wore that dress the night we got engaged. *I* mind."

And he had every right to. "I'm sorry, Will."

His nostrils flared; then his hold changed from firm to fierce. "You shouldn't have done this, Neala." That came out through clenched teeth. "Not tonight. Not in this dress."

"I said I was sorry. Look, I didn't know—"

"Shut up and dance."

Okay, so he was furious. She felt terrible for reminding him of the past, but she was determined to stand her ground. She would, too. Just as soon as Ryder stopped dragging her around the dance floor.

Only he wasn't exactly dragging her. There was the lure of the romantic music. The press of his hard body against hers. How long had it been since she'd danced in a man's arms? Years. She'd always been up on the stage, serenading the dancers, watching them sway together, aching with her own loneliness.

Here with Ryder, she found herself slipping away into a seductive fantasy. Dancing together, alone instead of in a roomful of people. Dancing in the dark, skin against skin, nothing to stop them from ending up in her bed, and taking the rhythm to another level.

Stop it. You're wearing his dead wife's clothes, for God's sake.

"I think I've had enough dancing for one night." Neal came to a stop and tried to extricate herself.

The thick fair brows lowered as he forced her to continue. "I'm not through with you yet. You're going back to the ranch."

She'd apologized, but she'd be damned if she was going to keep letting him pound his chest and wave his club. "I don't think so, Ryder. I've already shown my face, everybody knows who I am, so I'm staying and enjoying the evening with my date."

"Your date." He made a disgusted sound. "You won't be satisfied until you've got every man in town panting after you."

She gave him a thin smile. "You mean I missed some?"

"Don't push me, city girl. I've had enough of your mouth."

"Not yet, cowboy. You're about to find out how loudly I can scream."

His eyes turned to pure ice. "Want to find out how fast I can shut you up?"

"Excuse me, Will." Evan stepped up to them, compelling them to stop. "I was hoping to convince the lady to sing for us tonight."

She used the interruption to get out of Will's grip. He wanted war; he was going to get exactly that. "I'd be thrilled."

The stage was small, and already crowded with the band members playing. After climbing up and briefly running over her act with the musicians (who had performed many jazz gigs and luckily knew all of her songs), Neal stepped behind the mike. Everyone had stopped dancing by then, and was staring at her.

"Good evening, ladies and gentlemen." She ignored the whispers and concentrated on what she did best. "Anyone here old enough to remember Helen Kane?"

One of the elderly men sitting by the punch bowl called out, "Sure do. She was that Boop-Boop-a-Doop gal."

"The very first, even before Betty stole her act," Neala said. A couple of people laughed. "Here's a song she did way back in 1929—'I'd Do Anything for You.' "

She let the opening bars swell up around her, closed
her eyes, and let her voice drift over the crowd.

> *There's lots of things I don't like, sweetheart, it's*
>   *true,*
> *But then I change my mind with just one smile*
>   *from you;*
> *I loved you from the very start,*
> *Yes, I'd do anything for you, sweetheart!*

Neal's dark eyes opened slowly. Across the room,
Ryder watched her without blinking.

The band whirled into the transition and spun out
the faster cadence. Without a hitch she abandoned her
pose and went directly into her slapstick, teasing
dance, using her hips, kicking her feet, shaking her
head and finger at the audience in time with the music.

> *No, I don't like turnips, I can't stand turnips,*
>   *and I hate turnips, it's true!*
> *But if you say turnips, then I'd eat catnip,*
> *'cause I'd do anything for you!*

The ragtime beat and funny lyrics drew dozens of
eager couples onto the dance floor. As she sang, Neal
took the mike in her hand and eased her way off the
stage. She went as far as the cord would let her, play-
fully vamping her way in and out of the dancers, wink-
ing at the women and teasing the men. Someone's
wide-eyed toddler wandered up to her, and she
reached down to caress the round, soft cheek.

> *Sweetheart, can't you see*
> *what you mean to me!*

The little boy laughed and grabbed onto her skirt
with tiny, starfished hands. She bent and picked him
up with one arm without missing a note. Holding him
tucked on her hip, she sang the next verse to him as

he played with her hair. The toddler's smiling mother hurried over to rescue Neal, but it took plenty of coaxing and another full verse before the little boy let go. When Neal blew him a kiss, he made one last unsuccessful lunge at her, and that made everyone laugh.

Neal ran through all the verses, complaining about dancing, bananas, and weddings. As soon as she worked her way through the crowd to within a foot of Will, she focused all her attention on him. Or attempted to. After a minute, he turned and walked out of the hall.

Neal nearly stopped singing. Then, defiantly, she walked back up to the stage to let the last lines ring out.

> *Ooh, sweetheart, can't you see*
> *What you mean to little me?*

Neal let her voice fade out on a sigh, then fell silent and bowed her head. The band finished the final bars. Then thunderous applause made her jump.

Everyone on the dance floor was turned toward the stage, clapping, yelling, and whistling. Several people called out for more. Smiling, Neal held up her hand and, when they quieted enough, said, "Let's liven things up a bit, shall we?"

She counted off to the band, and launched into a sexy, swinging number that had everyone whirling around the floor. She kept the crowd dancing for another three songs, and would have enjoyed every minute if she hadn't spent half the time looking for Ryder.

Where is he? Why did he walk out like that?

She wrapped up the last number, then gracefully bowed and waited out the applause. She fanned herself with one hand. "Whew! I haven't had this much fun in years, but I've shown off enough for one night. Thank you, ladies and gentlemen."

Evan helped her down from the stage, and pressed

a cold drink into her hands. "It's plain lemonade," he said, bending close so she could hear him as he led her off to one side by the buffet table.

"Thanks, pal." She drank half of it, sighed, and smiled at her new fans. "That was fun."

A big shadow fell over her. "You always act like a stripper when you sing?"

She looked up at Will. *Now he comes back.* "It's harmless, Ryder. All part of the job. And none of my clothes came off." She glanced down, just to be sure.

"You like putting on the tease. I guess you have to, with that voice of yours."

That hurt. Neal's voice was the only talent she had, and she was proud of it. Ryder's clear contempt made her chin go up. He might not like it, but she was damn good, and she knew it. "Sorry it strained your ears. Everyone else seemed to tolerate the noise just fine."

Wendy appeared, flushed and a little unsteady. "Why are you still here?"

Neal wondered how much punch the younger girl had drunk. "I lost a glass slipper. Seen one anywhere?"

"You're not Cinderella." Wendy jerked a thumb toward herself, narrowly missing gouging her own face. "*I* was Cinderella."

"You were Cinderella," Neal said. "Okay. Whatever."

Evan took her arm and bent close. "Wendy played Cinderella for her senior skit night. And I think she's drunk."

"I think you're right," Neal murmured back.

"What are you telling her, Evan Gamble?" Wendy staggered forward. "Are you going to give her my photograph?"

They both looked at her, puzzled.

"Because I won't let you. No way, no how. Not even when Will and I get married. "It's *mine*."

"Must be some picture," Neal said.

He frowned. "I don't know what the heck she's talking about."

"You know exactly what I'm talking about." Wendy shook her finger at him. "The one with me and Will and Daddy and Starlight and you. And she can't have it."

"Honey, I think you'd better sit down." Will tried to steer her toward a chair, but she ripped her arm free.

"You don't get to tell me what to do yet, Will Ryder." She staggered forward to jab his chest with her finger, missed, and poked him in the biceps. "Not until we're married. Just wait while I take care of this; then I'll let you seduce me."

He stared down at her, obviously as baffled as Evan and Neal were.

"And you." Wendy whirled around, nearly fell, and then caught Neal's shoulder purely by accident. "You think you can come in here and shake your stuff in front of the whole town, and nobody's going to say boo to you? Well, *boo,* I say. Boo—boo—boooooooooo."

She's definitely had too much punch. Neal eased out from under her hand and took several cautious steps away from the younger woman. "You'd really better sit down for a little while, Wilma. You're turning green again."

"My *name* is *Wendy!*" The blonde lunged at her.

Neal avoided the punch by simply stepping out of the way. Wendy crashed into the buffet table, and ended up with her face smack in the center of a huge chocolate sheet cake. Another woman shrieked. A couple of men laughed.

"Shit." Neal tried to help the flailing, struggling girl up, and got splattered with chocolate icing. "Ryder—"

Evan grabbed Wendy at the same moment a hard hand clamped around Neal's arm. "Outside. Now."

Chapter 11

Everyone they passed stared. Will ignored them. Neal tried to free herself, but he had her through the back entrance and out in the dark before she thought to start yelling.

"Stop manhandling me."

"That was a cheap shot, lady."

"What are you talking about? The Prom Queen tried to punch my lights out—I just moved my face out of the way!"

"You pushed her to it." Will kicked the door shut behind them, then dragged her along the length of the building to the parking lot and his truck. "I'm taking you home."

"Denver is a long drive from here."

"Get in."

"Don't you think you ought to go back inside and pull Barbie out of that cake first?"

He was furious. So was she. He knew if he got her alone, they'd end up in the back of his truck, tearing each other's clothes off. Which felt like a pretty damn good idea. "Get in the truck, Neala."

"I came with Evan. I'm leaving with him, not you."

"Not tonight. You've done enough damage."

"That wasn't my fault. Besides, I'm not ready to leave."

He wanted that dress off her. He wanted her naked. He wanted her *now*. "You paraded yourself in front of the whole town, and embarrassed a naive girl who was so drunk she couldn't possibly have hurt you." She'd sung like an angel who'd fallen from the heavens, not that he planned to tell her that. "What more do you want?"

"Hmmmmm." She considered this. "A piece of that chocolate cake would have been nice."

But Neala was no angel. "Don't be a bitch."

She took exception to that. "Your jailbait girlfriend tried to break my jaw, and she's a naive girl, but I'm a bitch for defending myself?" To his amazement, tears welled up in her eyes.

"No. Don't start— Oh, hell." He reached for her.

She backed away. "Don't."

He was faster, stronger. "Neala." He got her in his arms. Caught her mouth with his. Delighted in the low, needy sound she made. He rested his brow against hers. "When are we going to stop this?"

"We haven't started anything. And according to your girlfriend, you're getting married, so you can't start anything."

"I'm not marrying her. Jesus, I used to baby-sit her for Dean after her mother died." He pulled her hair down and filled his hands with it. "She's a little girl."

"The little girl, if you haven't noticed, is twenty, blond, gorgeous, and wants you."

"What about you?"

"I'm not twenty or blond." She ducked her head to avoid his mouth. "Okay, I want you, but this isn't the time or the place."

"Then we'll make the time and find the place. Stop pushing me away."

Neal went very still; then she lifted her hand and touched his face. "Let's go."

He kissed her once, then swore. "Come on."

He'd opened the passenger-side door for her when Evan caught up to them.

"Will." He looked pale and miserable. "Wendy's in pretty rough shape. She threw up in front of everyone and now she's locked herself in the ladies' room and won't come out. I tried to talk to her, but all she wants is you. She won't let anyone else take her home."

Neal looked at him, then climbed back out of the truck. "Go back to her, Ryder."

"Take Miss Delaney back to the ranch, Evan. And keep her there."

"Well. That was a productive evening." Neal leaned her head back against the car seat and sighed. "God, that girl is wrecking my life." She glanced at Evan. "Sorry."

"Don't apologize. She's wrecking my life, too."

"How did she get so drunk so fast?"

"She started hitting the punch while you were dancing with Will. Five glasses in a row that I counted."

She winced. "Poor Barbie. Bad move."

"She didn't know what it meant to lose before tonight." Evan kept his expression a little too controlled. "She's been the local beauty all her life. Homecoming queen and prom queen and everything else. Like you said, it's time she realized she's not God's gift to men."

"Evan, I think your nose is getting longer."

He sighed; then he laughed. "Okay. I admit, I think she's the most beautiful girl in the world. No offense, Neal."

"None taken. Can't expect everyone to fall in love with me." She looked back at the empty road. No sign of Ryder's truck. Even though she knew he'd be taking care of Wendy and getting her home, it depressed her.

"You sure can sing like nobody's business. Tell me something—why aren't you out in Hollywood, making movies or records or what have you?"

"I tried out on Broadway. I wanted to star in musicals, like the ones I loved as a kid. *South Pacific. A Chorus Line. Cats.*" She smiled wistfully. "I'd have even settled for making the chorus line for an off-off-Broadway musical version of *Death of a Salesman*."

"Didn't you like Broadway?"

"Oh, I loved it. And they liked me. It's just my voice wasn't what they were looking for. I overpowered everyone I sang with. So unless they start casting for a musical one-woman show, no chance of my feet ever hitting those boards."

"What about that opera stuff? Don't you have to have a powerful voice for that?"

"You also have to learn French and Italian, and I barely got through high school Spanish." She yawned. "Plus the girl almost always dies in every show. It's too depressing."

An oncoming vehicle approached them, and its headlights made her squint. She sat up and held a hand in front of her face. "Idiot, why doesn't he turn off his brights—"

Evan turned the wheel hard to the right. "Hold on!"

The other vehicle roared past the driver's window, only an inch away. Then at the last second, the two cars collided. Metal scraped and sparks flew. The force sent Evan's truck off the road in a spin. Neal covered her head with her arms just before she hit the dashboard.

All at once, Evan wrestled the truck back under control and hit the brakes. Neal waited until they'd come to a full stop before she pulled herself up from the floor.

"Are you okay?" Evan took off his seat belt and helped her back onto the seat. After he made her move everything, he said, "Stay here." He got out and looked both ways down the highway before returning. "He's gone."

Neal winced as she flexed her arms. "If he comes back, beat him up for me, will you?"

"Let me see." He turned on the dome light and examined the rapidly darkening bruises on her forearms. "Damn, those are going to give you some grief in the morning."

"I'll survive." She looked through the windshield, but there was no sign of the other vehicle. "Though that idiot probably won't. What was he thinking?"

"I don't know; maybe he fell asleep at the wheel and just woke up." Evan leaned his head against the steering wheel for a moment. "God, that took a good ten years off my life. I swear, it looked like he was heading straight at us, deliberately."

"Maybe he was." Neal told him about the injection mark on her arm, ending with, "Someone around here doesn't want me to testify."

Evan put the truck in gear and slowly started back down the road. "I'll call it in to the sheriff. You'd better tell Will when he gets back to the house. Here." He took something from his pocket and handed it to her. "Keep this."

It was a cell phone. "You know Ryder doesn't want me to have a phone, Evan," she said slowly.

"Yeah, I know. Keep it anyway."

She didn't ask Evan in, and gave him a tender smile before kissing him on the cheek.

"Sorry about what happened with Wendy. This wasn't much of a date for you."

"You either." He patted her cheek fondly. "Good night, Neal."

She watched him drive off, then let herself in. It was a real shame Evan was in love with someone else, and aroused about as much passion in Neala as a younger brother would. She could have had a nice little fling with him and gotten rid of some of her frustration.

Frustration over a man who wanted her, but didn't love her. And that, she suspected, was going to rip her soul into shreds.

The damage to the side of the stolen car was minimal, but he'd still have to ditch it. That meant taking

the interstate and driving for hours until he hit someplace big enough to make an exchange. But he wasn't
willing to listen to any more of the Irishman's excuses,
and he had no intention of leaving Montana until he'd
taken care of Neala Delaney personally.

*I should have just stopped and shot the asshole she
was with.* He caressed the .45 sitting on the seat beside
him. *But that would spoil the reunion.*

J. R. hated the country. Had hated it ever since his
mother had dragged him out to live in it when he was
six, all in the name of love.

"Guess what, honey! Mommy's getting married!"

She'd met his stepfather at one of the rodeos she
was always forcing J. R. to endure. Rebecca Martin
had fallen in love before the show closed and hurled
herself into a whirlwind courtship.

"You be a good boy, J. R.," she said after the wedding, "and I know your stepdaddy will give you your
own pony to ride."

He hadn't wanted a pony. Hadn't wanted to leave
their home in upstate New York for the endless void
of empty fields and brooding mountains of the west.
Hadn't wanted an older brother—especially one who
was a foot taller and twenty pounds heavier.

He made his feelings clear in every possible way
he could.

Overhead, a sign indicated he had another fifty
miles to go before he reached Helena, but only two
miles until the exit for Tall Oaks. A fairly good-sized
town, he recalled. He'd once stolen one of his stepfather's precious horses and ridden all night to get
there.

He smiled as he remembered his stepfather's fury
when he'd picked up J. R. from the police station the
next day. The horse hadn't taken to J. R.'s riding crop,
and had never been the same.

As towns went, Tall Oaks was on the small side,
but it still boasted two Ford dealerships. J. R. concealed his damaged car in the back lot, removed the

small duffel bag from the truck, then went to inspect
what was available.

His stepfather had been a patient man, but after
three years, two ruined horses, numerous police visits,
and a wife who never stopped weeping, he'd had
enough. Then there had been the boarding schools
and the pathetic holiday visits, when his mother pretended to be glad to see him when she really couldn't
wait to see him go.

He found an older-model car he liked and released
the door lock by inserting a thin metal jimmy-strip
between the window and door panel. From the duffel
bag, he took out the body puller he'd bought for fifteen dollars from a parts shop and used it to pry the
ignition lock from the steering column. After tossing
the lock aside, he exchanged the body puller for an
ordinary screwdriver. J. R. inserted the slotted end
into the mutilated steering column, turning the screwdriver the way he would a key, and the engine started
at once.

As a teenager, he'd made every visit home as miserable as possible for his mother and her new family.
He also discovered how much he enjoyed taking what
they denied him. Shoplifting and stealing cars proved
even more fun than taking his stepfather's horses.
Then came the summer when J. R. had nearly been
killed.

"How could you?" His mother had stood beside his
hospital bed, pale and horrified. "How could you do
something like this?"

She'd never seen or spoken to him again.

He pulled out from the used-car lot and, after a
stop to take a license plate from another car on the
outskirts of town, immediately left Tall Oaks. For a
few minutes he amused himself with fantasies of returning to Sun Valley and finishing off Neala Delaney.

She'd try to sucker him again, of course. She'd
played him twice already, and a woman with her kind
of phenomenal body always assumed she could get

away with murder. Imagining her throwing back her
head to expose her soft, slim throat made him smile.
Such a pretty, perfect neck. It would take only a moment to wrap his hands around it and choke the life
out of her.

*And I will, as soon as she tells me about the deal
she made with the Chinese.*

Eventually Will coaxed Wendy to let him into the
ladies' room. She was covered with bits of cake and
brown icing, and began sobbing as soon as he closed
the door.

"Look what she did, Will." She wiped ineffectually
at her face and dress. "Everyone was laughing at me."

Molly appeared in the doorway with a roll of paper
towels. "Let me help."

"No, no, go away!" Wendy slid to the floor and
curled into a ball of misery.

Will took the paper towels and told the diner owner
he'd handle the cleanup. "But see if you can clear
everyone out of the hallway for me, Molly. No one
has to hang around and see her like this."

He wet a few paper towels and got most of the mess
off her face and hands, but her dress was ruined. The
girl didn't help by cowering away every time he
touched her.

He tried to find patience where there was none left.
"Honey, hold still so I can get this done."

"You'll still marry me, won't you, Will?" Wendy's
voice shook as she clutched at him with fierce hands.
"Daddy will be so angry if you don't. You still love
me, don't you?"

"Yes, sweetheart." He set his jaw as he thought of
some of the other things she'd said. Dean Lewis had
a lot to answer for. "I still love you."

Once Molly called an "all-clear" through the door,
he helped Wendy to her feet. "Come on, I'll take
you home."

Wendy wept through the entire ride, and he had to

pull off twice when her stomach rebelled. He held her head and spoke softly to her, trying to calm her down. He had to keep reassuring her that her life wasn't over.

"No one is going to laugh at you again. This wasn't your fault," he told her as he drove toward her father's front gate.

"What about Evan?"

"Evan?"

"Oh, stop the truck, Will, stop, please!" She clapped a hand over her mouth.

Things only got worse when they reached her house and found Dean Lewis on the front porch, waiting for them.

The sight of her father did more to sober Wendy up than anything Will had tried. "Daddy? What are you doing home?"

"Mother of God. Look at you." He regarded her dress with open disgust, then made a curt gesture. "Get inside and get yourself cleaned up, girl." He waited until she staggered off to the bathroom, then started on Will. "Mind telling me why my baby looks like she's been used to mop a dirty floor?"

"She had a little accident, Dean. Let's go inside and I'll tell you about it."

In his neighbor's study, Will briefly described what had happened at the dance, leaving out Neala's participation and the fact that Wendy had gotten drunk. Dean, however, was no fool.

"I can still smell the puke on her. Got into the punch, did she?" He didn't wait for Will to confirm it. "Damn, I never had a problem like this with her before."

"I'm sure she'll be fine in the morning."

"This gal you got out there at Sun Valley, she was at the dance too, wasn't she?"

"She was." Will knew Dean would hear everything by the morning, so he added, "They had some words. It won't happen again."

"I don't expect it will." Dean took out a cigar and lit it, then waved the lighted tip toward the highway. "Time you sent that gal on her way."

"She'll be heading back to Denver in a few weeks."

"That's not good enough, Will. In my day, we didn't stand for her kind around here. Women like that, we'd run out of town." Dean nodded toward the closed door. "Now she's done this to my baby. She needs to go. Now."

"That's not up to you, Dean."

"Where's your loyalty, boy?" Lewis puffed on his cigar as he prowled around the study. "I've heard this woman is easy on the eyes, but my daughter deserves better treatment from you."

"That's something else we need to talk about." Will noted the red flush starting to creep up his old friend's neck. "Wendy said something tonight about me marrying her."

"Jumped the gun on you proposing, did she?" Dean chuckled and clapped him on the back. "Well, you can make it up to her by taking her over to Helena this weekend. There's a jeweler there I know who'll give you a nice discount on your rings."

"Dean. I haven't asked Wendy to marry me."

The older man stopped smiling. "Well, what's holding you up, son? She's the prettiest girl in five counties, and she's been in love with you since she could walk. You won't find yourself a better wife or partner than my Wendy. Your father would have loved to live long enough to see this day."

"We've been friends for twenty-five years, Dean. You were the best man at both of my dad's weddings." Will chose his next words carefully. "In all those years we've known each other, have I ever said or done anything to make you think I would marry your daughter?"

"You were waiting for her to grow up, of course." Dean swung his hand in a casual wave, leaving an arc of cigar smoke hanging in the air. "I respect your restraint, son. But she's a woman now; there's no reason to hold back anymore."

There was no other way to put it but honestly. "Dean, I'm not marrying Wendy."

"You only need some time to think this through." The older man shook his head. "That's fine; Wendy can wait a bit. Just don't make her wait too long, Will, if you want to enjoy your children while you're a young man."

"We're not going to have children, Dean." Will turned his head, and saw Wendy standing in the hallway.

Her hair was still wet and tangled from her shower, and her face was the color of alabaster. "No. No." She rushed in, then came to a halt as she met her father's angry gaze. Instantly she composed herself. "I'm so sorry about what I did tonight, Will. Please don't let it upset you."

"Wendy—"

"I know Daddy's in a rush to have grandkids, but we can wait a few years. A man and his wife have to have time to get to know each other first." She turned and gave her father a brilliant smile. "You understand, don't you, Daddy? So there's nothing for the two of you to fight about. We'll get married, Will, and then in a few years—"

"I'm not marrying you."

Her eyes widened; then she produced a gurgle of laughter. "Of course we're going to get married. Daddy's going to sign the ranch over to us, and then we'll have the biggest cattle operation in Montana."

"Maybe you should think about that, Will." Dean stubbed out his cigar with an irritable gesture. "You turn down my daughter, you're losing out on a twenty-million-dollar merger."

"I don't want your money or your ranch, Dean."

"You don't mean that." Wendy tried to smile. "Besides, I've got my dress picked out already; it's white satin and organdy with pearls, and has a high lace collar with a cameo right here"—she touched her throat as tears began streaming down her cheeks— "and I promised all my girlfriends from school they could be my bridesmaids. So . . . so you see, we *have* to get married, because I know how much you love me. You said so tonight." Her voice rose to a shriek. "You said *you love me!*"

"You stop that caterwauling!" Dean came over, jerked Wendy around, and lifted his hand to slap her.

Will caught his arm. "No, Dean." He looked at Wendy. "I do love you, honey. The way I'd love a little sister. But we're not getting married."

Wendy stared at him for a full ten seconds, then ran from the room.

He gripped his neighbor's wrist hard. "Don't you try to hit that girl again. This isn't her doing."

"You misbegotten piece of shit." Lewis's red flush darkened to purple, and he jerked his hand free. "Get out of my house."

"I mean what I said, Dean. You keep your hands off her, or I'll be back for you."

As he drove toward Sun Valley, he thought about Neala's antics at the dance. Seeing her in Trish's dress hadn't been as bad as listening to her sing that ridiculous song. It should have made everyone laugh, but somehow she'd used her out-all-night-carousing voice to turn every silly word into a caress. He'd been forced to walk out before his neighbors saw how aroused he'd gotten. And still ended up standing outside, watching her whole act through a window like a starstruck teenager.

She was good. Better than good. Most of the men in town had been panting after her. But it was the moment when she picked up the little boy and sang to him that had hit him hard. *She'd be like that with our son. Our baby.*

The thought of Neala's slim body heavy with his child had been so enticing he'd nearly gone back in to sling her over his shoulder and carry her off to some silent, secluded spot in the woods where he could spend the rest of the night getting her pregnant.

Which he'd nearly ended up doing anyway.

Jake and Lou were back at their posts at the front gate, but he did not do more than nod as he drove up to the house. The lights were out, but he found Neala sitting alone in the dark front room as he went in.

"Is she okay? Did you get her home all right?"

He thought of Dean Lewis raising his hand, and Wendy's shocked eyes. "She'll survive." He closed the door and leaned back against it. "You sure covered yourself in glory tonight, city girl. What do you do for your next trick?"

"I disappear." She pulled her knees up and hugged them with her arms. "That should make you happy."

He tossed his keys on the side table, and the jangling crash made her jump. "You're not going anywhere, except to bed."

"I'm not tired."

"Pretend you are."

She rested her brow against her knees. "Give me a break, Ryder. I've had a rough night."

Somehow he was standing over her, snatching her up out of the chair, bringing her up to his eye level. It was easy to ignore the faint whimper of pain she uttered as he let his temper go. "I just had to watch an innocent girl who never hurt anyone go to pieces. Then I lost the friendship of her father, a man I've known and done business with and respected all my life. Before that, I got to watch you saunter around in my dead wife's clothes, and tease every man in town while you put on your little screw-me act." His voice leveled out at a shout. "And you've got the damned nerve to tell me *you've* had a rough night?"

She hung motionless between his hands. "Put me down, Ryder."

He didn't. He jerked her closer, until their eyes were only an inch apart. "Now you *listen,* city girl.

I've run out of whatever forbearance I can spare. You get your ass into bed and you stay there. From now on, you do what I say, when I say, or I'm going to take everything you've been throwing at me since you got here. Understand me?"

"I understand." Her voice was low and tight.

He put her down and watched her walk away. Something in the way she moved bothered him, but he shrugged it off. She'd survive. Neala Delaney was a specialist at that.

He didn't trust himself in the same house with her, so he drove up to High Point and spent the rest of the night there. In the morning, he came to a decision and called Kalen.

"Too many people know she's at Sun Valley now. I'm moving her out."

"There's something you should know, Will. Last night Neala's apartment building burned to the ground."

He closed his eyes. How was he going to tell her that? "How many dead?"

"None, but it was a close thing."

"Is that supposed to scare me, General?"

"Whoever is after her seems to have an affinity for gasoline and matches."

"I'm moving her today. End of discussion."

"It's your bonfire, Will," was all the general said before he hung up.

Despite her best efforts to cower under the covers for the rest of the week, aching muscles forced Neal out of bed at five a.m. A glance through the open doorway across the hall confirmed that Ryder had never come back last night.

He probably went out to beat up a steer.

Marks from his fingers mottled her upper arms, while larger, more painful contusions from the collision splotched the length of both forearms.

She put the kettle on the stove, then groaned as she

lifted her arms to take the tea from the cabinet. No more stretching for her for a few days. When she opened the box, a folded note fluttered out and landed on the counter. She opened it, and found it was a note in her uncle's handwriting, dated yesterday.

I figured you'd be the only one to see this if I put it here. No word from overseas but we can't wait any longer. Someone torched your place back in Denver. Everyone got out of the building okay, but this means they're serious. Pack your things. I'll be back tomorrow night for you.

The stunning news made her stand, numb with disbelief, until the kettle boiled and steam whistled sharply through the spout.

"They torched my apartment?"

She absently made her tea and huddled with it at the kitchen table, trying to sort out her panicked thoughts. Her arms throbbed miserably in time with her head. She was about to see if Bag Balm did anything for bruises when Jake knocked once, then entered through the back door.

"We're done for the night, and Lou was wondering if you could spare some— Miss Neal!" His Adam's apple bobbed as he gaped at her arms. "What happened? Did you fall?"

"I'm okay, Jake." No, she wasn't. "Evan and I were run off the road by some cretin last night. I hit the dashboard because I wasn't wearing my seat belt, which serves me right, and will never happen again." She wasn't going to vilify Ryder, no matter how richly he deserved it. "Would you mind getting me the bottle of aspirin out of the top cabinet over there? I can't seem to reach too well this morning."

Jake hurried over to get the medicine, while Lou appeared in the doorway.

"Jake?" He turned to Neal, and went still. Before

he could ask, she repeated what she'd told Jake. "We'd better take you over to see Doc."

"They look worse than they feel." She took two aspirin from the bottle Jake handed her and washed them down with her tea. "I just need to work out some of the kinks." Both boys had identical, skeptical expressions. "Guys, I'm fine, really. If I feel any worse I'll have Ryder take me to the emergency room." Unless he did something else and put her in one. "Go home and get some sleep."

She managed to keep up a normal front until the boys left, then trudged back to her bedroom and collapsed on the bed. Spending the rest of the day there had definite appeal, but she needed to get ready for tonight. She had just started to pack when someone hammered at the front door.

Slowly she trudged out to answer it. "If it's a Jehovah's Witness, I'm going to draw a pentagram on his face with indelible marker." She looked through the window and groaned. Almost as bad.

Wendy Lewis stood on the porch, dressed in a crisp plaid shirt and fitted black jeans. Her French braid bobbed as she used her fist on the door again.

"I know you're in there! Open up!"

She doesn't even have the common decency to have a hangover, the little witch.

Neal opened the door but decided not to waste a good morning. "You pounded?"

The younger girl jostled her to one side as she strode in. "Where is he?"

And Ryder thought *she* was pushy. "Out looking for a new club, I imagine."

A shaft of sunlight plainly revealed the dark shadows under her eyes. "I know Evan brought you home last night."

She's looking for Evan? Not Will? "Uh, Evan just dropped me off. Feel free to look under the furniture if you don't believe me."

Wendy chose to go through the house instead. Once

she'd checked every room, she circled back and confronted Neal. "It's bad enough you throwing yourself at Will, but you couldn't leave Evan alone, could you? You"—her eyes were drawn as Neal rubbed the side of her head—"just can't— What's wrong with your arms?"

She shook down the sleeve of her robe to cover the bruises. "Nothing. Just a couple of love bites."

Wendy clenched her fists and took a step toward her.

"I'm *kidding*." She sighed. "Look, are we done? Because I'm really not in the mood for a hair-pulling contest."

The younger girl stopped; then her expression cleared. "I know why you want me to leave. He's out in the barn, isn't he?" She didn't wait for an answer, but made an immediate beeline for the back door.

"Oh, for crying out loud." Neal followed.

Wendy stopped halfway to the barn, saw Neal's garden, then gave a sharp whistle.

In spite of her ire, Neal felt proud as she looked at the budding rows. "Pretty cool, huh?"

"*What* is *that*?"

"Future salad."

The girl paced the entire length of the patch. "Your rows aren't straight. Those tomato sprouts are too close to the cucumbers; they're going to choke each other out. Don't you ever weed it? Or can't you tell the difference? The other girl sneered as she stepped over one row to peer at another. "God, this is really pathetic."

"Hey." Alarmed now, Neal blocked her path. "Get out of my lettuce."

Wendy whistled again. "You've wasted all this seed for what? So you could play farm girl?"

If she doesn't like it, why does she keep whistling like a guy in a front-row seat at a strip joint?

Suddenly Neal knew exactly what to say. "Evan thinks I make a terrific farm girl."

She would have enjoyed the color Wendy turned, had a gigantic horse not come thundering around the house and run straight at her. Neal shrieked, forgot her aches and pains, and sprinted for the back door.

"Starlight, whoa, here I am." Wendy stepped right up to the towering monster, who came to an abrupt stop. She started rubbing his huge head and neck as if he were an oversized dog. "Good boy, that's my boy. She didn't mean to scare you."

"Me? Scare *him*?" At the door, Neal panted and pressed a hand over her pounding heart. "Aren't you supposed to tie that thing up?"

Wendy laughed. "You're afraid of horses. Oh, that's too good." With an odd smile, she turned and headed for the barn, leaving the horse right where he stood.

"Witch." Neal darted inside and rested her forehead against the window.

Okay, so I'm not crazy about horses. So my rows are a little crooked and I didn't get the tomatoes spaced right. I don't have to like horses. It's still a good garden. It's a terrific garden. She's just steamed about Evan.

That was when she saw the horse start toward the first row of plants.

"Hey. Hey!" She forgot fear, shoved the door open, and shouted, "Wendy, come and get this thing!"

"He won't bother you," the other girl called from the barn.

He might not bother her, but he certainly had despicable intentions toward her romaine.

"Starlight? That's your name, right? Well, don't even go there, pal." The horse turned its head as she forced herself to approach him. "That's right, I'm talking to you. Jesus, you're huge. No, no!" She yelped as the horse bent his head again. "You like oatmeal? I've got some. Boxes of it."

The horse snickered. There was no other word for it. Then he began delicately nibbling at a new sprout.

"Drop it. I mean it."

Starlight took a step forward to get at the next sprout.

"Okay, you asked for it." Neal swiped at his reins and gave them a tug. The big horse obligingly swung around and bumped her with his nose. "Don't do that. You don't want to see me drop dead of a heart attack. Let's go find your mommy. You can watch me acquire some more bruises."

For a moment, Starlight simply stared at her with his big, soft brown eyes. Then he snorted and let her pull him away from the garden.

"Heel. Good boy." Neal was covered with sweat, and shaking. She was also determined to beat Wendy to a pulp for this. "That's right, follow me."

She led the horse over to the barn, and nearly collided with Wendy as she came out the door.

"Here." She thrust the reins at the blonde. "Take him and leave."

"Starry boy, were you being bad?" From her tone, Wendy knew exactly what he'd done. She regarded Neal with mock pity. "You really are scared of him, aren't you? That's stupid." She rubbed her nose against the horse's with great affection and crooned, "He's just a big old marshmallow, aren't you, Starlight, baby?"

Neal sat down on a bale of hay. As attractive as the thought of giving Wendy a mud facial was, her knees weren't functioning properly, and she was fairly certain her breakfast was about to make a return appearance. "Evan's not here. Take the monster and go home."

"After we straighten things out. Woman to woman."

"Check back with me in a few years, when you grow up."

"I'm willing to forget what happened last night." Wendy ran her hand back and forth under Starlight's mane. "As long as you realize that Will Ryder is mine. I love him, he loves me, and we're getting married."

Did Evan know about this? No, he would have told her. Ryder must have proposed last night. A sharp, nameless pain shot through her chest while she carefully chose her words. "Congratulations. I'm sure you two will be very happy together."

"You just leave Evan Gamble alone. He doesn't need you."

Pain made her lash out without thinking. "What do you care what I do with Evan? Are you and Will planning on a threesome for the honeymoon?"

"No decent man needs you crawling all over him."

That did it. Neal got up and let a seductive smile spread across her face. "Gee, Barbie, he seemed to like what I did to him last night at the dance. Whoops, I forgot; you were getting up close and personal with the sheet cake."

"I still owe you for that." She let go of the horse and gave Neal a hard shove. "And stop calling me *Barbie*."

"Good." She shoved back. "Now I have a legitimate reason to kick your ass."

"Wendy!"

They both reacted, whirling around to see Will Ryder stalking across the yard.

"Here's your chance to show your fiancé how grown up you are, Barbie." Neal faced her opponent once more. "Come on, take another shot. I wouldn't mind ruining all that nice orthodontic work of yours."

But Will was already there, and got between them fast. "Neala, cut it out."

It hurt her arms to push him aside, but somehow she managed it. "Wait your turn, Ryder."

Chapter 12

He'd driven out, not worried about how he'd convince her to leave. All the arguments in the world wouldn't budge Neala; he'd learned that much. No, he'd give her one minute to say whatever she had to; then he'd pick her up and throw her in his truck. Jake and Lou could bring the rest of her things up to High Point later.

Catching her about to start whaling on Wendy Lewis convinced him he was doing the right thing. So did seeing the bruises Evan had told him about.

"It's over, Wendy. Take Starlight and go home now."

"Will." Her voice quavered as she turned her tear-filled gaze to him. "I just stopped by to see how Miss Delaney was doing. But from the moment I got here, she's been, well, just *awful* to me."

Neala rolled her eyes. "Brace yourself; the manure's starting to get pretty thick."

Will didn't spare her a second glance. "I'll deal with Ms. Delaney, honey."

"Yeah, honey." She lifted a hand and inspected her manicure, then flicked her fingers in a royal gesture of dismissal. "Be a good girl and scoot home to Daddy."

The blond girl forgot about her tears and substituted an appalled look. "Will, are you just going to stand there and let her speak to me like that?"

He didn't have the time or inclination to be patient now. "Wendy, *go*."

With an audible sob, she mounted her horse and rode off without another word.

Neal sat down suddenly, as if her legs had given out. "That wasn't very nice."

"You should know. Let me see your arms." He didn't wait for permission, but took her by the wrists and examined the injuries closely. "Evan told me you weren't wearing your seat belt. This could have been your face. You might have lost some teeth."

"Yeah, well, I didn't." As she displayed them for him, she tugged at his grasp. "Are you finished, or do you want to pick up where you left off last night?"

"You're packing." He tugged her to her feet. "I'll help you."

"You pack. I'm going back to bed."

"You can sleep later." He held on and led her back into the house. "Where's your suitcase?"

"I sold it to gypsies."

Will found it, put it up on the edge of the bed, and went to the bureau drawers. Inside was a jumble of unattractive garments and an eye-popping assortment of silky lingerie. A white lace thong got snagged on his thumb, and he had to shake it off before he started fingering it.

She wears thongs. Lace thongs. He glanced at her.

She was smiling. "Like my underwear?"

"It's cute."

"It's also staying where it is."

She continued to argue with him, of course, the whole time he was throwing her clothes in her suitcase; then as she reluctantly dressed in the jeans and T-shirt he tossed to her. She even kept it up after he hustled her into the truck and drove down to the highway.

"Aren't you listening to me?" She turned around to watch the ranch house disappear through the rear window. "I can't go now. Lou was bringing me some new oregano plants. The tomatoes need spraying. And I have to water my cucumbers every day or they'll dry up and turn into pickles."

"Calamity, I've never had a spanking fetish, but you're making me develop one." He took one hand off the wheel and held it out. "Give me the phone, please."

"What phone?"

"The one Evan gave you last night."

She folded her arms. "I left it back at the house."

He gave her a lazy smile. "I can pull over and perform a body search. Won't bother me a bit."

With a sullen scowl she took the cell phone from her jacket and slapped it into his palm.

"Good girl." He reached across her lap to open the glove box, shoved it inside, and slammed it shut. Now came the hard part. "I'm sorry I got out of hand last night. I lost my temper, and I didn't know you were hurt."

She didn't say anything.

"I'll send Jake and Lou to look after your garden. In the meantime, you'll be safer with me."

She still didn't say anything.

Will realized he was getting the silent treatment, and grinned. "It'll be interesting to see how long you can keep this up, city girl."

She made a rather pointed finger gesture, and turned toward the window.

"Maybe later." He pulled out from the yard and started down the drive. "You know, I think I'm actually going to enjoy this."

He stopped enjoying it after the first ten minutes. Her silence was so complete it was unnerving.

Will never realized how much he liked hearing the sound of her voice, the way she said his name. In the beginning, Neala's constant teasing and flirting had riled him to no end, but now that he'd gotten used to it he couldn't bear the unnerving way she ignored him.

He dealt with it by telling her about High Point, and how his father had started out in the cattle business.

"My family has been living in these mountains since the end of the Civil War, but Dad was the first to buy enough land to make a go of it. He worked the rodeo circuit for ten years, until he'd won enough prize money to take the gamble. Said putting down the first payment was the high point of his life, so naming the ranch that seemed a good way to remember it."

Will looked out at the land his father had slowly accrued over a lifetime. "My mother grew up here, too. She and Dad were high school sweethearts, and when he left she promised she'd wait for him. When he came back, the first thing he did was marry her."

The vague memory of his mother was always bittersweet, the blur of her pretty, thin face and the touch of her gentle hands superimposed over trips to the hospital, and endless nights listening to his big, strong father quietly weeping after she died.

He wasn't going to tell her about that—he'd already said more than enough. Neala said nothing at all. She only sat and pressed her cheek against the window. He looked at the terrible bruises on her arms, and reached out to take her hand.

"Look, city girl, I know you're scared. Trust me, in a few weeks—" He stopped as he felt her fingers, limp and unresisting. He slowly braked to a stop, then leaned over to look at her. "I'll be damned."

She'd fallen asleep on him.

He smoothed a piece of hair back from her cheek. "Didn't know I was that boring."

He put the truck back into drive. That was when a very wide-awake Neala wrenched open the door and jumped out of the truck.

Neala waited until she heard him shift gears before she wrenched open the truck door and leaped out. As soon as her feet hit the rocky ground, she ran for the trees.

She had no choice. Dragging her feet, arguing, even harping about her garden hadn't helped. There were no traffic lights for him to stop at on the highway. Her uncle would be back at Sun Valley by nightfall, and she had no way to contact him. She couldn't let him drag her off to High Point. Then she'd remembered how she'd gotten away from the drug lord: by pretending to faint.

New clusters of weeds dragged at her legs, and the pines rustled with faint whispering sounds. Behind her she heard a masculine shout, then heavy footsteps pounding the ground.

I can lose him in the woods. I'm smaller and skinnier; I can dodge things better.

She never got the chance. Despite her desperate efforts to cross the last ten feet to the tree line, a hard arm snaked around her waist and lifted her off the ground.

"You're fast," she panted when he turned her around in his arms.

"You're not." Without bothering to put her down, Ryder swiveled and carried her back to the truck. He pushed her in and fastened the seat belt over her. "Will you behave now, or do I have to jam the lock on the door?"

She pushed out her lower lip and tried to look defeated. "I'll behave."

He turned off the highway and took a side road that appeared to lead up into the mountains. Neal spotted a small sign that read HIGH POINT RANCH in front of a turnoff, and surreptitiously curled her fingers around the door handle again. As soon as he stopped at the gate, she'd try again.

Will drove straight past the turnoff and kept driving up the mountain.

She made a startled sound. "Hey—you missed it!"

"Missed what?"

"Your ranch."

"We're not going to High Point."

"We're not?" Neal looked ahead as the front of the truck began to slope noticeably upward. Dense forests of lodgepole pine formed a wall on either side of the road. "Then where are we going?"

"You'll see." He slowed down as he approached a blind curve, and Neal decided this was her last chance.

This time she didn't hit the ground running, but landed on her knees. She didn't stop to check the damage as she scrambled to her feet and plunged into the trees.

He grabbed her just as he had before, only this time she fought him, and kept fighting as he hauled her back into the truck. "You're not getting away from me, Calamity. Accept it."

"Let me go!"

She gave him as much trouble as she could, which made it difficult for him to drive. Finally he yanked her over and clamped her twisting body against his side while he steered with his free hand.

"I've got at least seventy-five pounds on you, city girl, and I can wrestle a steer down to the ground in three seconds. Give it up."

She strained and pulled against his hold. "We'll just . . . see about . . . that."

"We're on my mountain now." He nodded toward her side of the road, where the trees had been replaced by a narrow strip of rocky shoulder. "Be still or we'll end up at the bottom of a cliff."

"Can I push you off one?" His serious tone made her slump back in defeat. "What do you mean, *my* mountain?"

"It's Ryder's Mountain."

"They named a mountain after you?"

"My father."

Will drove higher and higher, until Neal winced as her ears popped. Patches of pristine white snow dotted the increasingly sparse line of trees on the mountain. Just when she was going to ask if he meant to dump her at the peak, he slowed and turned onto a narrow

dirt trail barely wide enough to accommodate the
truck. That led through the trees to a pass, and then
a hidden valley.

He stopped in front of a small, neat log cabin.
"We're here."

"I can see that. The question is, why are we here,
and is there a bathroom in this wooden shack?"

He helped her out of the truck and led her into the
cabin. "Bathroom's through there." He nodded
toward an interior door. "I'm going to unload the
truck."

"Unload . . . ?" She watched him walk back out.
At the same time, a small, gray-haired woman
emerged from the other room. "Are you the new
baby-sitter?"

"Not unless Mr. Will gives me a raise," the older
woman said with a ferocious frown.

Ryder reappeared with Neal's suitcase. "Neala, this
is Beatrice Knudson, my housekeeper."

Neal nodded politely. "Hello, Mrs. Knudson. I'm
leaving." She whirled around and headed for the door.

Ryder caught her easily. "No, you're not."

A sniff got added to the frown. "Pitiful, seeing two
grown people carrying on this way."

"Miss Delaney"—Ryder cautiously released her—
"is going to behave herself."

Neal resisted the urge to drive her elbow into his
ribs. "Mr. Ryder is delusional and, as of right now,
committing a felony."

"I brought up everything you had on the list, Mr.
Will, and enough meals for a couple of weeks."

"Weeks?" Neal looked around the cabin, then went
for the front door again. Ryder planted himself in her
path. "No way, Ryder. Sun Valley was bad enough."

Beatrice removed her apron. "I'm too old to be
chasing a young thing like her down the mountain."

"You won't have to. Just call my cell phone if she
tries anything." He put his hands on Neal's shoulders
and guided her past the housekeeper. "Would you

mind making us some breakfast? Miss Delaney will be having hers in the bedroom."

"He's keeping me here against my will," Neal threw over her shoulder, along with a pleading look. They were both women; surely the housekeeper would be on her side.

Beatrice's sparse gray brows rose. "Then I'd advise you make yourself comfortable, young lady."

Neal allowed him to hustle her into the next room. As she took in the rustic decor and wide, quilt-covered bed, Will shut the door.

"It doesn't have to be this way, now, does it?"

She sat down on the edge of the bed, and traced a fingertip over the tiny stitches in the quilt. "Think again."

"You're acting like a spoiled brat, city girl. Is that how you want me to treat you?" Will came to the bed, and her fingers tightened until dents appeared in the fabric beneath them. "I'm about ready to turn you over my knee as it is. Look at me."

She looked. Instead of launching into a tirade, Will dropped down onto one knee beside her. "You can trust me; don't you know that?"

She knew, but said nothing.

He cradled her face and stroked her cheek with his thumb. "How much longer will you keep fighting me?" He wasn't talking about keeping her on the mountain. "I won't let anything happen to you."

Molly's insinuation about Trish Ryder echoed in her ears, and she touched the now-fading mark on the inside of her elbow. She wanted to believe him more than anything in the world. "Do you remember what you said to me, right after the fire?"

He sat back on his heels. "I said a lot of things."

"You accused me of doing drugs. But I don't, and I never have. But according to Molly, your ex-wife did."

The kindness in his eyes became remote fury. "I'm not going to discuss Trish with you."

"If you really want me to trust you, we have to talk about this. Did she die of a heroin overdose?"

"Yeah. She did."

"Trish didn't like needles, did she?"

He went to say something, then halted and stared at her. "No. She hated them. When we got the blood test to get married, she fainted on me."

"I see." Neal swallowed. "Not someone you'd expect to become an IV-drug user."

"I never thought about it at the time." He slowly rose to his feet. "You're right. She would never have injected herself voluntarily."

"Neither would I. Which brings us back to the one thing your dead wife and I have in common. You." She got up and held out her arm again. "Did you do this to me, Will?"

"No." He went very still, but kept his gaze locked with hers. "I didn't inject you with drugs. I didn't kill Trish, either."

"I want to believe you."

"If I were trying to kill you, Neala, you'd be dead already."

"Maybe you don't want to kill me. Maybe you're only trying to keep me in line. Control me."

"I don't need drugs to do that." He brought his hand up and traced the shape of her lips with one of his long fingers. "Do I?"

She wasn't going to give him the satisfaction of a no. "Then who did it? What did they use? And why?"

"Whatever it was, it sure made you talkative."

"That's an understatement." Her mouth hitched as she recalled her behavior. "I can't believe some of the things I said. I never . . ." She trailed off as her eyes widened. "Marc."

"The marine?"

She nodded. "We were engaged when he joined up. He went overseas to Serbia-Croatia and was shot by a sniper the second week he was there. He was only twenty years old." She touched the mark on her arm. "I never talk about him. Not even to my sister."

"But you told me. You didn't even hesitate."

"Ryder, you don't know me very well, but trust me: I never confide my deepest, darkest secrets. To anyone. It was the drug—it must have been responsible for the way I acted."

He looked skeptical. "You think someone gave you sodium pentothal?"

"I'd guess something more like rohypnol. The 'date-rape drug.'" When he gave her a blank look, she added, "One of the clubs I worked at passed out FDA bulletins about it. It became so trendy that the manager prohibited female employees from accepting any type of beverage from patrons. One of the main side effects is that it makes you abandon all your normal inhibitions." She gave him a grim smile. "Sound familiar?"

"Yeah, it does. All the more reason you're staying up here for the duration."

"I can't. Take me back down to Sun Valley."

"The bit about watering your cucumbers didn't work for me, Neala. You want to tell me why you're so anxious to go back to that ranch?"

"I miss weeding, too."

"Is this how it's going to be?" His fingers tightened. "Because I can keep you locked up in here until April."

She glanced at the window, saw the keyed lock on the frame, and bit her lower lip.

"If you're thinking about breaking it, don't. It's twenty miles down the mountain, and not worth getting lost in the woods."

"In *your* opinion," she couldn't help saying.

"I'll check in on you later. Don't give Beatrice a hard time." Out he went, locking the door from the other side.

Neal waited until his footsteps died away, then buried her face in the plump pillows on the bed and shrieked with frustration.

The housekeeper unlocked the door a half hour later, carrying a tray and looking rather annoyed.

"What's gotten into you, girl? Way I hear it, Mr. Will's only trying to keep you safe."

"I can take care of myself."

"So you city folks are always saying. Bunch of them come out here every summer to stay at my sister's dude ranch, then fuss about cable for the television and phone lines for their computers and beepers that don't work."

Fascinated by the grumbling old woman now, Neal grinned. "Are we really that bad?"

Beatrice gave a disdainful snort. "Half the time I don't know whether to shake you people's hands, or plug you into a wall socket."

She laughed. "I guess we city folk don't know how to sit back, relax, and smell the manure."

"That's another thing." The housekeeper set the tray on the bed beside Neal. "Never in my life saw so much fuss made about that. All God's creatures have to do their business; what do they expect? But let them get a little horse pucky on their designer boots, and you'd think the world was coming to an end."

Neal's personal exposure to horse pucky made her bite her tongue on that subject. However, the smells from the tray were delicious, and her stomach rumbled in response. "Is that a Spanish omelet, Mrs. Knudson?"

"Beatrice. And it's western." The older woman set the tray down beside her. "Eat now, before it gets cold."

"Would you mind leaving the door open?"

"Mr. Will said to keep it locked until he gets back."

Neal surreptitiously crossed her fingers. "I'm not going to make a break for it."

"He said you'd say that, too."

She sighed her defeat. "You know something, Beatrice? Men are snakes."

The prim mouth bent around the edges as the housekeeper went to the door. "Don't insult the snakes, now."

Neal devoured the delicious breakfast, then paced

the room until lunchtime, when Beatrice brought her a huge seafood salad and a couple of magazines. No amount of coercion would sway the housekeeper, however, and Neala remained locked in the bedroom until the sky began to darken.

Her uncle would be frantic when he didn't find her at the ranch, but she couldn't tell Ryder that. She went to the window just in time to see Jake and Lou arrive, then leave, taking Beatrice with them.

Neala Delaney was proving to be the most bull-headed, baffling woman Will had ever known.

Staying on the mountain solved one problem—namely, keeping her presence concealed—but created a whole set of new ones. He didn't trust her not to hot-wire his truck, so he was forced to ride back up to the cabin on Blue. She refused to do anything but sit in the bedroom and brood. Her silence went from annoying to unnerving.

Although she could have overpowered Beatrice with little effort, his unwilling houseguest hadn't tried to make a break for it while the older woman was at the cabin.

After Jake and Lou took his housekeeper back down to High Point, he took Neal's dinner tray in. "Feeling better?"

She sat up, got to her feet, and went to the window.

"Back to not talking to me?" He came up behind her. He didn't touch her, but stood close enough to feel her flinch. "Do you think you can keep it up for six weeks, Neala?"

She pressed her brow against the glass.

"One word will ruin the whole thing, won't it?" He touched her then, sliding his hand under her hair to caress the back of her neck. "I guess it's better than holding your breath until you turn blue."

He moved her hair aside and pressed his mouth to the back of her neck. She curled her fingers against the glass but didn't resist.

"It's hard, isn't it?" he murmured. With the way he had her crowded, she could certainly feel exactly how hard he was. "All you have to do is relax and let me take care of you."

He wasn't talking about keeping her safe anymore, and wondered if she realized that. He put both his hands on her, rubbing the tense muscles of her shoulders, easing her back until all the gaps between them disappeared. Her body heat permeated his clothes, warming his skin.

He continued to use his hands on her, petting and stroking her the way he would a nervous mare. A few times his arms brushed against her breasts, and her hard little nipples scraped over his skin.

"Feel it, Neala?" he said, right next to her ear. "I've wanted you for weeks, the same way you've wanted me. I've never wanted like this. I can't wait, and neither can you."

He knew her body's response now. If she so much as twitched an eyelash he would have her. But Neala only remained motionless in his arms.

"I won't force you. But soon, lady, real soon, you'll wake up in the dark, wanting me. You'll call my name, and I'll come to you. And then"—he slid his hands down to her hips, and moved her against him—"we'll dance in each other all night long."

He bent his head, and lightly raked his teeth down the side of her neck. Then he let her go and watched her grip the windowsill with white-knuckled hands.

"Call me if you change your mind."

The operative returned to Sun Valley to find it deserted, and immediately performed another fruitless search of the house. This time every possible hiding place was examined—even to the point of ripping open every box and container in the kitchen cabinets to see if she had secreted it there.

Where could she have hidden it? Did she carry it

with her now, or had she left it somewhere else on
the property?

Through the kitchen window, the operative regarded the crooked rows of budding plants behind
the house.

Of course, the garden.

The girl had left a shovel outside the back door,
which the operative put to good use. Digging up row
after row of the sprouting garden also served as a
pleasant method of dispelling frustration—until it became apparent the girl had not hidden the microdisk
in the soft soil.

The operative then relieved a little more frustration
by using the edge of the shovel to hack apart every
single plant Neala Delaney had coaxed from the
ground.

When the girl did not return to Sun Valley, the
operative reluctantly returned to town. Tracking her
down would have to wait; the diner had already begun
to fill up with the regular dinner trade, and a dozen
orders waited to be filled.

An opportunity arose when Will Ryder's foreman
came in for a meal, followed shortly by Wendy Lewis,
who immediately stalked over to his booth near the
service counter.

"Evan!"

Evan Gamble didn't appear happy to see the blond
girl. "Afternoon, Wendy."

"I went to see your girlfriend today." The girl slid
into the booth across from him. Temper flushed her
cheeks, and strands of hair had straggled from the
usually neat ponytail she wore. "I was going to let her
apologize for what she did to me at the dance, and do
you know, that woman tried to pick a fight with me."

"Did she?" Ryder's foreman didn't sound too
concerned.

"Yes, she did. Thank goodness Will showed up. He
had to pull her off me." Evan muttered something,

and the blond girl reared back. "That's not funny. She could have hurt me, you know."

The young man rubbed the back of his neck. "So why are you telling me this, Wendy?"

"I think you should know the kind of woman she is. She made a complete fool of herself at the dance. Plus she's been making eyes at Will since she got here." The girl tucked a strand of hair behind her ear. "Not that I'm worried about him, of course."

"You just can't accept it, can you?" Evan shook his head sadly. "Will Ryder's not in love with you."

"You think he's got feelings for that bimbo from Denver?"

"I'm telling you that you haven't got an icicle's chance in hell of marrying my boss." Evan reached over and touched her hand. "Give it up, Wendy, before you make a fool out of yourself again."

"That wasn't my fault." The girl's face grew pinker, but she let her hand rest in his. "She pushed me into that table." She bent her head. "You're not going to see her again, are you?"

"I don't even know where she is." Evan released her hand. "Will said he was moving her out of Sun Valley this morning."

As Wendy gaped, the operative found an excuse to move closer by refilling the coffee cup of a ranch hand wearing a brown Stetson and mirrored sunglasses. "He didn't take her up to High Point, did he?"

"No. He didn't think she'd be safe there, either." Evan settled his hat back on his head as he got to his feet. "You may not like her much, but Neala's life is in danger. Someone already tried to kill her once."

"I don't know why Will has to be involved. There's no place around here he can hide her besides High Point."

"I'm sure he'll figure something out." Evan held out his hand as the blond girl slid out from the booth. "You need a ride home?"

"No, I've got Starlight tied up outside." She gave

him a cautious smile. "Why don't you come out and say hello? He misses you."

"The only thing he misses are the sugar cubes in my pocket," Evan told her as he went with her.

Hiding a satisfied smile, the operative moved back behind the counter to fill another order, and accidentally knocked over a silver-handled cane propped next to one of the stools.

"That's okay." The ranch hand with the mirrored sunglasses reached down to pick it up before the operative could. "I've got it."

Neala knew she couldn't stay. Not another night. Telling Will the truth about what had happened in the senator's suite was too tempting.

God, if I did, would he even believe me?

They'd find out she had it soon. Some government bright boy would eventually question why the Chinese had bothered to burn down her apartment building. She knew her uncle would never betray her—nor the other two people who'd staked their lives on her silence—but he didn't know where she was. Once he found her missing from Sun Valley, he might do anything.

She had to use her teeth to strip a wire out of the lamp's electrical cord, then folded the wire and used it to pick the window lock. Cold air poured into the bedroom as she eased the window up. She stuck her head out first, then climbed over the sill and jumped to the ground.

She landed more heavily than she would have liked. She stayed where she was, crouched over, listening. No sound of footsteps from inside the cabin. He hadn't heard. She could get to the truck and get out of here.

Fifteen minutes later, she swore softly. His truck was gone—Will must have figured she'd try to steal it again. That meant she had to walk, or . . .

Neal looked over at the horse standing in the center

of the clearing. That was how he'd gotten here—on horseback. For a brief moment she heard Agent Selbrook laughing in the back of her head as she spotted a saddle sitting on the small porch in front of the cabin.

"If it came with a saddle, it has to be friendly," she muttered under her breath. "All I have to do is climb on it and ride down the mountain. Will and Evan ride horses. *Wendy* rides horses. I can ride this horse."

The big chestnut horse had a blaze of white on its nose, which flashed as it lifted its head and whickered softly.

If it's Will's, it has to be the best horse in Montana. She grabbed the saddle, which was surprisingly heavy, and lugged it along with her to the center of the clearing.

"Hi, there." She tried for a quiet, reassuring tone. "Want to go for a ride, big, um, girl? Boy? I don't weigh as much as Ryder. I don't think I weigh as much as this saddle."

The horse made another, softer sound, and shuffled around, presenting her with a view of its hindquarters.

"Talk to the butt, huh?" Neal looked down at the saddle. With all the straps and buckles on the thing, she'd never figure out how to get it on correctly. She'd read about people riding bareback. Surely the horse wouldn't mind. "Here, horsey. Come here, horsey."

The horse walked around in a half circle, sniffed at her, then started nibbling at some grass at her feet.

"Good horsey. Nice horsey." She saw a large rock nearby that would serve nicely as a stool. "Over here."

As she went over and stepped up on the rock, the horse followed. Awkwardly she gave the big neck a couple of pats as she sized up the angle. The rock wasn't high enough; she'd have to grab something and pull herself on.

"Is that hair on your neck really sensitive?" She gave it an experimental tug, but the horse didn't twitch. "Guess not. Okay, here goes. Nice and calm now. No stomping me into the dirt."

She grabbed a handful of mane, and pulled herself halfway over the horse before remembering she'd have to get one leg on one side, and one on the other. Readjusting made her bump her nose hard on the horse's neck.

"Jesus." She pushed herself back up, and suddenly she was sitting on the horse's broad back. Glancing down made her stomach roll as she saw how high off the ground she was. "Now what do I—"

The nice, calm, nonstomping horse swung around and gave her an evil look out of one eye.

"Hi, it's just little old me. You're not going to get mad or anything now, are you?"

It snorted, and took a couple of quick steps to one side.

"Stop, I mean, whoa. I don't know how to steer you without the stuff they hitch around your head." She tried to pat the animal's neck again, but her hands were trembling, and the horse became even more agitated. "This was a really bad idea, wasn't it? Tell you what, I'll get down now."

She never got the chance. The horse reared up, making her slide backward and swipe at his mane. Neal screamed as she lost her grip and went flying backward through the air.

He woke up at the sound of a ruckus outside the cabin.

"Blue?" He went to the window. His horse was in the center of the clearing, and something was on his back.

Then Blue bucked, and a woman screamed.

"Neala." He yanked open the cabin door and raced outside.

Blue was already making an indignant circuit of the clearing. Will saw a small, still shadow on the ground and ran over to find Neala curled up and unconscious in the grass. Her mouth was bleeding, and so was a small cut on her cheek. He knelt down and gently ran his hands over her limbs.

"Neala? Can you hear me?"

Blue trotted over and bumped Ryder on the shoulder.

"It's okay, boy." He left her only long enough to calm the horse and check him over. Blue was agitated, but otherwise unharmed.

"Simmer down, Blue. She's fine."

He lifted her carefully and carried her back into the cabin. When he set her down on his bed, her eyelids fluttered and she groaned. "Damn." She pressed trembling fingers to one side of her skull. "That hurt."

"I bet it did." He pulled a bandanna from his pocket and wiped the blood from her face. "We don't take kindly to horse thieves around here."

"I'm not a horse thief. I'm a political prisoner."

"Well, Miss Politics, you can't ride my horse. Especially bareback."

"Why not? I got up there and everything."

"No one has ever ridden Blue but me."

"No wonder he got upset." She squinted as he used his flashlight on her eyes, then checked her nose, mouth, and both of her ears. "Something wrong with my makeup?"

After making sure there was no permanent damage, he cleaned the cut on her cheek and some abrasions on her palms. "You're going to have one mother of a headache when you get up tomorrow. Who's the President of the United States?"

"Me." She chuckled weakly at his frown. "Just kidding. That Shrub guy, what's-his-name. George."

Relief brought with it a surge of fury. "You stay the hell away from my horse from here on out, city girl."

"One ride was plenty, thanks." She drifted off.

He carried her back into the bedroom, but this time left the door unlocked and stretched out beside her. Watching her sleep was subtle torture, but he couldn't

tear himself away from her side. Especially when she
began to dream, and started moaning and twisting in
her sleep.

"Mom . . . Mom, don't go . . . please don't go. . . ."

"It's okay, Neala." He pulled her into the curve of
his arm.

She strained away. "Stop . . . oh, God, don't hit
her. . . ." She groaned and tried to hold her hands in
front of her face. "They'll know what happened . . .
self-defense . . . how can you ask me . . . ?"

"Shhhh." He stroked her brow with one hand. "It's
all right, lady, I'm here. Don't be afraid."

"Will?" She turned toward him, then curled into a
ball. "No, can't . . ."

"Can't what, sweetheart?"

She mumbled some more, then said, "Wish I
was . . . what you wanted. . . ."

He let the low laugh out. If he wanted her any
more, he'd explode. Then he realized what she was
saying. Tenderly he brushed her hair back away from
her face. "I know, baby. I wish you were, too."

Chapter 13

Kuei-fei was a devout woman, T'ang Yin thought as he watched her arranging the small shrine in the bedroom. She bowed low before a photograph of a tiny infant, praying softly in Chinese. Then she began to light the candles, one by one, as she did every night.

"My wife." He didn't wish to disturb her, but what he'd learned was too important. "Po sent word. Jian-Shan has left China."

Her slim back went stiff. "With Po's permission?"

"No."

She stood and turned toward him slowly, moving as if in great pain. "He has been kidnapped. There will be ransom demands. Po will pay them, of course."

"No. There was no kidnapping. He left of his own will. He . . . he left a letter for his father. It was he who turned the information over to the senator's wife. Apparently they became lovers some months ago, when she visited Beijing with her husband."

"I see." She bowed her head, and lifted one small hand to cover her mouth.

"There is nothing I can do, Kuei-fei. Even if I found him, Po has given me explicit orders. He has betrayed the tong. He must die."

"I understand, my husband. Please excuse me while I pray for my son. I am in great need of prayer now."

"Of course."

Kuei-fei waited until the door closed, then turned to her altar. Her son, her only, beloved son. He had been lost to her for thirty-two years. Po had kept her only long enough to impregnate her, then whisked the baby away immediately after his birth. Jian-Shan still believed his mother died giving life to him.

She had been scheming ever since, seducing T'ang Yin into noticing her, trusting her, then marrying her. As his wife it was simple to steal and hide away the needed money. She developed her influence over him gradually, until he trusted her with everything. She kept careful note of every illegal act, gathering it for the day she would have enough to force the tong to set her son free.

Now Jian-Shan had betrayed Po, bolted, and in doing so placed a death warrant on his own head that no amount of blackmail could ever lift.

She lifted the photograph, staring at it. Then, with great deliberation, she used it to smash the shrine to pieces.

The man beside her shifted, moving his hand from her arm to her waist. Neal turned and curled into his warmth, hoping it would melt away the faint pounding beneath her skull. The feel of his bare chest under her palms made her mouth curve.

If only I didn't have this damn headache.

Memories of why her head hurt eventually filtered in through Neal's drowsy contentment, and she opened her eyes. Ryder's square chin rested a half inch from her nose. One of his arms lay draped over her, along with one of his long legs. His hand spanned her waist just beneath her rib cage, and as she shifted back his fingers tightened.

He opened one eye. "Go back to sleep."

"I can't. My head is about to explode."

"Come here." He pulled her over to him, and moved his hand up under her hair. "Don't move. This works."

His chest didn't make much of a pillow—the broad

muscles were too hard—but whatever he was doing to the back of her head was magical, and she snuggled up to him as best she could.

"Are you mad about the horse thing?"

"Yeah."

"I didn't hurt her, did I?"

"Him. No."

He didn't say anything for a while, and she nearly fell back to sleep under the hypnotic, soothing motions his fingers made on her scalp. Then, almost hesitantly, he asked, "Don't you think it's time you trusted me, Neala?"

Inexplicable tears burned beneath her eyelids, and she sniffed them back. "I'm not helpless. I can take care of myself. I always have."

"What about your mother?"

She scowled. "What about her?"

"You called out for her last night."

"A momentary aberration." The tears receded as she opened her eyes and stared past his head at the wall. "Sometimes I have dreams about her singing. She worked in clubs, too."

"So she taught you everything you know."

"Hardly." Neal rolled onto her back. "She liked to sleep all day so she could be fresh for her act, then stay out until dawn partying with whoever was boyfriend of the month."

"Not your style."

"I sure as hell wouldn't dump my kids so I could run off to Las Vegas with a piano player."

He propped himself up on one elbow to look down at her. "She abandoned you?"

"When Laney and I were teenagers." The bitterness made her voice harsh. "She packed up her costumes, told me we were old enough to take care of ourselves, and left. I haven't seen her since."

He began rubbing her scalp again. "That must have been tough."

"We survived."

"What about your dad?"

"I don't know who he was. Some sax player she shacked up with for a few months. There were a lot of them." She closed her eyes as she felt her stomach roll. "Ryder, let go." When he did, she pushed herself up and stumbled off to the bathroom.

Will knocked on the door a few minutes later. "You okay?"

"Wonderful." She spit the mouthful of water out in the basin. "I love throwing up first thing in the morning."

"Let me in."

"I don't need any help puking, thanks." She finished washing her hot face and leaned her head against the rough door frame. "Give me a minute, will you?"

She scrounged through the medicine cabinet and found a tube of toothpaste, and cleaned her mouth out with that and her finger. Once she'd gotten rid of the horrible taste, she dried her face off and opened the door.

He was standing right outside. "Go lie down until your stomach settles."

"I'm okay." She brushed past him and went out through the open door into the front room. "Where's your cell phone?"

"You can't call anyone."

"Unless you'd like to be the reason for a very ugly international incident between the United States and China, you'd better let me talk to some people."

"Honey, I know you've got a sore head, but spare me the dramatics."

As she paced around the cabin, Will made up an ice pack and handed it to her. "Put this on your head. I'll make us some coffee."

She immediately pressed it to her temple. "I despise coffee."

"It's coffee or water."

"I love coffee."

A few minutes later Neal grimaced at the mug of

steaming brew he handed her. "I should report you
to Amnesty International for inhumane treatment of
a prisoner."

That didn't seem to phase him. "Be sure to tell
them it's Ryder with a *y.*"

"I'm not kidding around anymore, Ryder." She
took a sip of the coffee and told her stomach it was
only for the caffeine. "I need to talk to these people
today."

"Tell me why, and I'll see what I can do."

A little voice inside her head chirped up at once:
He's never going to believe you. "I can't tell you; that's
why they call it national security. You can't go around
telling people this stuff; the nation won't stay secure."

"Then I can't help you." He removed a coin from
his pocket and tossed it to her. "Maybe you should
make another decision."

Heads I tell him, tails I don't.

She flipped the quarter, and it landed with a small
smack on her palm. Washington's dignified profile
stared up at her.

"All right. The senator who I saw get killed was
involved with the Chinese. They made some illegal
campaign contributions to get him to vote their way
on an international trade bill. He went over there a
few times, too. Is that enough?"

He made a rolling gesture with one hand.

"The real reason I was in his suite was to meet his
wife. She gave me something she brought back from
China for safekeeping, and no one knows that I have
it. Not even the feds." She winced and touched her
lip, which had cracked and started bleeding again. "I
have to tell the government about what she gave me."

"Where is it? What is it?"

"I can't get into details."

"Lady, I'm not giving you my phone until I hear
more."

"I just have to make a few calls. Let people know
about this. That's all."

"To who?"

"My uncle, and a number overseas."

"Overseas where?"

"China." She took a gulp of the coffee. "Maybe Japan."

"That doesn't sound like it would be good for national security, either. How did you get mixed up in all this?"

She thumped the mug back down. "I was working for my uncle. He's a government agent."

Will lifted a brow. "Is he now?"

"Yes, he is. I told you that before. He talked me into playing courier for him and the senator's wife. If I'd left Denver that night like I'd planned to, he'd be sitting here instead of me." She eyed him. "And before you ask, I was leaving Denver because I found out my employer is an organized-crime boss."

"A crime boss."

She sighed. "He's also the guy who's on trial for murdering the senator."

"I see." Will tipped his chair back and rubbed his chin. "You know, honey, I'm kind of partial to reading Tom Clancy myself, but even he would have a hard time handling a plot as complicated as yours." He rose and went to the efficiency-sized kitchen on one side of the cabin. "How do you like your eggs?"

The inner voice turned instantly, gleefully vicious. *I told you he wouldn't believe you.* "Sprinkled with aspirin, please."

He didn't believe she was serious until she took two spoons and crushed the aspirin tablets up herself. She ate what he fixed her, cleaned up the plates, then started back for the bedroom.

"Hold it."

She paused, then turned around.

"You've slept enough."

"You have something else for me to do?"

"You can stop sulking." He gestured toward the bookcase. "Read something."

She wandered over without much enthusiasm. "Got any copies of *Cosmo*?"

"*Field and Stream.*"

"Pass."

She silently investigated everything in the cabin. There wasn't much to see. Some simple chairs, a table, and an old sofa. The bed. The fireplace. The kitchenette. And ten years of *Field and Stream*.

Will left her and went outside. Through the window, she watched him pace the length of the porch. Then he sat on a rocking chair and stared at the mountains.

She remembered everything she'd said to him under the influence of the drug. She knew what he was feeling. He was right: they couldn't go on like this much longer.

She got a change of clothes and went back into the bathroom, then took her time preparing for the inevitable.

It felt good to wash her hair, shave her legs, and dry off after the shower. She wished she had something nicer to wear, but Agent Selbrook's inventory didn't leave much choice. Looking like a very clean bag lady, she left the bathroom and neatly stowed her dirty clothes out of sight.

Will came in the doorway and gave her a long look. "You're wet."

"I took a shower." She went in and sat down on the bed to brush out her hair.

"Why?"

She gave him a shrug. "I wanted to be clean." *For you, thickhead.*

He came a little closer. "I took a shower last night, before you woke up."

"I know. I smelled the soap."

By then he was right in front of her. His hands were two huge knots. The front of his jeans was at her eye level. There was a lot to see.

"You're pretty calm about this." He sounded upset. No, he sounded almost wrathful.

"Sure." She lifted her face and smiled a little. "No big deal. Like you said, it's been brewing from day one."

He grabbed her and hauled her off the bed until her feet dangled. "It's more than that. It's been eating me up inside. Every day. Every night. Until I can't take a breath without wondering what it would be like, tasting you."

Maybe he didn't want it to be casual. "You don't have to wonder anymore. Just kiss me and—"

He stopped her voice with his mouth. With his tongue. With the edge of his teeth. He didn't kiss her so much as ravage her. Some inner beast beneath his skin had finally clawed its way free, and it was going to take what it wanted.

Neala dug her fingers into his thick, sun-bleached hair, and pulled until his mouth left hers. She gave up trying to be cool and let him see exactly how she felt. Every single screaming nerve ending of it. "Did I mention I'd like your hands on me, too?"

He already had the neckline of her ugly blouse twisted in one fist. "You'll get them." He yanked, and tore the blouse open from throat to waist.

Neal hadn't bothered with a bra, and she now arched her exposed breasts into his hungry hands. "Excellent."

He shoved her down on the bed, on her back, and stood there looking at her for a moment before stripping the loose jeans from her body. His eyes never left the sight of her green satin panties as he kicked off his boots and stripped out of his clothes.

Neal propped her head on her hands to watch him. When he got down to his skin, she forgot how to blink. There was so much of him, all muscular and golden skinned and ready for action. Especially the thick, erect shaft rising from the darker blond hair between his thighs.

"Like what you see?"

Speech was unimaginable, so she settled for a nod.

He removed a condom from the pocket of his jeans, sheathed himself, and came to stand over her.

So he'd stopped at a drugstore somewhere along the way to the mountain. She didn't know whether to be pleased or annoyed. "You came prepared."

"I always do." He curled his fingers around one of her ankles. "Take the panties off."

She did, as slowly as she could. When she lifted her knees, the satin fell against his hand. He slipped it off the rest of the way and, instead of throwing it away, brought it up to his face.

Why was he doing that? "Do I pass inspection?"

The panties dropped to the floor. "Oh, yeah."

She couldn't help cringing a little as he got on the bed. He noticed, too. But he didn't grab her or jump on her. He sat beside her, his gaze intent on her face as he took her hand in his. His grip was so tight it was almost painful. "If this is another one of your games, tell me now."

"I'm naked and in your bed, Ryder. Does it look like I'm playing with you?" She brought his hand to her breast, pressing her engorged nipple against his palm. "Of course, if you want to play with *me,* then—"

She never got the rest out. He rolled over and slid over her, pinning her beneath him, taking her mouth with his. His hands went everywhere, kneading her breasts, shifting her hips, stroking her thighs. Everywhere he touched her, a slow, hot ache began to spread. One of his legs separated hers, and he rubbed his thigh against her. He reached down and did the same with his fingers. One side of his mouth curled as she lifted her hips and sank her fingernails into his shoulders.

"You're wet, Neala. Soft and hot and wet." He kissed her mouth again. "How long have you been thinking about me touching you?"

"You want that in hours, days, or weeks?"

He reached down and positioned himself. When the swollen head of his penis nudged her, she had a mo-

ment of doubt. He was huge, and she'd been living
like a nun. Then he was pushing into her, stretching
the tight inner muscles, forcing his way in an inch at
a time.

"Hold on to me."

Neal closed her eyes and held on. The burning,
stretching sensation got worse. God, it had been so
long, too long. This hurt almost as much as losing her
virginity had. Then she felt their body hair mesh, and
felt the sound he made. She opened her eyes, and
flinched when she saw his expression.

"Ryder?"

He was so tense his face looked carved out of stone.
"Don't move." Slowly he slid back an inch, then forward again, testing the fit. At the same time, he
reached down between them and used his fingertips
to gently stroke her clitoris. "Relax, baby. I'm going
to make it easier on you, real fast."

The discomfort did ease away as he kept his movements slow and shallow. The clever touch of his fingers
brought back the ache and need, until it swept away
the hurt and left her needing more. She bore down,
clenching around him instinctively.

He went still. "Don't do that."

"Doesn't it feel good?" She did it again.

He groaned, and rested his forehead against hers.
"It feels great. Knock it off."

"Not a chance." She moved under him, restless
now, needing more, wanting all he had to give her.
"Ryder, please!"

He swore, then caught her mouth with a bruising
kiss as he withdrew and pushed back in, hard and fast
and deep. She cried out and clamped down on him a
third time.

"Jesus." He began thrusting into her without restraint, using long, powerful strokes that made her
twist under him as she met each one.

Neala's head fell back as wild pleasure streaked
through her, and she clutched at him. He pulled her

knees up, slamming his hips into hers, until the ache became everything and she was lost in a dark, relentless storm of sensation.

"Will!" She went taut as the need exploded into incredible, screaming pleasure. "Oh, God!"

He slid his hands under her, curled them over her shoulders, and held her still. His thrusts became deeper, wilder, and he never looked away from her face. Not even when he buried himself as deeply as he could, and found his release.

He held her as she slept, their bodies still interlocked. For the moment he was content to stay inside her, hold her, and try to understand what had just happened.

It had pissed him off, the way she'd been so matter-of-fact in the beginning. He'd wanted to scare her, shake her out of her damned complacency. Ripping her shirt hadn't frightened her. Making her take off her panties hadn't intimidated her. But when they were both naked, and he'd reached for her, the fear in her eyes had been plain.

Not as casual about this as you want me to think you are.

Taking her had been even more of a revelation. She was wild and responsive to his touch, but when he began entering her he found her as narrow as a virgin. His penis stiffened inside her as he remembered sinking slowly in, that first time. Getting caught in a vise would have been easier.

Will had nearly stopped right there, but she worked herself around him, trying to adjust their fit, and he knew she wanted it as much as he did. He'd just have to hang on to his self-control. Then she'd found the pleasure in it, and went wild on him.

So much for restraint.

Having Neala should have put an end to craving her, but he wanted her now even more than before.

He pushed gently into her, then remembered the condom and carefully withdrew.

And suddenly saw what had happened.

"Shit."

A sleepy voice said, "Hey, you." Her slim hand reached blindly, trying to grab him. "Come back here and finish what you started."

"We have a problem." He stripped the remains of the condom off and discarded it before turning back to her.

"I know." She grinned and rolled onto her back. "Come here and take care of it."

"The rubber didn't hold up."

She blinked, then sat up and checked herself. "Uh-oh." She glanced at him. "I don't suppose you've ever had a vasectomy?"

He shook his head.

"Okay." She let out a long breath. "I haven't had sex in at least a year, and since then I've been tested clean for everything"—at his look, she nodded—"I have to for my insurance, every year. So I know I'm not carrying any STDs. You?"

"I had my annual checkup just before you got here. I'm clean, too."

"Okay. That's one obstacle down. Okay." She thought for a moment. "Damn. Might as well be honest: I'm in the middle of my cycle. The timing, um, sucks."

"What if you get pregnant?"

"Then we're having a baby." She lifted her chin and eyed him directly. "Don't even bring up the *A* word. I'm Catholic, it's my body, and I love children."

"You do?" He took her in his arms. "How would you feel, having my kid?"

She touched his mouth with her fingers as her grin reappeared. "From the way Mom described labor pains, probably like castrating you with a rusty knife."

He eased her back onto the pillows, and kissed her

stubborn chin. "We'll see. I don't think the rest of those condoms are going to hold up any better."

"What's that saying about spilled milk? Does it mean the same thing when it's—" She bit her lip as one of his fingers pushed into her. "Oh, don't tease me now."

"I'm in no hurry." He used another finger to penetrate and stroke her. "It's been more than a year, hasn't it?"

"Why?" She looked down, made a face. "Did it grow back?"

"Just about."

"You'll just have to suffer, I guess."

He threw his head back and laughed as he whirled over, putting her astride him. "So make me suffer, honey."

She lifted up and sank back down, impaling herself on him. Will's spine bowed as his breath hissed out. The feel of her on him, with nothing to mask the slick, satiny friction, made him clamp his hands on her hips.

"Yeah. That's how I like to be tortured."

She obliged him by dancing over him, sliding her hips up and down, caressing him with slow, exquisite movements. She refined the torment by lightly raking his chest and arms with her nails as she moved. Will gritted his teeth but resisted the urge to hold her and thrust hard up into her body.

She sank all the way down, until the soft curve of her buttocks brushed the top of his thighs, and stayed there. "Will." Her eyes were half-closed as she bent down and pressed her lips to his, then lightly bit the tip of his tongue. "It feels so good, you inside me like this. Do you like it?"

He hated it. He loved it. "Still a tease."

"Uh-uh. I deliver." She rolled her hips gently. "Maybe I'll stay like this for a while. I like feeling you inside me."

"The hell you will." He braced her against him with both arms and rolled over, forcing her legs wider, thrusting himself deeper. "You want me inside you?" He couldn't stop, had to have all of her. "Here. Here's what you want. Can you feel me? I'm in you now, baby. Do you want me to stop?"

"I feel you," she said, and gasped as the tip of his penis nudged her cervix. "Don't stop. Please."

He gave her what she wanted, taking them both higher, farther than before. When she came to him, she came screaming, clawing at him, and he poured himself into her. Then he held her trembling body in his arms, and whispered her name against her mouth, over and over.

J. R. got out of the car and leaned heavily on his cane as he looked at the sprawling prosperity around him. His mother's multicolored Impatiens still crowded around the entire base of the porch. Trish's hybrid rosebushes, however, were gone.

Ripped them out the day I left town with her, I bet. Did you tear your hands up on the thorns when you did that, big brother? Or did you just mow them down with one of your tractors?

"Well, now." He limped halfway over to the house, expecting to see his stepbrother appear any moment. "Seems old Will has done pretty well for himself since the last time I visited the old homestead."

High Point did seem a little deserted. At this time of day, there should have been men all over the place. Yet the only thing that moved was the sun-shaped weather vane on the peak of the roof.

The same roof J. R. had tried to shove Will off of when he was thirteen. His leg throbbed even harder at the thought of that particular childhood memory.

He always was the luckiest son of a bitch I ever knew.

As he went up to the front door, J. R. regarded the house thoughtfully. Ryder didn't move his main beef herds until mid-July, so his men weren't out on a cattle drive.

Where had he hidden Neala Delaney?

The gaunt woman who answered the doorbell gave him an unsmiling, suspicious look. "Yes?"

"I'm looking for Will Ryder."

"Mr. Ryder isn't here, and I don't know when he'll be back. Who are you?"

He'd forgotten how blunt these yokels could be. "I'm Bob Ryder—Will's cousin, from California. I was in the area and thought I'd drop by and say hello."

"Like I said, he isn't here." Some of the mistrust in her sharp eyes cleared. "You want to leave a message for him?"

"Actually, I need to speak to him about some horses. Is there any way I can get in touch with him myself?"

She hesitated, then pulled the door open wider. "Come inside. I'll give the foreman a call, see what he can do for you."

"Thank you, I'd appreciate it." He took his hand off the gun in his pocket as he walked past her. "I'm sorry for being a nuisance."

"You city folks always are." The housekeeper didn't specify if she meant *sorry* or *a nuisance*.

A half hour later he sat drinking coffee with Evan Gamble, who was open, friendly, and still wouldn't tell him a damn thing about where Will could have taken the girl.

J. R. was getting impatient, and went for the direct approach. "Look, if Will's still in town, where is he?"

Again the foreman's expression became guarded. "He's gone to take care of some business. I can probably get a message to him for you, if it's important."

J. R. checked his watch. "I guess it'll wait until he gets back."

"I don't know how long he'll be gone," Evan said, frowning. "How do I get in touch with you, Bob?"

J. R. pretended to look shocked. "I usually stay here at the house. At least, that's what I did the last time I passed through town."

The foreman seemed suspicious. "I've never heard Will mention you before."

"He probably didn't." J. R. knew enough about his stepbrother to bluff his way through. "We only see each other every couple of years, when he makes a buying trip out to my place. Last time was, what, two years ago? He purchased some Morgans from a breeder I introduced him to."

"I remember. But he made that trip three years ago."

J. R. let his eyebrows rise. "Was it? Time flies."

"That it does." Evan seemed to be making his mind up. "All right, I'll try to get hold of Will. In the meantime, make yourself comfortable." Evan put on his hat as he went to the door. He paused, then looked back. "Cousin, right?"

He smiled. "Yeah. His dad was like a father to me."

After the foreman left, he prowled discreetly around the house. He was just going through Will's files when a young blond girl strode into the study.

"Will, I want to talk to you. Is she—"

J. R. smiled at her. "Hello, sweet thing."

She peered at him, then took a step back as she recognized him. "Jeb? What are you doing here?"

"Looking for my brother, same as you."

She shook her head. "I can't believe it. How long has it been?"

"Ten years, give or take. You've grown up to be a real beauty, Wendy." He closed the file drawer. "So why are you still hanging around this place?"

"Will and I are engaged." She watched him sit behind the desk, then eased into the chair in front of him. "I'm hoping we'll be able to have a June wedding."

Just how many women was his stepbrother juggling? "I didn't know that. Congratulations."

"It's sort of . . . unofficial at the moment. We've had a few problems, but Will and I are working them out."

"Are you sure about that?" He hesitated, giving her

a sympathetic look. "I understand he's taken off with some woman."

Tears filled her eyes, making her look even younger than she was. "She's been trying to steal him from me since she got here, and now . . . and now . . ." She covered her face with her hands. "Oh, God, my daddy's going to be so furious."

"There, now." J. R. awkwardly patted her shoulder. If the pampered little brat didn't stop whining soon, he'd probably end up clipping her with his fist. "I'm sure you two can straighten this all out. Where could they be shacking up? Maybe I can go and talk some sense into him."

"Evan was right." Wendy jumped to her feet. "I have to go, Jeb." With another sob she raced out the back door.

Chapter 14

Evan drove out to Sun Valley later that day to close up the house. He wasn't happy about the man claiming to be Will's cousin staying back at High Point, and warned Beatrice to keep a close eye on him before he left. On the way to the other ranch, he tried calling Will's radio and cell phone several times, but got no answer.

Evan had a feeling he'd want to know about the unexpected visitor. As he debated what he should do, he spotted Wendy's horse, Starlight, tethered out at the front of the ranch house.

"What's she doing back here?" He got out of his truck and went to Starlight, who was still lathered from a hard ride. "Wendy?"

There was no answer, so he hurried inside, to find her sitting in the kitchen, weeping.

"Wendy? Honey, what is it?" Then he looked through the back window, and his smile faded. "You spiteful little witch."

He strode outside and walked along the perimeter of what had been Neal's garden. Every single plant had been trampled, ripped out, and destroyed. The destruction was so meticulous it made him sick. He turned and saw Wendy standing at the back door. "Nice work."

Her small nose went up in the air. "I didn't do it."

He didn't believe her. "Do you know how much

work she put into this? What it meant to her?" Evan
strode over, grabbed her by the arms, and shook her.
"Is that why you had to tear it up? Because she cares
about something besides herself, and you don't?"

Wendy's eyes went wide. "I didn't touch her pathetic little weed patch. Let go of me."

"I should whip the daylights out of you for this
stupid stunt." Evan shook her, making her hair fall in
her eyes. "That's what you need."

She shook the hair away. "Just try it, Evan Gamble,
and my daddy will make sure you never work in this
county again."

"Well, then. Might as well get my ass in a sling for
the right reason." He jerked her up against him. Her
shocked stillness made it easy to cup her face with his
hand and take her mouth. Evan poured his frustration
and anger into the kiss, letting her feel every ounce
of it.

Slowly Wendy's arms crept up around his back. Her
young body shuddered, and he lifted his head.

She was flushed and beautiful and everything he had
ever wanted. And still acting like a spoiled sixteen-
year-old Prom Queen. With a curse he shoved her
aside and strode far enough away so he wasn't
tempted to touch her again.

She followed him anyway. "Evan? Why did you
do that?"

"I lost my temper." He wasn't going to apologize.
Not this time. Not for kissing her.

"I meant . . ." She looked at her toes, then back at
him. "Why did you push me away like that?"

He stared at her. She couldn't be serious. "For
God's sake, Wendy! Forget about it!"

"But . . . I liked it." She shuffled closer, reaching
out to him. "Did you? Did you like kissing me?"

"Yeah." He laughed bitterly. "I loved it."

"So?" She gave him her come-hither smile, the kind
she habitually used to enslave every man she met.
"Why don't you kiss me again?"

"You're supposed to be in love with Will Ryder, remember?"

Her face darkened. "He's with her. Besides, I don't want him anymore."

"It figures. I hate to tell you this, but you don't get me as a consolation prize, honey." He walked past her and headed for his pickup.

"Evan! Wait!"

He slammed the door shut and started the engine. Wendy appeared at the window and pounded a fist on it. He rolled it down. "You can't do that to me and then just leave."

"That's exactly what I'm doing. Go home, Wendy. Go home to Daddy." He glanced at the ruined garden and shook his head. "You've done more than enough damage for one day."

He backed up and drove away. One last look in his rearview mirror showed Wendy standing there, still staring after him, her fists clenched at her sides.

Sean circled around the house, staying out of sight while he waited for the Lewis girl to leave. It took her a few minutes. She swore and kicked at the dirt and even spooked her own horse. The sound of his hooves hitting the dirt as he shied and tugged at the post served to snap her out of her rage.

"Damn, Starlight, I'm sorry." She put her arms around the horse's arched neck, and soothed him with her voice and touch until he calmed. "I guess we'd better go home and face Daddy. He isn't going to like this, is he?" She mounted the horse and rode out through the back meadow, eventually disappearing around a cluster of aspens.

Finally.

He went in through the front door that no one had bothered to lock, but found no trace of Neal. He repeated the search he'd performed last night, but failed once more to turn up the microdisk.

Where is she? Where did she put it?

He pulled out his cell phone to call Grady, then hesitated. If he reported her missing, Grady might send in the heavy artillery. If Grady hadn't moved her himself. If he had, why hadn't he said anything?

He put the phone back in his pocket.

As he tried to figure out his next move, he paced the length of the kitchen. Surely no one had found her yet. Certainly not J. R., who had promised him one million dollars to execute the woman whose testimony would put him on death row.

"Damn it, girl, where are you?"

"She's not here, George." Molly stepped into the kitchen. "But I am."

Sean considered his options. Lying was always number one on the list. "Miss Hatcher. Glad to see you. I was looking for the lady who lives here."

"You were searching the house, and you couldn't possibly know the lady who used to live here. Or could you?"

"I met her just the other day. Beautiful girl." He tried to look sheepish. "Can't blame an old man for trying."

"Trying, no. Handing me a bunch of lies, yes." Molly peered at his face. "She doesn't much look like you at all, except around the eyes. Is she your daughter?"

"She's no relation to me at all—"

"Give me a break, George. I want to know who you are, what you're doing here, and how that girl is involved with you. Or I'm calling the sheriff and telling him I've found the burglar who ransacked this place a few days ago."

Sean doubted Molly could convince the law he was a burglar, but he couldn't take the chance of being arrested. "I'm not her father; I'm her uncle. Her mother was my only sister."

"Now that makes sense. That why you ducked out of the diner the day she came in? Didn't want her to see you?"

"Something like that. Where is she?"

"I just ran into Evan Gamble. Seems Will Ryder came here and took her away. He's not the best person for her to be with right now, I think."

"Why?"

Molly told him about the fire and the mark she'd found on Neal's arm. "Will Ryder's first wife left him for his brother, Jeb, but she came back a year later." She pushed her glasses up on her nose. "The day she did, she died of an overdose, right here in this house."

"That doesn't mean Will Ryder killed her, or wants to hurt my Neal."

"That's just the thing, George. You see, Will's brother Jeb lives in Denver. He owns a couple of night clubs, and I'm pretty sure Neala was involved with him before she came here. And there's no one Will hates more than Jeb."

"Tell me about this place."

He held her in his arms and nuzzled her hair. "The cabin? I built it a couple of years ago. I come up here when I need to get away from the ranch for a day or two."

"No wonder it looks like a bachelor pad."

"I wanted to build one for me and Trish, but she didn't like it up here."

"Women have this thing about electrical outlets," Neal said. "We need more than one, or we go through withdrawal."

"The only thing Trish wanted was a way out." He made a harsh sound. "My stepbrother finally gave her what she wanted."

Neal propped herself up on one elbow. Her dark hair fell in wild disarray over her naked breasts. "Your stepbrother? The one who . . ." She hesitated.

"Yeah, the one Trish ran off with. Jeb hated this place. He hated the farm, too. Dad had to put down two horses he'd ruined. My folks sent him off to boarding school, thinking he'd be happier there. He just got angrier and more destructive every time he came home. The last summer we spent together, he nearly killed me."

"He what?" She rolled over and looked into his eyes. "He tried to kill you?"

"Yeah. He liked to smoke, and after he'd started a couple of fires by tossing his butts around, my father grounded him for a couple of weeks. That night Jeb got pissed off and crawled out of his bedroom window. He climbed up onto the roof of the horse barn. I saw him sitting up there, tossing lit matches down and laughing when he saw the hay catching. I went up after him."

Will didn't say anything for a minute, then tucked her in closer.

"When I got out there on the roof with him, he started shouting at me and wrestled with me. I got him pinned, and made him agree to come inside and settle down. Only when I was helping him up, he tried to push me off the roof."

"How high was it?"

"The roof? Four stories off the ground."

Neal took in a quick breath. "Jesus."

"I managed to hold on and swing myself back over the edge. When I did, he tried to kick me in the face, lost his balance, and rolled off." Will rubbed his face with one hand. "He broke his back, and was never able to walk right again. He tried to blame me for it, but a couple of the hands had witnessed what had happened. After he got out of the hospital, my folks sent him back to school, and never let him come home again."

"God. That's terrible." She snuggled against him, her hands stroking him. "Your poor stepmom."

"It shattered Rebecca, and she never forgave him or herself." He held her, needing her warmth more than ever. "After she died, I think that's why Jeb came back and broke up my marriage. Revenge for what happened on that roof. Revenge for everything."

"Don't think about him anymore." Neal rubbed her

cheek against his chest. "He's out of your life, and you never have to see him again, right?"

"I hope not. I think if I do, one of us is going to end up dead."

He fell asleep with her in his arms. Some time later, the ringing of his cell phone woke him, and he eased out of Neal's arms to put on his jeans and take the call outside. He scanned the deserted clearing as he answered it.

"Ryder."

"It's Kalen." Grady sounded annoyed. "Where the hell are you?"

"Up at my cabin. We need to talk."

"Yeah, well, me first. J. R. showed up at High Point."

Will sat down on the porch chair. "I thought you were going to give me plenty of warning."

"Yeah, well, you've been warned. He's waiting for you to come home. Get Neal and head back down there."

"You're telling me you want me to hand her over to Jeb?"

"Hell, Will, you knew this was how it was going to work. My men are on the way, but I need to keep him there until they arrive. J. R. wants Neal."

"My stepbrother wants her dead."

"You'll be there to make sure she doesn't get hurt. Once my people have him back in custody, he'll make the deal and hand us the Chinese on a silver platter. Then I've got Shandian by the balls."

"Screw the deal." For some reason, the image of Trish's body popped up in his mind—only this time, she had Neala's face. "You wanted J. R., well, now you know where he is. Go get him."

"Get her off that mountain or you're going to blow the entire setup."

"She doesn't know he's my stepbrother. He'll try to kill her the minute he sees her."

"T'ang and his wife will be out of the country in forty-eight hours, unless I get the indictments. I can't get those without his cooperation. Which I can't get if he rabbits on us again."

"Goddamn it, you'd better not let him get away this time!" He heard a sound from inside the cabin, and lowered his voice. "I'll call you later."

The sound of Will's voice woke her up, and she stretched lazily before sliding out of the bed. Her leg knocked into a small side table, and she caught it before it fell over.

"Clumsy." She set it up right and went to close the small drawer that had fallen open. The sight of a photo inside made her stop and pull it out to investigate.

It was a picture of two boys, one large and blond, one shorter and darker. The big one was Will, judging by the startling hair and eyes. He'd been a good-looking kid. The shorter one was dark and scowled at the camera.

Who's Mr. Attitude? The stepbrother?

She turned the photo over. *Will and Jeb* was written in an elegant feminine hand.

After she got dressed, she walked over to the window and saw the back of Will's head. She went to open the window, then heard what he said and froze.

"I thought you were going to give me plenty of warning."

Warning about what?

"You want me to hand her over to Jeb?"

Jeb? Will said something else she missed; then she gave him her full attention.

"My stepbrother wants her dead."

Why would his stepbrother want her dead?

"Screw the deal. You wanted J. R., well, now you know where he is. Go get him."

His stepbrother. Jeb. J. R. She watched him without

blinking. Two of her fingernails split as she dug them into the windowsill.

"She doesn't know he's my stepbrother. He'll try to kill her the minute he sees her."

No, this couldn't be right. J. R. couldn't be Will's stepbrother. She backed slowly away from the window.

He said something else, then, "Goddamn it, you'd better not let him get away this time!"

She bumped into the edge of the bed, and gasped.

J. R. was his stepbrother. Of course, that was why they'd brought her here. Why they wanted her to stay at Will's ranch. Why Will had gotten involved. J. R.— no, *Jeb*—had wrecked his marriage, taken off with his wife.

Naturally Ryder would jump at the chance for revenge. And now she had to ruin it.

Neala waited until he ended the phone call before she walked out onto the porch. "Hey."

He gave her a worried look that almost, but not quite, melted her heart. "What are you doing up?"

"I was listening to you talk to your friend, the general." Yesterday she would have laughed at his stunned expression. Now it only made her want to cry like a lost child. "If this situation wasn't so sad, it would almost be funny."

He sat in silence for a full minute before getting to his feet. "My stepbrother is a killer."

"He could be." She shrugged. "I really have no idea."

"What are you talking about?" He came over and clamped his hands on her shoulders. "He murdered Colfax."

"Here's the punch line, Will." She took a deep breath. "I lied. J. R. didn't kill the senator. I lied and I framed your stepbrother for the murder."

What she'd said didn't make sense. It couldn't, not with what he knew about her. Slowly he dropped his hands. "No."

"Yeah, I'm afraid so. I set him up." Her dark gaze remained intent on his face. "If there had been any other way, I wouldn't have done it. You have to understand that."

They could have been standing in the center of a November blizzard and Will wouldn't have felt colder. The only word left in his mind came out of him with a wrench. "Why?"

"If I'd told the truth, it would have gotten two more people killed." The color was gone from her face, but she managed a smile. "I have to wait until I know they're safe."

Will reached and took her cold hand in his, then led her back inside the cabin. When she would have slipped away from him, he put an arm around her. "No, don't pull away from me." He guided her to a chair at the table, then pulled up another close to hers. "Tell me exactly what happened."

"I went to the senator's hotel room to meet Karen, his wife, and pick up something for my uncle. We had to hide in the bedroom closet when the senator came in unexpectedly with J. R. We heard them arguing, then the sound of a scuffle." She looked down at her hands. "Karen was terrified. She thought J. R. was going to beat him to death. I slipped out and opened the bedroom door. I watched J. R. leave. The senator was unconscious."

"But he was still alive." She nodded. "Who came in after my stepbrother?"

Neal took a deep breath and lifted her gaze to meet his. "No one else came in."

Will tensed. "Did you kill him, Neala?"

She shook her head. "Karen did." Her lips trembled. "It was self-defense, Will. He was trying to strangle her, and I couldn't get him off her. I tried, but he was too strong, and then she grabbed the knife . . . and then . . ." She gave up and burst into tears.

"Come here, baby." He lifted her out of the chair

and onto his lap, into his arms. He held her slim body against his and stroked her back as she curled her hands in his shirt and cried. "Let it out, just let it go."

Gradually she stopped sobbing, but he let her rest against him and didn't push her to give him the details. Whatever she had been through in that hotel suite, it had been enough. He wouldn't force her to relive it again, not until she was ready to tell him.

Neala pushed back and wiped her face with her palms. "Sorry. I'm not usually such a wimp but I . . . I never saw anyone die before."

She had no idea how tough she was. "It's okay, sweetheart. We'll work it out together."

She curled against him for a moment, then slowly detangled herself and rose to her feet. "After J. R. left, the senator regained consciousness. He was so angry. I tried to talk him into going to a hospital—he hit his head on one of the tables, and he was bleeding a lot—but he wouldn't go. He kept shouting at Karen, blaming her for the whole mess."

He watched as Neala began to pace around the small kitchen. "Why would he blame her?"

"He said it wouldn't have happened if she'd shown up on time, like he'd told her to. He slapped her; then he raised his fist, like he was going to punch her. That's when I got between them and told him to back off. Colfax laughed at me." Her pacing became more agitated. "Then he knocked me out of the way and went after Karen. He started beating her."

She stopped at the window and looked out at the meadow. "Karen told me later that he'd been abusing her for years, and she'd never fought back before. He assumed she never would, but he was wrong." She gripped the windowsill with both hands. "She finally found a reason to fight back that night.

"Karen shoved him back and told him she was leaving him. She pulled up her sleeve, and I saw cigar burns on her arm. She said she'd gone to the hospital, and

they'd taken pictures. She'd given the police a state-
ment, saying he'd done that to her. She was going to
divorce him and send him to jail.''

"That was when he tried to kill her," Will guessed.

Neala nodded slowly. "He grabbed Karen by the
throat and started to strangle her. I tried to get them
apart, but he kicked me away. He backed her into
the table where room service had set up their dinner.
Somehow Karen got hold of one of the steak knives.''

Will went to her, and turned her to face him. "She
stabbed him with it."

"Yes. She had no choice. It was absolutely self-
defense.''

"Neala.'' He touched her cheek with the backs of
his fingers. "If this is what really happened, why didn't
you tell the police the truth?''

"This is where it gets complicated. Karen had met
and fallen in love with another man. It happened the
last time she and the senator made a state visit to
China. Her lover also happens to be the son of the
tong leader. He'd given her a microdisk with intelligence—enough to expose the senator's illegal campaign funds and bring down his father's operation and
two other Chinese tongs involved in forming an
American-based triad. The only problem was, she had
to leave her lover behind in China, and she had to go
back and get him out—that night. Despite the years
of abuse she'd suffered, she was sure she'd be charged
with her husband's murder, and held indefinitely.''

"So you made a deal.''

"I called my uncle, and he agreed to help her. In
exchange for the microdisk, he would protect both of
them from the triad. I agreed to blame J. R. for the
senator's murder until I had to appear in court and
testify under oath. Karen gave my uncle the microdisk
for safekeeping, and as a good-faith gesture.''

"You and your uncle never told Grady about the
microdisk.''

"We were waiting until we knew Karen and her

lover were safe. It was all part of the deal." She pressed her hand against the glass. "I'd give anything to know if they're still alive, if they've gotten out of China all right. Then this could all be over."

"It will be, soon." Will covered her hand with his. "I'll call Grady; he'll know how to locate them."

"No." Her head whipped up. "You can't do that. He'll sacrifice Karen and her lover just to get the microdisk."

"Honey, even you have to admit you are in way over your head on this one. Grady needs to know J. R. didn't kill the senator, and that the Chinese are involved. He'll want the microdisk, too, but he won't sacrifice anyone." When she would have spoken, he rested a finger against her lips. "Trust me. Kalen and I go back a long way. He'll do the right thing."

After Will went out on the porch to call the general, Neala took the half-dollar from her pocket and stared at it for a minute. Despite his assurances, she didn't trust General Grady to do anything but what was necessary to get the microdisk. Will thought she was out of her league, but in reality, he was.

I can't let them die. Not after going through all this. Heads I stay, tails I go find Uncle Sean. She took the half-dollar from her pocket and flipped it. It landed on tails.

Sometimes I'm a lucky girl.

She placed the Kennedy coin on the bedside table, then looked around. The only ways out of the cabin were through the front door or the back bedroom window. Silently she opened the window and climbed out.

Circling through the woods to get out of eyesight took a few minutes. Then she tried to get her bearings. There was the dirt road that led out through the pass. She'd follow that, keeping herself hidden in the trees.

Neala had to wipe her face on her sleeves several times as she made her way down the mountain. Trying not to cry kept her so preoccupied, she never saw the shadow following her.

Sean walked into the deserted diner and went to the counter, where Molly was waiting. "No one seems to know where this cabin is."

"Did you go to High Point?"

"Yeah." And had nearly had a heart attack, seeing Jeb Ryder had already arrived there. "We've got to go up on that mountain and find them."

"There's only one way we can do this." Molly shut off the coffee machine and turned off the grill. "I'll round up everyone in town, and we'll get them to go with us and help us look."

"And they'd do that? For my Neal?"

"People around here take care of each other." Molly was already heading for the phone. "You go on over to the Shoofly. I'll have everyone meet there first. Oh, and George, I wouldn't mention what I told you about Will Ryder. I don't know for sure if he means to hurt her."

Sean bent over and kissed Molly's cheek. "You're a goodhearted woman, Molly Hatcher."

She smiled up at him. "Tell me that again when I put you on double shift tomorrow to make up for lost business."

Within a short time, three-quarters of the population of Lone Creek had assembled inside the Shoofly Bar and Grill. Most of the men brought rifles, and surprisingly some of the women, too. At a nod from Molly, Sean got up on a table and whistled to get everyone's attention.

"Most of you remember my niece Neala from her singing at the town dance. She's in trouble, and I need to find her. She witnessed the murder of Senator Colfax of Colorado, and the man she saw murder the senator is here, in Lone Creek. His name is Jeb Ryder. He means to kill her, too."

"Excuse me. Let me through, please," Wendy Lewis

pushed forward until she stood in front of Sean's table. "Mister, I have to tell you something. I saw Jeb out at High Point today. I'm afraid I told him that Neal was with Will."

Evan appeared beside her. "You saw Jeb?"

"You did, too." She glanced at him. "He said he spoke to you."

Evan realized who she was talking about, and hit his forehead with his palm. "Damn, I knew there was something wrong with that guy's story."

"I guess we both messed up." Wendy reached out and shyly folded her hand around his before she turned to Sean. "We'll help you look. Evan knows that mountain better than anyone here."

Angry voices rose in agreement, and Sean clapped his hands a couple of times to dispel the ripple of reaction. "Someone else has been after her, too. I don't know in what kind of condition we'll find her. She may be drugged or disoriented. Don't hurt her. If you can't convince her to come with you, fire off three shots and we'll come to you."

"You can climb down off that table now, George, or whatever your name is." The crowd parted to let Sheriff Walton through. He didn't look happy. "Just what do you think you're doing, stirring folks up like this?"

Sean folded his arms. "I'm trying to find my niece before this murdering bastard does."

"Some of these folks will likely end up shooting each other." The sheriff turned toward the crowd. "If you're serious about looking for this girl, leave the rifles home."

"We've got a right to protect ourselves, Caleb," someone shouted. Several other men agreed.

Sean spread his hands. "You can't put them all in handcuffs, Sheriff."

"No, mister, but I have a pair that should fit you right nicely."

"Why don't you go with us instead, supervise the search?"

"Searching on foot isn't the way to find someone on that mountain." Caleb gestured to Evan. "You remember how we located those lost hikers last fall?"

A slow smile spread across Evan's face. "I sure do, Sheriff."

Caleb nodded. "All right, then, that's how we'll do it this go-round, too. But the first one of you who doesn't follow my orders gets to spend a night scrubbing the floor of my holding cell."

Neal got as far as the highway, then flagged down a passing truck and hitched a ride. Fortunately the trucker was a decent man, and even joked with her about being stranded in the middle of nowhere.

"So I was saying to my wife, breaking down in Death Valley ain't so bad, long as you like tumbleweeds, cactus, and snake—"

They were approaching the gate to Sun Valley, so Neal interrupted him. "I'm sorry, but this is where I get off."

"Right." The trucker came to a slow stop. "You going to be okay, miss?"

Her life was in ruins. "I'll be fine. Thanks."

She climbed out of the cab, then started the long walk up to the house. Jeb would be coming for her soon, along with Grady, so she had to make preparations.

One more look. Just to see how big the radish plants grew.

She might have seen the shadow coming up behind her if she hadn't walked so quickly around the house. When she saw the comprehensive destruction, she stopped in her tracks.

My garden.

There were hoofprints all around the ravaged plants, in the soft soil she'd worked so hard to prepare. Apparently Wendy had gotten even with her for whatever she'd done. Neal walked around what had been the only real thing she'd ever made with her own hands, then bent to touch a torn, wilted leaf.

"The bugs probably would have eaten everything anyway." She straightened and gazed around. There wasn't a single thing left to be salvaged. It was all gone. "Or I'd have eaten a bug stuck to something."

She didn't know why she felt so frozen. It wasn't like she really liked digging in the damn dirt, breaking her back every day pulling out weeds, and spraying that awful garlic juice all over everything. Gently she picked up a small, smashed tomato, and closed her fingers over it. It hadn't even turned red yet. It had never had a chance.

Neither had she.

Will was hot, tired, and ready to strangle the first person who looked sideways at him. He was also scared out of his mind.

He'd sat for a while after talking to Kalen, then gone in to tell Neala what the general intended to do. That was when he saw her lucky coin on the bedside table, and the photo she'd left on the empty bed.

She bolted on me.

He walked a half mile around the cabin before realizing she'd gotten too far ahead of him to find her on foot. He went back for Blue, and rode down to the highway in time to see her climb into the cab of a semi.

Damn it, why can't the fool woman trust me?

He couldn't follow them on horseback, but he'd left his truck hidden halfway down the mountain, only a few yards off the road. Once he got to the truck, he dismounted and slapped Blue's rump, sending him galloping off to High Point.

Back on the road, Will caught up with the truck in a few minutes. He planned to pull her out of the truck the moment the trucker stopped. Only when he stopped it was at Sun Valley, and Neala got out and walked up to the house alone.

He parked his truck at the gate and walked up to the house on foot. For once he didn't care about what he owed Kalen or Jeb. Neala belonged to him, and it was high time she realized it.

He slipped into the house, and found the woman he wanted to strangle standing at the counter, calmly making a cup of tea.

"Neala."

She didn't shriek or jump or even bother to turn around. "Hello, Ryder. What are you doing here?"

"Did you think I wouldn't come after you?"

"No, just not this fast." Now she turned around, and he saw the knife in her hand. "What did the general say?"

"He wants the microdisk you took from Karen Colfax. Put the knife down."

She looked down as if she'd forgotten she was holding it. "Sorry." She set it aside. "I'm a little scared."

"Is that why you ran?" He pushed a curl back from her cheek. "I would never let anyone hurt you, Neala."

"You don't have a choice, big brother."

Will turned to see Jeb standing in the kitchen doorway, holding a gun on them. "Shit."

"I wouldn't try anything, big brother. A couple of my men are waiting just outside the front door." His cruel smile widened. "Hello, songbird. Long time, no see."

"J. R.," she said, her voice flat.

"I have to apologize for making you wait, but I had a feeling Will would catch up with you. Couldn't resist the opportunity for a double reunion." He gestured with the gun. "Outside." To Will, he said, "You stay here."

"She's not going anywhere with you."

"On the contrary, brother. She's coming back with me to Denver so she can clear the murder charge against me with the district attorney. Who, I imagine, will toss her pretty little ass in jail for obstruction of justice."

Will took a step toward him. "No, Jeb."

His stepbrother held out his hand. "Come to me, Neal, or I'll shoot him in the head."

"Please, Will," she whispered. "I'll be all right."

He sensed someone behind him, but before he could turn something slammed into the back of his head. He tried to reach for Neala, but fell into the darkness instead.

Chapter 15

Neala had two choices—try to wrestle the gun from J. R.'s hand, or try to jump from his car while he was doing seventy. Both would probably get her killed.

"Did you miss me while I was in jail?" J. R. asked her as he reached over and caressed her hair with the hand holding the gun. "Or were you too busy screwing my brother?"

"I'm sorry about what I did." Getting shot would be quicker, and probably less painful. "Were you serious about taking me back to Denver? Or are you going to kill me?"

"Why would I kill my alibi? I have better things to do with you." He rubbed a thumb across her cheek. "Much better things."

She swallowed hard against the surge of bile in her throat. "I'll tell the Denver D.A. everything." She tried to inject some enthusiasm into her voice. "I'll do whatever you want; just leave Will alone."

"Are you offering me another exclusive agreement? You reneged on the last one."

"I was scared." She held out her hand, and was pleased to see it didn't shake when she rested it on his thigh. "We could have some good times together."

"Maybe we can. You'd do anything for my stepbrother, I think." He considered that for a moment.

"All right, songbird, you can start by telling me why the Chinese are after you."

Her blood ran cold. "I don't know."

"I think it's because you have something they want. Like this microdisk you took from Karen Colfax."

He must have overheard her talking to Will. "I don't have it. My uncle does."

He wound some of her hair around the cold gun barrel. "I need that microdisk, Neal. I have the feeling it'll be my new insurance policy with the triad. Where is it?"

"I told you, my uncle—" She yelped as he yanked the gun down, pulling her hair with it. "My uncle has the microdisk. I don't."

"You're starting to really annoy me now, songbird." He cocked the gun and rested it an inch away from her left eye. "I don't need you to clear my name with the D.A. as badly as I need that microdisk. So I'll give you one more chance before I spray your brains all over the inside of this car. Where is it?"

Neala's fingers itched for a coin; then the irony kicked in. She couldn't leave Montana without the microdisk, and she certainly couldn't let J. R. kill her. No one else knew where it was. "It's at the cabin up on the mountain."

She sat back and began to plot, but the drive took far less time than she expected. She kept an eye on the rearview mirror, constantly hoping to see Ryder's black truck appear.

If only I'd trusted him. She realized she wouldn't be in danger now—and wouldn't have put Will in danger—if she had. By running away to Sun Valley, she'd practically handed J. R. what he wanted. Now all she could do was hope that Will was all right, and would somehow come to her rescue one more time.

Come on, Will. Think the way I do. Find us.

The door to the cabin was still open, evidence of how quickly Ryder had left to come after her. It scared her to get out and march into the cabin at gunpoint. Scared her even more to see that the coin was gone. She sat down on the bed and let her head rest back against the carved headboard.

J. R. closed the door and looked at her. "So where is it?"

"It's gone." She closed her eyes and sent a prayer for God to watch over Laney and Will for her. "Someone took it."

Something cold touched the side of her head. "No, songbird, that's not what I want to hear." He yanked her off the bed. "Get it."

As she turned, she saw a fleeting shape move behind J. R.'s car. For an instant she forgot to control her expression as joy burst inside her heart.

He found us.

Will regained consciousness as one of Jeb's men was dragging him out the front door.

The bigger of the two holstered his weapon and cracked his knuckles. "The boss wants us to work him over good," he said to the one dragging Will. "A going-away present, he says. Stand him up."

Will stayed limp as he was dragged to his feet and braced against the wall.

"Heavy son of a bitch," the smaller man said. "Face or belly?"

"Both."

He opened his eyes and caught the thug's fist just before it connected with his ribs. "Does my stepbrother know he's got morons on his payroll?"

Both men glanced at each other, then at him. "What did you say?" the knuckle cracker growled.

"I said"—Will used his left elbow to break the shorter thug's jaw—"Does my stepbrother—"

As the knuckle cracker dove for him, Will caught his arm, pivoted, and used the momentum to fling him head-on into the shorter man. As their bodies collided, he reached up and slammed their heads together.

". . . know he's got morons—"

The shorter man slid down the wall beside the door and crumpled over, unconscious. Will caught the bigger one as he staggered backward, spun him around, and administered a pulverizing roundhouse punch squarely to the other man's nose. The knuckle cracker reeled backward, then slipped and landed on his back. He lifted one arm, then slumped back and went motionless.

". . . on his payroll?"

Will reached down to remove the smaller man's gun from his holster, and tucked it in the back of his belt. Then he retrieved the other weapon from the knuckle cracker and checked the clip before glancing at the unconscious men one last time.

"I guess not."

He circled around the house, but J. R. and Neala were gone. When he came back around to the front of the house, a long, official-looking car sat in the drive.

Will lowered the gun in his hand as Kalen Grady emerged, along with a group of armed men in protective gear and bulletproof vests. "You're a little late, General."

"Will." Kalen, who wore his Armani suit like body armor, surveyed the situation. "Where're J. R. and the girl?"

"He just took off." Will started for his truck.

"Wait a minute, Will. Let the federal marshals have a look."

Kalen's marshals quickly fanned out to search the immediate area, then returned. "No sign of them, General, but there are tire tracks leading out to the access road."

"The cabin. We've got some catching up to do," Will said, and grabbed his old army buddy by the front of his jacket. "Later, when I come back to knock the shit out of your sorry government ass."

Kalen didn't blink. "Keep wrinkling my suit, and I'll have to return the favor."

Will slowly released his hold. "I'm going after them."

"We'll join you."

*   *   *

Will crossed the last hundred yards to the cabin in a crouch, and used Jeb's car as cover as he tried to get around to the back window Neala had used twice to escape.

"Look who's here, sweetheart." J. R. dragged Neala out of the house, holding her in front of him. Will went motionless as he saw that his stepbrother had the business end of the gun pressed under Neala's chin. "Come on out, big brother, or I'll blow her goddamned head off."

Slowly he stood up.

"Drop the gun, big brother."

He let the weapon slip from his fingers. "Don't call me that. I was never your brother. I tried to be, for Rebecca's sake, until you broke her heart."

"You mean, when you broke my back."

"You did that to yourself, Jeb. You were a mean, sneaky little bastard who couldn't win unless you cheated." He swung a hand toward Neala. "Holding a gun on a woman, now that really makes you a big man, doesn't it? Only you can't shoot her."

"I don't need to shoot her." J. R. flung Neala away and leveled the gun at Will's chest. "I can shoot you."

"Go ahead. You won't face me on even ground; you're too much of a coward. So do it. Shoot me."

"I don't need a gun." He pocketed his weapon and swung his cane in a vicious arc as he came toward Will. "I've been looking forward to this for a long time."

Will moved quickly for his size, but Jeb was an experienced street brawler. The cane, which turned out to be reinforced steel, caught Will in the side, and sent him staggering.

"Ever since my mother dragged me to that ranch, I've wanted to see you bleed."

"Too bad you only had the guts to try it once." Will circled back, keeping his hands up. He deflected another bone-cracking blow with a fist, and felt the skin split. "You might have gotten something out of it."

"I got Trish, didn't I?" Jeb laughed, and brought the cane down hard on Will's shoulder. Will fell to one knee. "A little money, a little sweet talk, and she was all over me."

Will rolled to the side to avoid a second blow to his head. "You used her."

"I did you a favor." Jeb drove the end of his cane into Will's stomach. "What's the matter, big brother? Getting old? You're not putting up much of a fight."

No, he wasn't. He was waiting for the right moment. "Why did she come back here?"

"I have no idea. Maybe she felt guilty about the kid." He chuckled as he kicked Will over. "You didn't know she was knocked up when she left you."

He stared up at his stepbrother. "No. She never told me."

"She didn't know if it was mine or yours. I made her get rid of it." J. R. planted his boot in the center of Will's chest. "Then I let her run back to you. Notice anything different about her when she came home?"

The moment arrived, and Will didn't waste it. With one blow he knocked the cane from J. R.'s hand, and followed through with a punch that laid him out flat on his back. "You sick bastard."

J. R. shoved himself up, but Will tackled him, and the two grappled. Rage gave Will the edge, and soon he was hammering his stepbrother, until J. R.'s face became a battered, scarlet mask.

"Will." Neala tugged at him. "No more. Please. It's over."

He shoved his stepbrother's limp body away from him and got to his feet. He would have taken her hand, but his were covered in blood. There was no blood on her, but she was dead white, and shaking uncontrollably.

"Did he hurt you?"

"No. Did you steal my lucky coin?"

He forgot about the condition of his hands as he pulled her into his arms and held her tightly. She probably couldn't breathe, but he needed this, needed to feel her warm and alive in his arms.

"Put me down and let's go inside." Her teeth were chattering as he set her back down, and she tugged him toward the cabin. "I really have to make some phone calls this time."

"Bitch."

Will turned to see J. R. back on his feet, weaving unsteadily, aiming the gun in his hands at Neala's face. Will forgot about caution, forgot about everything except his woman as he lunged in front of her.

"No!"

A trio of shots rang out as Neal screamed. Will watched as the front of his stepbrother's chest burst open in three places. Jeb fell face-first into the grass, and didn't move again. Behind him stood a familiar figure.

"Hello, Will. Sorry to barge in like this."

"Molly?" He stared at the owner of the town diner. Molly kept her pistol pointed at Will's heart. "Neala, give me the microdisk, or I'll do the same thing to him."

"It's not here." Neala tried to put herself between Molly and Will, but on the first step Molly fired a shot at her feet.

"Don't move. Not another inch. Where is it?"

"I have it," Will said, ignoring the panicked look Neala gave him. A distant, familiar rumble made him focus intently on Molly. "Mind telling me who you plan to give it to?"

"Not at all. My superior, Mr. T'ang, at Shandian."

"You're good." Will clenched his fists as he stared at her. "I would have never guessed it was you."

"You've been working for the Chinese?" Neala gaped. "All this time?"

"I don't just work for them, my dear. I've had a couple of operations over the years, but"—the older woman removed her dark-tinted glasses, revealing the distinctly Asian cast to her eyes—"as you can see, I *am* Chinese."

"It's not Molly, is it? More something like Mah-Lee, I'll guess." Will heard the noise drawing closer, and tensed. He had to keep her distracted. "You've been here almost three years. Did they send you to keep tabs on J. R.?"

Molly shrugged. "It's the way things are done." She changed her grip on the pistol. "Give me the microdisk."

The rumbling got even closer. "Come and get it."

Molly changed her aim and pointed the gun at Neala. "Do you want to see how slowly I can kill your girlfriend? It'll take five shots. Five very painful shots. I'll save the last for you."

"Will." Neala didn't blink. "I love you."

Shock rippled through him, and he glanced at her. The only thing that kept him away from her in that moment was Molly's gun. "City girl, you pick the damnedest times to tell me things."

Molly looked around as the rumble became an approaching roar. "What is that?"

"Thunder," Will said. He needed another distraction. "Come here, Neala." He held out his arm.

"Don't move, or I'll kill you."

"You'll kill us anyway." Neala went to him. "I'm sorry about this."

Will bent to kiss her head, then murmured, "Run for the cabin. Now."

But Neala saw what was coming around the edge of the pass into the clearing, and couldn't move an inch.

As wide and dark as a seething river, a huge mass of moving bodies poured into the clearing and headed straight for them. Their weight shook the ground as their hooves pounded over the grass, flattening it in an instant. The frantic, almost piercing sounds the cattle made pervaded the air, and clods of dust and dirt flew up all around them. Keeping pace with the herd were dozens of men and women on horseback, riding on the fringes as they drove them forward.

Stampede.

Molly jerked around. "No. They weren't supposed to come this way!"

"Now!" Will pushed Neala toward the cabin.

She stumbled away, looking back over her shoulder to see Molly firing directly at the stampeding herd, and several of the lead cattle fell, only to be trampled beneath the pounding hooves of the ones who followed.

Evan jumped his horse out in front of the cattle, making a path for himself by swinging a coil of rope at the nearest steer's head. He rode straight toward Will, holding out the other arm.

"Go!" Will shouted, reaching up for Evan's arm as he bent down to pull Will out of the path of the frenzied animals. At the same time, Wendy appeared on Starlight, trying to do the same for Molly. But the diner owner dropped her pistol and darted away from the girl, trying to make it to the trees.

Wendy shouted, "Molly, no!"

The stampede reached the cabin just as Neala made it inside and slammed the door shut. Faced with a larger obstacle, the herd at first piled up against the front of the cabin, then abruptly changed direction. A moment later the riders were driving them toward the trees.

Evan circled around in time for Will to see the Chinese operative stumble and fall. Molly screamed and tried to scramble to her feet as Wendy made another, desperate attempt to recover her. The blond girl's hand briefly touched, then was torn away from, the diner owner's clutching grasp. The cattle were too many and too fast for Wendy to make another attempt.

Molly disappeared under the thundering hooves.

After the federal marshals arrived, and Molly was taken by helicopter to the trauma center in Billings, all Neala could do was sit inside the cabin and try to process everything that had happened.

I'm just glad it's over.

Will had disappeared with Evan and the other townspeople as they herded the cattle back down the mountain. Unconsciously she took up a post at the window, watching for his return. Although she didn't know what she was going to say to him when he did.

Sorry for lying through my teeth about everything, big guy. And not trusting you. Want to try this again?

Someone touched her arm, and she turned away from the window.

The big, gray-haired man grinned. "Hello, darlin' girl."

"Uncle Sean."

She started sobbing then, and didn't stop, not when Sean took her into his arms, not when he ushered her back to the bedroom, not when he made her lie back with a cool washcloth draped over her forehead. She fell asleep weeping soundlessly, and woke up to the sound of angry voices.

Her uncle was sitting beside her bed, reading *Field and Stream*. She pulled the washcloth from her face and sat up. "Hey."

"How's my best girl feeling?"

"Still a little woozy. Did Laney really get married?"

"Yes, she did."

"Is he nice?"

Sean snorted. "In my opinion, not particularly. He's big and mean and doesn't say much, but he loves her half to death and won't let her out of his sight."

"Good. Then he'll keep her out of trouble." The voices outside the bedroom door got deeper and angrier. One of them was Will's. "Is everything okay out there?"

"Your landlord and my boss are hashing things out." Sean winced as something large and heavy skidded into the other side of the wall, then fell into pieces. "Or they might be doing a bit of furniture rearranging."

"Sounds more like face rearranging." Neala hauled herself off the bed and marched to the door.

"Are you sure you really want to be going out there?"

She flashed a grin back at him. "I'm sure."

Outside the door, a chair lay in a dozen pieces. Will and a red-haired man stood on opposite sides of the kitchen table. Will wasn't shouting. "I said, she's done with it."

The red-haired man *was* shouting. "Don't make this into something personal, Ryder."

Neala folded her hands and cleared her throat. When both men looked at her, she smiled. "You're not breaking furniture over me, are you?"

"The general is leaving."

"Not until I get the microdisk and an explanation from Ms. Delaney as to why she never thought to mention it to the agents who escorted her from Denver."

"No wonder Uncle Sean's hiding out in the bedroom. Sit down, both of you." Neala pulled a chair up to the table and waited until the two men sat down beside her. "Now, let's see if we can do this in a civilized way, before someone ends up in the hospital"—she looked at Kalen—"or prison"—she turned to glare at Ryder—"okay?"

"Will told me you said Karen Colfax killed her husband in self-defense."

"She did. Here's how it happened." Neal calmly recited the facts. "And I'm not giving you the microdisk until I know they're safe."

"All right." Kalen sighed. "I'm willing to go for the self-defense. I'll even provide witness protection for Karen Colfax and Jian-Shan when they return to the United States." When Neala's eyes widened with shock, he gave her a faint smile. "Satisfied?"

"You'd do all that? For them?"

"Of course. Would you like it in writing?"

She slowly shook her head. "I just never thought you'd try to help them. That's not what intelligence agencies do."

"We like to break up the tedium of murder and mayhem with an occasional act of kindness. However"—he held up one hand—"there is one condition."

"Name it."

"Give me the microdisk right now, or I throw everyone in federal prison."

"Will." Neala's lips quirked. "Do you still have my lucky coin?"

Will fished it out of his pocket and handed it to her. "You going to flip for this decision, too?"

"Not this one." Using her thumbnail, Neal pried at the edge of a hidden seam, and carefully popped off one face of the coin. "There you go, General." She removed the thin, delicate wafer of silicon that had been hidden inside the Kennedy half-dollar. "One microdisk chock-full of intelligence, safe and sound."

Kalen smiled. "Ms. Delaney, your government appreciates this." He glanced at Will, then rose to his feet. "Colonel Delaney?"

Sean appeared in the doorway, looking rather pleased with himself. "Yes, General?"

"Your retirement papers are on my desk back in Washington," Kalen said. "I suggest we go and discuss why I shouldn't burn them and toss you in Leavenworth for the balance of your existence."

On the way out, Sean bent and whispered, "One down, one to go. Good luck, darlin'."

Will waited until the men had left them before he reached over and pulled Neala out of her chair and onto his lap. "What do I have to promise to get what I want from you?"

"The usual—the moon, the stars, a lifetime supply of nail polish remover."

"Calamity, you're coming back to High Point with

me, and you're staying. The hell with your manicure. I'm marrying you."

"I am not a mule. I might not like your ranch. And the condition of my nails is very important to me, Ryder."

"God, I love you." He took her mouth with a bruising, ferocious kiss. "You win. I'll do whatever you want. I'll sell the ranch and move to Denver. I'll get a city job. Whatever you want. Just don't leave me. Stay with me." He ran his hand over her flat stomach. "Have this baby with me."

"You don't know if I'm pregnant."

"Let's just say I've got a feeling, Calamity."

"Well, then, I'll have to stay, won't I?" She curled her arms around his neck. "Wild Bill."

Epilogue

Evan Gamble paced up and down the deserted corridor. He didn't know what else to do.

A slim, red-haired woman and a huge, dark-bearded man stepped off a nearby elevator and, after consulting a wall sign, walked toward Evan. A tiny baby wrapped in a blue blanket lay cradled against the man's chest.

The redhead gave him a cautious smile. "Mr. Gamble? I'm Laney Tremayne, Neal's sister. This is my husband, Joe, and our son, Matthew."

"Nice to meet you. I'm Evan." He shook hands with them both and briefly admired the sleeping baby.

Laney glanced down the corridor. "How's it going?"

"I'm not sure." Evan shuffled his feet. "They've been in there for nine hours." A young blond woman in a floral dress walked out of another elevator, and he waved at her. "Over here, Wendy."

She came over and smiled at the Tremaynes as he made introductions. "I know Neal will be glad to know you're here."

"It'll probably be a while. I need to feed Matthew, so we'll be in the waiting room down the hall," Laney said. "When they come out, will you let us know?" Evan nodded. "Thanks."

Wendy watched them go. "Well? Anything yet?"

He rocked back on his heels. "Nothing so far." His gaze went from her perfectly groomed hair to the pretty pink sandals she wore. "You look nice."

She gave him a faintly ironic look. "Just *nice*? That's not what you said when you left this morning, Mr. Gamble."

He leaned forward to murmur against her ear, "As I remember, you were naked this morning, Mrs. Gamble." He grinned and pulled her into his arms. "Now, like that, you look fantastic."

Wendy laughed and kissed him. Two months of being married still hadn't made a dent in the thrill she felt when he touched her. "I love you."

Evan pressed her close. She did love him. Enough to move out of her father's house for him. Enough to marry him, despite all the threats Dean Lewis had made about disowning her. Enough to get a full-time job training horses to add to their income. And she loved him just the way he was—a hired hand, working at High Point, with dreams of having his own ranch someday.

Only now it was going to be theirs.

She pulled back. "How long has it been?"

He checked his watch. "Almost ten hours."

"Poor thing." Wendy closed her eyes and shuddered. "And what Will must be going through."

What Will was going through was coming to a crisis, a few doors down the hall.

Neala closed her eyes. "I'm going to kill you. Slowly. With a big, sharp knife. And guess where I'm going to start?"

"Easy now, Mrs. Ryder."

She looked at him. His face was white, his hair soaked with sweat. He looked terrified, which almost—*almost*—made things equal. A moment later she decided she was wrong. Only ritual disembowelment would make them even.

Will's voice shook as he reached for her. "Hold my hand, honey. Breathe."

"I don't want to hold your hand. I don't want to

breathe. I want to see you dead." She took a deep breath and screamed as loud as she could.

The woman kneeling before her looked up. "One more time, Mrs. Ryder."

"One more time, my ass!" She turned her face and glared at her husband. "And you—if you so much as put a pinky on me for the next ten years, I will geld you. Just like they do horses."

"I can see the head, Mrs. Ryder," the midwife said. "One more push and you'll be a mom. Come on, you're doing fine. One more push now; let's do it."

"You're not doing anything but catching!" Neal snarled, then gathered the last of her strength and bore down. The stretching, ripping sensation became overwhelming, and she screamed again. Then a huge pressure forced its way out of her body, and she collapsed.

A small, angry voice cried out in the stillness of the delivery room.

"Mr. Ryder, Mrs. Ryder. You have a son."

As she looked up at her husband, Neala watched the fear and tension disappear from his face, replaced by disbelief, awe, then a slow, beautiful smile she felt down to her bones.

"Oh, my God." Will took the baby in his big hands, and placed him tenderly against Neal's breasts. "Look at what we made, sweetheart. Here's our boy."

The pain of labor and exhaustion from delivering vanished the moment Neala touched their son for the first time. He was squirming and damp and still crying, but he was alive and in her hands and squinting at her with his tiny, bewildered eyes.

She held him and looked down at him until her eyes blurred; then she blinked and lifted her face. There were tears running down her husband's face, tears of joy and wonder, just like hers. "He's beautiful. Oh, Will. He's just so beautiful."

"When we get him cleaned up, he'll look even better, I promise." The midwife pulled down her mask and smiled at both of them. "Congratulations."

"He takes after you," Will said, gently touching the wet, dark hair on the baby's small skull.

She eased him into the cradle of her arm. "He does not. He's red and slimy and— Oh, my God, would you look at the size of his . . ." She dissolved into weak laughter. "Well, Daddy, looks like he really takes after you."

Will bent down and kissed them both. "Then he'll love you for the rest of his life."

The bad guys have been vanquished and love has triumphed over evil in *Paradise Island, Dream Mountain,* and *Sun Valley.*

Or has it?

As the Shandian Corporation and its bosses unravel, see what's in store for T'ang Jian-Shan, General Kalen Grady, and Colonel Sean Delaney.

Don't miss Gena Hale's new trilogy of adventure and romance

Gena Hale

PARADISE ISLAND

Paradise Island makes an ideal refuge for marine archaeologist Luke Fleming—until the day he finds a barely-clad woman washed ashore on a raft. She claims she has amnesia. He's sure she's just out to seduce him. But he can't deny the heat between them...

0-451-40982-5

To order call: 1-800-788-6262

S450/Hale

Second in the trilogy by

GENA HALE

Dream Mountain

Stranded in the Colorado wilderness with a
very handsome, very paranoid stranger,
Delaney Arlen must decide if they are
doomed to be enemies or destined to
be lovers.

"Nonstop adventure, gnarly intrigue, lots of
laughs...and a hunk. What more could you ask?"
—Catherine Coulter

0-451-41003-3

To order call: 1-800-788-6262

JANET LYNNFORD

COMING FROM ONYX IN AUGUST 2002

SPELLBOUND SUMMER

An enchanting tale of two very different souls brought together one spellbound summer...

Confronted by a temperamental Scottish laird while collecting clay from his property, artisan Angelica Cavandish finds herself in the midst of a war over disputed land—and in a personal battle for the heart of a warrior.

"Lush and sexy...brings the romance of the Scottish countryside to life." —Tess Gerritsen

0-451-41052-1

To order call: 1-800-788-6262

S426/Lynnford

F 1.4081/18

PENGUIN PUTNAM INC.
Online

Your Internet gateway to a virtual environment with
hundreds of entertaining and enlightening books
from Penguin Putnam Inc.

*While you're there, get the latest buzz on
the best authors and books around—*

Tom Clancy, Patricia Cornwell, W.E.B. Griffin,
Nora Roberts, William Gibson, Robin Cook,
Brian Jacques, Catherine Coulter, Stephen King,
Ken Follett, Terry McMillan, and many more!

**Penguin Putnam Online is located at
http://www.penguinputnam.com**

PENGUIN PUTNAM NEWS

Every month you'll get an inside look at our upcom-
ing books and new features on our site. This is an
ongoing effort to provide you with the most
up-to-date information about
our books and authors.

Subscribe to Penguin Putnam News at
http://www.penguinputnam.com/newsletters